The Devil
Wears Tank Tops

The Devil Wears Tank Tops

Angela Corbett writing as
Destiny Ford

Printed in the United States of America

Dedication

For the women who
aren't afraid to show a little shoulder.

And for the mouse who met my mother,
and gave me the mouse-tie story.
There was a photo, though I've been threatened with
"no more cookies for life" if anyone ever sees it.

Chapter One

Some days I love being a reporter, other days I hate it. Then there were days like today.

"Gary Smith's chickens got out again! I'm tellin' ya! We can't just have chickens runnin' around willy-nilly in the middle of the street chasin' kids and cars. They're birds, not dogs!" Norm Crane, Branson's resident rabble-rouser was standing at the podium in front of the Branson Falls City Council, trying to incite chicken-hate furor.

Jessie Green, a Branson Falls City Councilman, pounded his fist on the table. "Dang those chickens!"

Dale Call, another council member, barely looked up over his brown, plastic-rimmed eye glass frames as he raised his hand and said, "Second."

All of the commotion in the room stopped as everyone's heads swiveled simultaneously in Dale Call's direction.

Finally, Councilman Mark Brady spoke up, "Shoot, Dale! That wasn't a motion! You can't dang chickens!"

I sat listening to the ridiculous discussion, and taking notes. City council meetings weren't usually this lively and I could generally browse the celebrity gossip sites on my phone in between discussions about the latest tractors, or whether ATVs should get their own lane on the road. But thanks to the chickens, today's meeting was more animated than usual.

"First, people start tryin' to take our guns away, then men start marryin' men, and now chickens are runnin' citizens off the road. This country is goin' to heck in a handbasket!" Norm threw his hands in the air, exasperated.

I stared at Norm through his outburst, trying to figure out what in the world gun rights and marriage equality had to do with chickens. No one else seemed to be able to make the connection either. "We'll talk to Gary about constructing a better cage," Councilman Brady said.

Norm huffed and crossed his arms over his chest. "Well, I guess that'll have to do. In the meantime, I'll just pray for the second comin'. Nothin' else is gonna stop the madness."

My eyes were huge as I watched the crazy back and forth in utter disbelief. I'd considered skipping the meeting and going home to binge watch TV shows on Netflix. Now, I was happy I'd been there to witness it all in person instead of asking one of the other reporters to cover the meeting.

Suddenly, Councilman Brady remembered me sitting in the back of the room and the blood drained from his face. "You listen here, Kate," he said, pointing at me with a stern look, "that chicken thing? That's off the record."

I smiled dutifully, and nodded my head. *The Branson Tribune* certainly wouldn't want to be the cause of a scandal by reporting that people were upset about chickens crossing roads. Though, I was mighty tempted to ask our graphics guy to make a comic about it for the opinion page. I was also pretty sure everyone in the meeting would get the council's message back to Gary Smith and every other person in town before tomorrow morning, let alone the *Tribune's* next printing in a week.

Brady adjourned the meeting and I gathered my things, smiling at June Tate, a Branson resident who'd been sitting next to me. She'd come to complain about increased traffic by her property. Her house sat next to a highway, so there wasn't much the city council could do. "I'm sorry they couldn't help you," I said to June, noticing her white shirt under a matching lavender skirt and jacket. She looked very put-together in the business attire.

She shrugged. "We bought the house before the highway was there. I guess we should have moved before it got so busy." She was in her sixties and she and her husband had lived in Branson Falls all of their lives. "I just don't know why it's picked up so much during the last six months."

"Well, if it's only happened recently, maybe it will slow down again too," I offered, trying to make her feel better. With the population growing in Branson and neighboring towns, I had a feeling it probably wouldn't be getting better.

June fanned herself as she stood. It was August in Branson, and still hotter than the ninth circle of hell. The city council met in a building that was constructed sometime around the extinction of dinosaurs, and didn't have central air, or even a swamp cooler. "Aren't you dying of heat?" I asked, looking again at her very professional, but stifling layers. "I don't know how you can stand it. The less clothes, the better I say."

"I agree."

The deep voice brought me, and everything south of my navel, right to attention…even though I wasn't particularly happy about it. June looked at him the same way as every other woman on the planet…well, every other woman except me: with complete adoration. "Dylan Drake! I thought I saw you sneak in," June said with a warm smile. June had seen him sneak in and I hadn't? Observant reporter fail.

"What are you doing at the meeting tonight?" June asked.

Drake gave his winning politician's smile, practiced over years of working in the Utah House of Representatives. "Well, when I heard you were going to be here, June, I cancelled all of my other plans."

June waved a hand in front of her face, blushing. "You're such a charmer, Dylan." I did a double take at the use of his first name. Most people—me included—called him Drake because that's what he'd been known as on the football field. June put her hand on his forearm. "If I was thirty years younger, you'd be in trouble." She gathered her things. "I better get home before Paul burns the house down trying to cook dinner." She glanced at me, eyes twinkling. "You two have a nice night."

I wrinkled my nose at that twinkle, and wanted to correct her and say there would be no "two" of us at all, but she was surprisingly spry for a sixty-something year old, and already out the door. I turned my attention back to the man who'd snuck up on me—something he did frequently. His thick, dark hair framed his perfectly sculpted square jaw. Broad shoulders filled out a grey polo shirt and his black slacks draped over his lower body like fabric temptation. I shook myself out of the haze he almost always seemed to create in my head. I blamed it on his serious excess of testosterone. My ovaries just needed a minute to calibrate with the new hormones in the air. Eventually, they'd calm down and get blood back to my brain.

"Hey, Drake," I said, picking up my own things and trying to avoid eye contact. Locking gazes wouldn't help my ovary situation. But once I had my purse, camera, phone, and notebook, there was nothing else to do unless I wanted to start folding up chairs. I took a deep breath and looked up at the six-foot-three extremely attractive giant in front of me.

His smile was slow and deliberate as his eyes trailed over me, taking in my teal ruffled skirt that fell four inches above my knee, and my lacy grey tank top showing a bit of cleavage—none of which met Branson's conservative dress code. I was a rebel. Drake didn't seem to mind the rebelliousness at all—at least, not when it came to my clothes. "Katie," he said, his eyes coming to rest on mine. "Will I see you at the parade this week?"

I stuffed my notebook into my purse and searched for my keys as I answered, "Probably not."

"You're not covering it?"

"No, I am. But I'll be reporting from the parade route, not a float."

Drake's brow lifted. "That's a bad move on Spence's part. He'd get a lot more *Tribune* subscribers with a pretty girl in the front seat."

I fought back a blush. Because as much as I didn't want Drake's flirting to affect me, it did. When I was younger, I'd dreamed about him saying things *exactly* like that to me. Now, I knew his reputation—even if my ovaries hadn't gotten the memo. "I'm making it a goal to not draw attention to myself."

I tried to skirt by him, but he laughed and followed me outside to my car. A move that would undoubtedly start the Ladies'—Branson's version of *The Real Housewives*, with less money, perms, talon-like fingernails, and the ability to ruin a person's reputation in less than an hour flat—gossip phone tree. You know, because they didn't already have enough information to terrorize me with. As a prerequisite to becoming a Lady, you generally had to be perky, pretty, and popular in high school. I was none of the above, and I would never want to be a part of their gossipy group.

Drake gave a hearty laugh. "Good luck with that. Do you know who your mother is?"

"Ha, ha, Drake," I said with my best glare. "I'll also be avoiding you."

His lips slid into a hurt frown. "That's not nice, Katie."

I tried my best not to be nice to Drake. He pushed every single one of my buttons, both good and bad and I had a hard time managing him, and my completely conflicted feelings about him. My strategy so far had been constant offense that bordered on hostility. I'd learned it in elementary school. "I assume you'll be on a float, fake-smiling and waving to people, trying to get votes for something?" Drake was Branson's district representative for the Utah House of Representatives. He was also a lawyer. I despised him on both counts.

He shook his head. "You're confusing me with the Branson Falls pageant royalty."

I smirked. "Am I? Because around here, everyone seems to think you're Branson's version of Prince William."

His mouth widened into a grin. "And you would make the perfect Princess Kate."

My stomach fluttered and my eyes narrowed in anger at my tummy treason. My stomach wasn't supposed to flutter for Drake, regardless of how obsessed I'd once been with him. Drake's five years older than me, but he'd been my teenage crush. Though he claimed to remember me from our youth, I didn't buy it for a second, and he'd never given me any proof to back up his claim.

"Nope," I said, shaking my head. "That would never happen. I couldn't stand to wear the panty hose, and I'm far too opinionated. I'd offend people left and right, and probably start wars." He laughed, and I got in my dark blue Jeep Grand Cherokee. "Night, Drake."

He leaned back on his heels. "I'll see you soon, Katie."

"You know that's not my name," I said.

"You'll always be Katie to me."

I shook my head as I pulled away. I could see him grinning in my rearview mirror all the way to the end of the street.

Frosted Paradise, the pastry shop with my favorite doughnuts in the universe, was already closed, so I decided to stop at the grocery store on the way home instead. Every situation could be made better with comfort food, and an encounter with Dylan Drake practically required carbs. Plus, I thought maybe if I gained enough weight, he'd stop talking to me completely. That would certainly make my life easier.

I was pulling into a grocery store parking spot when I heard a loud explosion. People pushing grocery carts to their cars stopped in their tracks, looking around, some even ducked. I jumped out of my Jeep, searching for what might have caused the noise, but couldn't see anything. Less than thirty seconds later, another explosion sounded. People started yelling to take cover from the unknown threat as an eerie, flickering orange light began glowing west of town. "Forever in Blue Jeans" started singing from my phone—the Neil Diamond ringtone assigned to my boss, and publisher of the *Branson Tribune*. "Spence! What the hell was that?"

Spence's voice sounded tense. "Not sure yet. The only info I have is that it happened at the sugar factory."

"I'm on it." I hung up, pulled out of the parking lot, and started for the sugar factory in the industrial area of town.

The sugar factory was surrounded by other industrial plants making everything from diapers to yogurt. Most people in town were employed at one of the factories. Whatever had happened had sounded serious, so I hoped everyone had gotten out of the building safely.

I pulled in behind several fire trucks, and ambulances. My friend, Officer Bob, was on the scene. "Hey, Bobby," I said, lifting my camera to take some pictures of the firefighters battling the blaze. It was already hot, and the heat from the fire was making the men battling the blaze even hotter. Taking photos of muscled, sweaty firefighters is definitely a job perk.

"Kate," Bobby said, glancing at me before turning back to watch the burning building. Flames were shooting out of every window on the bottom floor.

"Do you know what happened yet?" I asked, taking out my notebook and pen.

He stared at the scene, light from the flames coloring his pale skin. "Not sure; it's too soon to tell. But if ya want my guess, I'd say sugar explosion."

I lifted my pen from the paper and rolled my eyes. "Seriously, Bobby. If you don't know yet, you can just say so."

He winged a brow, amused. "I'm not kiddin' Kate. It's a factory full of sugar. I'd bet sugar exploded."

I narrowed my brows, still not believing his story. "How?"

"Sugar dust is highly flammable, Kate. Don't you watch the Science Channel?"

I widened my eyes in surprise. "I wasn't aware there were shows dedicated to sugar."

He hooked his thumbs through his belt loops. "All it needs is a little spark, and poof! Dust explosion."

I had no idea that was possible. "What do you think would have caused the spark?"

Bobby shrugged. "We won't know till the firefighters can get in and investigate. No one was in the building that we know of, but it could've been vandals, or someone goofin' around who didn't know the trouble they could cause. I suspect it was a piece of machinery, though. With that much dust, it wouldn't take more than a tiny spark."

"But there were two explosions," I pointed out.

Some firefighters rushed by with more hoses as Bobby nodded. "The secondary explosion. The first explosion probably caused the second by putting more dust in the air."

The Devil Wears Tank Tops

The fact that I was getting this lecture by Bobby—who'd slept through even the most interesting classes in high school—kind of made me feel like I should have paid more attention in science.

Other Branson residents had started showing up. They'd undoubtedly heard about the explosion on their police scanners—which assisted in their efforts to be as nosy as possible.

"Was anyone hurt?" I asked, concerned.

"Don't think so," Bobby said. "The workers were all home when it happened, but there's a chance someone else could've been inside."

"Well, I'm glad the employees are all accounted for at least."

Bobby nodded.

"Is the owner of the factory here?"

Bobby reached in his pocket and pulled out a piece of gum. He offered me a stick, but I declined. "It's Kory Greer," he said, unwrapping his gum and putting it in his mouth. "We called him, but he's out of town right now. I can email you his contact info."

"Okay, thanks." I'd have to call him when he got back. I stayed on the scene for almost an hour, snapping photos and talking to residents, the fire chief, and other factory workers. I got some quotes, and then called Spence to update him.

"The fire is almost contained now," I said, after explaining the situation. "They're not sure what caused it yet, though. I also want to talk to the owner, so I'll follow up on both of those things."

"Thanks for covering it," Spence said. "I didn't know sugar could be so dangerous."

"Me either," I answered, stuffing my notes and camera back into my bag on the way to my Jeep. "Now I need food."

"I'll bring treats in the morning."

I smiled. "Then I'd have to kiss you."

Spence laughed. "Could you do it in front of the Ladies? Because that would really help my reputation."

Spence is gay, but I was the only person in town who knew about it. I snorted. "Yours, but not mine." The Ladies already thought I was sleeping with Hawke and Drake, and seemed to have suspicions about Spence as well. I didn't need to add to those theories.

I hung up, and drove back to the grocery store. After a sugar explosion, I needed carbs even more than before. A Drake encounter mixed with fire was a stressful combination.

I made my way to the cookie aisle and found it crammed full of people—a surprise considering a whole building had just exploded. An event like that usually caused the entire town to descend upon the area of news, though, thinking about it, the number of people at the fire had been surprisingly small in comparison with other town news-making events. The residents also hadn't been at the city council meeting and had to deal with Drake's pheromones, so I knew their reasons for needing treats must be different than mine.

I pushed through the crowd until I could see what all the fuss was about. People were gathered around a sample tray and someone handing out cookies.

The Devil Wears Tank Tops

Normally, I'd be the first in line for free sugar, but there were far too many people there for me to wait for samples when I could get plenty of other treats in less occupied aisles.

I wandered to the bakery section and found some freshly made sugar cookies. If my mom knew I was buying store-bought, it would send her into conniptions, but I didn't think it would be very nice to knock on her door at nine at night and ask her to bake—though she would have done so happily. Since I hadn't been gifted with her domestic genes, store-bought would have to do tonight.

"They're not as good as your mom's." I looked up to see Annie Sparks standing next to me, looking at the baked goods selection. I'd met Annie soon after I moved back to Branson Falls. She was a local EMT, and often on duty during my mom's misadventures. She was a member of the Mormon Church, but she wasn't as zealous as the majority of other Branson residents. With her jet black hair, multiple ear piercings, and out-of-the-church thinking, we'd become fast friends. I never felt judged by her, and in a small Utah community like Branson Falls, that's rare.

"I needed comfort food and didn't want to wake my mom."

"Ah, that time of the month?"

"No, but I just had a run-in with Drake."

Annie grinned. "So you're carb loading for later?"

My mouth fell open. "No!" I hissed, my voice barely above a whisper. "You can't say things like that here, Annie! Lady Spies are all over the place." I waved my arms around in a circle, looking up for the location of security cameras.

Annie laughed.

"What are you doing here?" I asked her.

"Grocery shopping."

It was practically the middle of the night. "At nine o'clock?"

"It's usually the best time to do it. Most people are home with their kids, and Rich is busy watching some sport on TV." Rich was Annie's husband. They didn't have kids—yet—proving them to be rather defiant Mormons. I was surprised they hadn't been called into church for a lecture about replenishing the earth. "Tonight's kind of crazy, though," Annie said. "It took me five minutes just to find a parking space. I thought they were having a spontaneous sale on something, but nope."

I nodded. "I was surprised, too. Especially since there was just an explosion at the sugar factory."

"I heard about that!" Annie said. "Do they know what caused it?"

"Not yet. Bobby thinks it was sugar dust."

Annie tilted her head thoughtfully—like sugar explosions made sense, and I felt even dumber for not knowing what seemed to be common explosion facts. "It's weird so many people are here instead of at the factory," Annie pointed out.

I'd also noticed the sheer number of people in the store and wondered about it. "Yeah, I thought that was strange, too," I said. "Usually people love being the first to know what's going on...especially when it has to do with something flammable. But it seems like everyone is here instead. I think most of the bottleneck is in the sample aisle."

"Ah," Annie said, nodding her head. "That makes sense then. I usually avoid the store on sample day. It's as bad as trying to find a parking space in Salt Lake City during a Utah Jazz game."

I picked up the box of sugar cookies and placed it in my basket with the non-fat, organic milk I'd grabbed earlier. "I guess I've never been here on sample day, but I'll avoid it in the future."

"Good plan," Annie said, grabbing some cookies herself and then steering away from the table and following me to the check-out line. "Hey, Rich and I wanted to invite you to dinner this weekend if you'll be around."

I thought about my completely blank social calendar confirming that I was, in fact, the most boring person on earth before saying, "Sure, that sounds great! And the fair will be over, so hopefully things will have calmed down a bit."

Annie laughed. "Well, your mom will still be around, so there's probably no chance of that happening—ever."

I laughed with her, as my items were rung up. "That's probably true."

"I'll text you the dinner info in a couple of days."

"Sounds good," I said, taking my bag. "I'll talk to you soon."

I was pleased with myself for adding an event to my social calendar that didn't involve work, happy I had a friend, and even happier that it was one who wouldn't get offended if I accidentally slipped and used a swear word—a real one, not the imitation swears most people in town utilized. I went home to my DVR, and a box full of frosted happiness.

I pulled into my house—a rental that I could only afford because I was living in one of the smallest cities in Utah. I loved having my own space, though, and the cream colored siding with royal blue shutters made me happy. I pulled into my matching detached garage, and walked through the backdoor into my kitchen. The countertops were square and the color of eggshells, the floor was a cheap ceramic tile, and the walls were lemon-yellow. The color forced a minuscule level of perky into me every morning. My pot of coffee didn't hurt either.

I threw my bags on the table and walked into my IKEA decorated living room. I'd recently added some bright blue vases my mom brought over after telling me my house was in dire need of some personality. I knew this was in response to whatever show she was currently obsessed with on HGTV. I was worried I'd come home one day to a missing wall or two. Personally, I felt like my house already had personality—it was Scandinavian, like IKEA.

The Devil Wears Tank Tops

I sat on my soft beige couches, put my food on the coffee table, and flipped on Netflix. I was half-way through my box of sugar cookies and had seen Jax Teller's ass two times in as many hours—a win on all accounts—when my phone started playing "Sweet Caroline," the ringtone that indicates the call is from someone I don't know. It had a Branson prefix, but I didn't recognize the number. I paused *Sons of Anarchy* and answered, "Hello."

"Kate, it's Bobby."

"Hey," I said, pushing my brows together. I'd just left him at the sugar factory a few hours ago, and hadn't seen any other explosions recently, so I wondered why he was calling. "What's up?"

His voice sounded grim. "I thought I should let you know. A body was found in the factory."

"Oh no!" I gasped. "Do they know who it is?"

"Not yet. It'll take some time to identify."

"But all of the workers were home, right?"

"Yeah, we've confirmed that so it must've been someone else."

I really hoped it wasn't someone in town that I knew, but I felt bad regardless. I didn't like to think about people dying, and death by fire would be a horrific way to go. "I'll get my stuff and be there in about ten minutes."

"You don't need to come down," Bobby said. "The area's been sealed off, and I gave you all the info we have right now. I'll call you when we know more."

A sudden sadness washed over me for the person who had died. "Thanks, Bobby. I appreciate the call, and your help." I put the phone down on the coffee table, and couldn't help but think about how short life really is.

Chapter Two

There was enough glitter and crepe paper traveling down Main Street to supply a craft convention. And a lot of it—the glitter at least—was being worn by women who weren't even Vegas Showgirls. Some of the horses were wearing it, too, and a few even had sparkly, painted hooves. I lifted my camera and took a picture; the horses' pedicures were better than mine.

I got some shots of the crowd in between parade entries. A float that was supposed to be a giant seagull, the Utah state bird, went by. Instead of a peaceful bird, however, this particular rendition resembled a pterodactyl, and the kids sitting under it looking miserable in the August heat didn't help the perception.

As a cute kid, I'd loved riding in the annual county parade. Whether I was singing on a float, sitting on a trailer throwing salt water taffy, or riding on top of a fire truck, I'd loved the attention. The parade marked the beginning of the last sweet days of summer freedom. By the following week, all the cute kids waving from the floats would be grumbling on their way back to school, and parents all over town would breathe a sigh of relief to have eight kid-free hours back in their day.

As an adult, though, the parade held a lot less novelty. I got enough attention around my hometown of Branson Falls, Utah; I didn't need to participate in the parade and invite more. I'd probably get eggs thrown at me—and since I'd already had eggs thrown at my Jeep recently, I definitely wasn't interested in being egged myself.

I'd managed to talk my way out of riding in the parade with the argument that someone needed to actually report on the parade for the *Branson Tribune* and take photos, and as the editor, that someone should be me. Then, Spence had gotten a car dealership in Salt Lake City to donate a bright yellow Viper convertible for the *Tribune* to use in their parade entry.

Spence was driving it.

I was pretty bitter about that.

I would have gladly drawn the attention if it meant I got to pilot a sleek, 640 horsepower V-10. Spence had waved as he drove by me, air conditioning blowing full blast, a smirk on his lips. I wanted to flip him off, but that would have caused even more gossip about me, so I stuck my tongue out instead—a move that I belatedly realized probably held more innuendo than my middle finger.

The Devil Wears Tank Tops

Officer Bob was riding on a police motorcycle behind Spence's Viper. I waved at Bob, and he waved back. It had been two days since the explosion at the sugar factory, but the body still hadn't been identified. Rumors were running rampant about who it might be. I'd checked, and all of the workers were accounted for, so it wasn't a factory employee, and there hadn't been any missing person's reports in town.

I wasn't patient, and waiting for information was not one of my strengths. If Bobby didn't get back to me soon, I'd call and bug him about it later this week.

As I walked along the parade route and took photos, I noticed a woman shield her daughter's eyes from me and whisper something in her ear. The little girl listened to her mom, then with a sharp scowl and finger-point in my direction, the girl said, "Bad lady!" She must have seen me stick my tongue out at Spence for his supercar stealing. As a rule, I tried not to take name calling personally, but when it came from a toddler, it was a bit more insulting than usual. And I'd been getting odd stares from people all day.

I frowned as I thought about it, and pulled my wavy brown hair into a messy bun on the top of my head. It was too hot even for a ponytail. Hair reined in, I sat down next to Kim Jordan, a girl I'd known in high school, to eat my banana flavored popsicle. The popsicles had been a parade staple every year since before I was born. They were handed out by the local grocery store, and were one of my favorite parts of sitting in the sweltering August heat surrounded by people and asphalt. Heaven knows, I wasn't there to see the horses poop, or watch the cleanup crew on four-wheelers with pooper scoopers behind them.

I leaned over to Kim, who was attempting to stop her son's cherry popsicle from soaking his shirt. "Can I ask you a question?"

With red, sticky liquid dripping from her hands, she finally gave up and let the popsicle win. Her toddler son grinned in triumph then promptly wiped his face with his shirt. She rolled her eyes and turned toward me. "Sure," she said, "as long as it doesn't involve keeping kids clean, because I have no advice about that."

I laughed. "I think you're doing a great job. Plus, they really seem to have a mind of their own." It was something that terrified me about having children. That and the thought that the kid might be a boy and I'd have to deal with hormones, or a girl and I'd have to deal with hormones. And the chance that they'd inherit my mom's disaster tendencies and the stress would shorten my lifespan significantly. I sighed inwardly, thinking it was a really good thing I didn't have kids.

"Yes," she said, glancing down at her son who now bore a strong resemblance to Elmo, "they definitely do." She looked back at me. "What did you want to ask?"

Thinking about the absolute terrors of childrearing had almost made me forget. "Is it just me, or am I being glared at? By everyone."

Kim looked at me, her eyes quickly taking inventory. "I'm not sure. Have you made anyone mad recently?"

I snorted. "A better question would be who haven't I made mad?"

She laughed and took the other half of her son's popsicle for herself. "Things have definitely been more entertaining since you came back to town. It's kept The Ladies occupied, so a lot of people are appreciative of that."

I tilted my popsicle in her direction. "I aim to please."

She licked a drop of cherry ice before it could fall to the grass. "You know about the Facebook group, right?"

I pushed my brows together. "What group?"

"The one the Ladies started about you."

I dropped my popsicle. The loss of my sweet, banana flavored treat made me even madder than I already was. "You're kidding me!?"

She winced. "Sorry. I thought you knew."

"How long has it been up?"

"I got invited to it a week ago. It's a private group."

As if it wasn't hot enough, now my blood was starting to boil. "How many people are in it?"

She tilted her head back and furrowed her brow in thought. "I don't know the exact number, but there are quite a few."

I pursed my lips, trying to stop the string of profanity from exiting my mouth. When I calmed down, I managed to grind out, "Great."

"They mostly just post where you've been, and what you've been doing."

My lip curled involuntarily. "Like a bunch of Lady Stalkers."

"At least they're not being as obvious about it now," Kim offered.

Ever since I'd moved back to Branson, the Ladies had decided my life—and love life, particularly—were Priority One. I kept hoping someone, or something, more interesting would grab their attention, but so far, it hadn't happened, which was a surprise when they had fodder subjects as juicy as Hawke and Drake. I wasn't used to the small town scrutiny, and didn't like it. What I did, and who I did it with, was no one's business. Sometimes I felt like I really needed to move back to the city. "I'd rather have them patrolling my house. I'd finally identified most of their cars."

Kim laughed. "I'll let you know if anything horrifying is reported."

"I'm sure that won't take long," I said with a roll of my eyes.

We watched a dance team swinging their hips down the road. The girls were covered in more sequins than Cher—and the glittery accessories were just as strategically placed. It always surprised me how Branson's strict modesty codes didn't seem to apply to the dance team or cheerleaders.

A few tractors went by and I recognized the Paxtons' combine from a recent incident when it had been stolen and my mom, in a misguided attempt to help, had tried to assist the thieves. I waved, and the Paxtons waved back. My mom still had the photo of her posing with the combine on her fridge. Farm equipment model wasn't something on most people's bucket list, but my mom had added it—and checked it off.

As the last tractor passed, Opie Vargis, wearing a clown costume, drove by on his four-wheeler, pulling a wagon advertising his company, C.T.R. plumbing. C.T.R. stands for "Choose The Right." It's a motto taught to every Mormon kid. They even have rings with a shield and the letters to wear as a reminder. Using the motto in a business name just seemed wrong. Like they were trying to convey their trustworthiness based solely on their religious beliefs. Any student of history would know that never turned out well.

I noticed the four-wheeler driving a little erratically. But this was a parade; he was supposed to weave from one side of the road to the other like someone crazy— or drunk. Even though drinking, along with other fun things like watching R-rated movies, drinking coffee, swearing, or having premarital sex was strictly against the rules of the Mormon Church.

I'd moved to Branson Falls as a child and like so many kids who aren't religious in Utah, I'd joined the Mormon Church because I wanted to fit in. I attended half-heartedly until I was old enough to ask questions, and then I'd been asked not to come back. I didn't mind, though; the religion worked for some people, but it wasn't right for me. I respected their right to their beliefs, and hoped they'd respect mine.

I pointed the clown out to Kim. "Opie's really taking his role seriously."

Her brows pinched together. "Yeah. I noticed that too. I wonder what's up?"

I shook my head. "Who knows. Maybe he had too much sparkling apple cider before the parade." If someone had managed to spike that, I wanted to know who it was, and I wanted to give them a high-five.

She laughed. "Maybe. The sparkling apple cider really isn't that bad."

My lips lifted. "You just think that because you've never had a nice glass of Moscato."

Another dance team went by wearing more glitter and sequins than the last, and less fabric. The speakers on the truck in front of them pounded out songs with a lot of bass and indecipherable lyrics. The music was blaring so loud that I almost didn't hear the commotion. The screaming from a few houses down alerted me, though. I turned to see that the C.T.R. clown, Opie, had crashed right into a lemonade stand in front of a house.

I ran over and pushed my way through the crowd gathered around the stand. The clown was on the ground. My friend Annie was giving him CPR. Not to be confused with the name of his company. I heard sirens in the distance. Luckily, the police station was only a few blocks away and with all the traffic blocked off for the parade, they were able to get to him fast. It was also lucky Annie had been in the vicinity.

Annie was still doing CPR when the ambulance arrived. They stabilized Opie quickly and Annie jumped in the back. "Is he okay, Annie?" I asked.

Annie shook her head slightly. "He has a pulse, but barely. And he's not breathing well. I think he had a heart attack."

They loaded him into the back of the ambulance and took off.

I got pictures of the aftermath and asked what the eyewitnesses had seen. "He plum lost control!" Lee Paulson said. "Just slumped over and drove right into the lemonade stand. Thank the good Lord my little LarLee was in getting drink refills, or she would have been plowed straight over."

I nodded, thinking that LarLee was seriously going to hate that name when she grew up—if she didn't already. I silently thanked my parents for giving me a normal moniker, and not some weird name combination. I suspected that like many kids in Utah, LarLee came from a combination of her parents' names: Lee, and his wife Skylar. "I'm glad LarLee is safe. Did you see anything else strange?"

He shook his head. "He was clutchin' his chest before he drove into the stand. Looked like a heart problem to me."

The other eyewitnesses concurred.

After the commotion was over, the parade ended abruptly. On my walk back to the *Tribune* office, where my car was parked, I heard some people commenting on Opie's condition, but most were just expressing their concern over his health and hoping he'd be okay. I agreed. My grandpa had died from a heart attack, so I understood their worry, and hoped the doctors would be able to help him.

Chapter Three

The parade is the kick-off for the county fair celebrations. There's a rodeo, carnival rides, livestock auctions, booths to peruse, and enough greasy fair food to make your internal organs run away in terror. One of the more popular events is always the fair competitions. People enter everything from pies, to quilts, to artwork. The items are judged, and winners sent on to compete at the state fair level.

I always enjoyed walking through the buildings to see what people with far more talent than me had made. My mom usually walked around with me. I think she secretly hoped I'd acquire everyone's domestic and crafting abilities by osmosis.

I stood outside the building where the food was being judged, waiting for her. We usually went there first because she wanted to chat with everyone about her lemon-drop cookies, the legendary, grand prize fair cookie winner every year for the past ten years. She was the queen of cookies, and she loved the attention.

I checked my watch. The heart attack story had put me behind by about thirty minutes, but I'd texted her to let her know. Even with my text, she was fifteen minutes late. That was unlike her . . . unless there'd been an incident. I took a long, deep breath. I *really* hoped there hadn't been an incident.

There hadn't.

Yet.

But there was about to be.

When I was nine, Mary Ann Boggs had written, "Rosses are red, violets are blue, I turned out perfict what happened to you" in my yearbook. I'd returned the favor by writing, "At least I can spell, you stupid butthole."

That had resulted in a phone call from Mary Ann's mom berating my dirty mouth and questioning my mom's parenting abilities. Despite my attempts to show my mom the yearbook signature to prove I had just cause for my profanity, and Mary Ann actually *was* a stupid butthole, my mom didn't see things my way. She'd turned into a red-faced, female fury in a pink checkered skirt and pantyhose. I maintained that the pantyhose were probably the biggest part of the reason she was so angry, and had she not been wearing them, my sentence might have been less harsh. But, thanks to the demon who invented hosiery, she'd washed my mouth out with soap—I still hadn't forgiven her—and told me never to use that word again. I had, and much worse, but I tried to be careful about swearing in her presence. It was the one time I'd seen her truly out of her mind with rage in my whole life.

Until now.

Sophie Saxee, whose adventures entertained Branson residents almost as much as my love life, was stalking across the fairgrounds like a female Moses, parting crowds with her expression alone. People knew what she was capable of, and didn't want to be caught in the crosshairs. Frankly, I didn't blame them.

She caught my eye, and started stomping in my direction. I measured the merits of leaving and pretending I didn't see her with what would surely be a lecture—and probably attempted spanking—when she eventually found me. I was fairly certain I could outrun her, but I decided to hold my ground, mostly because I was intensely curious at what could have caused a butthole-grade expression. I was pretty sure it wasn't me . . . at least, I hoped not. I mentally reviewed the previous week and couldn't think of anything exceedingly heinous.

"In all my years," she fumed, coming to a sudden stop in front of me. Her face was bright red and she was shifting back and forth on her feet like a barely contained bomb. "I've never dealt with such horrid manners."

I narrowed my eyes. "What's going on, Mom?"

"Ridiculous nonsense! That man is a . . . a . . ." She looked to me, her eyes pleading for help. I had plenty of words to offer, but didn't want my mouth washed out with soap again. "A NINCOMPOOP!" she yelled, happy to have found a sufficient descriptor. "He doesn't know cookies from toilet paper!"

"Who?" I asked, completely befuddled.

"That *gosh darn* idiot judging the cookies!"

I stepped back, out of her rage circumference. "Gosh" and "darn" were *big* words for my mom. They were imitation swears that, when combined, imitated the worst possible swear next to the F word. Mom rarely used the imitators, and *never* used the actual words. She'd just put two imitators together. This was the word equivalent of an explosion. "What happened?" I asked, putting my hand on her shoulder, trying to soothe her.

"I'll tell you what happened," she said, her eyes squinting as she folded her arms over her chest, shoulders back and head high. "Ryan Miles, and all the other dumb judges, have no taste buds. *That's* what happened."

I stared at her, everything suddenly sinking in. "Are you saying your cookies didn't win?"

"My. Cookies. Didn't. Win." She ground out. "And the *gosh darn* ones that did win are a new entry!" She was so angry, she sputtered the words. "A *new* entry! Can you believe that nonsense?"

A debutante winning was almost as much of a travesty as my mom's loss. If there's one thing that can always be counted on in small towns, it's tradition and heritage. To have a newcomer overtake the reigning ten year champion was unheard of. She was a legacy, and her legacy had just been squashed. If I didn't calm her down soon, there was no telling what she'd do next.

I didn't think it was possible, but my mom's face seemed to be getting even redder. "Maybe we should leave," I said, really hoping she'd agree to go home and relax in the shade of their beautiful, red-hued garden with a nice iced tea.

Her eyes darted around the fairgrounds like a laser looking for its target. "Leave?" she said, her voice getting more and more shrill with each syllable, "*Leave?*" She stomped her foot. "Leaving is the last thing I'll do. I'm staying *right* here, and I'm going to find those usurpers!" She grabbed my hand and started dragging me into the building with all of the vendor displays.

The building was packed. At first, I thought it was just busy in general. The mostly empty booths told me otherwise. The commotion, and all of the traffic, seemed to be centered on one area. And my mom was dragging me straight to it. I looked at the festive blue sign above the booth: *Saints and Sinners Cookies. So good, you'll think they're a sin.*

My mom saw the tag line at the same time I did. "Saints and Sinners? So good you'll think they're a sin? *Sin*!!!" she shrieked. My eyes widened. This had escalated *way* past a butthole reaction. I didn't think I would have gotten this level of anger even if I'd called Mary Ann the F word. "I'm not a sinner! And my cookies are far better than this doo-doo!"

People toward the back of the crowd turned to stare at her like she was nuts. Given the crazed look in her eyes, I'd probably have agreed with them. "Mom, why don't we go outside and get some air. Maybe even go home and see how Dad's doing?" And, I thought privately, find a valium, or tranquilizer—anything to calm her down.

"These people *stole* your heritage, Kate! They're the cookie prize thieves! They entered their horrible treats in the fair, and," she screeched, flailing her hands in all directions, "they got a *gosh darn* booth!" A vein on my mom's neck looked like it might pop. "The lemon-drop recipe has been in our family for years! These…ninnies," she hissed, waving a hand in the general direction of the booth, "don't know who they're messing with! They're evil. Eeevvviiill!"

Judging by the size of the line, and the glares my mom was getting for insulting the cookies, it was clear not everyone shared my mom's sentiments. Some seemed ready to defend the Saints and Sinners Cookies. I tried to pull her away before something unfortunate happened. "Mom, maybe we should go. There's nothing you can do here."

"Heya, Katie!"

I turned and saw Ella, the volunteer archivist for the *Tribune*. She was seventy-five, but had the mind of a fourteen-year old. She was holding a bag of Saints and Sinners Cookies in one hand, and a chocolate covered cookie in the other. Judging by the gleam in her amber colored eyes, she looked mighty happy about her purchase. "Hey, Ella."

Out of the corner of my eye, I saw my mom staring at Ella's cookies, and I swear steam started coming out of her nose like she was about to turn into a real-life cookie scorching dragon. I grabbed my mom's upper arm to try to hold her in place, and then turned back to Ella. "How are you?"

"Great, now! Finally got my cookies." She held up a bag that looked heavy enough to make her fall over. I had no idea what she planned to do with all of those cookies, but I hoped the answer wasn't eat them, or she'd probably end up in the hospital. "Best darn cookies I've ever had."

My mom had been maintaining until that point—to a degree—but with Ella's declaration, Mom lunged straight for Ella. Ella yelped as my mom grabbed the cookie bag from Ella's hand, threw it on the ground, and started jumping around, stomping it to a hundred little pieces.

"Hey!" Ella cried, looking at the cookie destruction.

"Mom!" I yelled.

Using her crazy eyes again, she parted the crowd, an impressive feat. "What are you going to do?" I asked.

She looked at me over her shoulder, her face screwed up in fury. "What am I going to do?" she asked, her voice rising with each word. "I'll tell you what I'm going to do! I'm going to buy some of those cookies, and figure out what the *fudge* everyone sees in them!"

My mouth fell open at the word "fudge" and what swear it represented. She'd never used such an aggressive imitation swear in my whole life. She marched to the front of the booth, and demanded her gosh darn cookies.

The Devil Wears Tank Tops

After some whispers and flat out insults from people on the way back to the car—I swear I heard the word "hussy" in there, which really wasn't fair considering a. I hadn't been involved in the cookie debacle at all, b. hussy didn't apply to the situation, and c. I wasn't a hussy, despite what everyone said—I got my mom to her car without further incident. Although she refused to let me take her bag of cookies from her. Demanding to know what would put them above her status as cookie queen, she was determined to go home and dissect them, piece by little piece.

I gave up, and texted my dad to give him a summary of the events. Thanks to his police scanner, he'd already heard about his wife trying to kill cookies. I imagined he was probably making a strong drink. Which was a totally unapproved coping mechanism for most people in Branson, but my parents weren't Mormon, so they could get away with it. Plus, even if they had been, I was fairly certain God would forgive my dad the alcohol since my dad was the one who routinely had to deal with my mom.

After I dropped my mom off, leaving her 'crazy' in my dad's capable hands, I stopped and got some cheese smothered breadsticks from *Sticks and Pie*. I drove home, looking forward to my couch. It had been a long day, and I had cherry chocolate chip ice cream in the freezer, and a *Sons of Anarchy* episode waiting for me on my Netflix queue. The thought of bad boy Jax made me think of the bad boy in my own life and I shivered, despite the heat. I could totally justify Hawke's potential contract killing if he had an ass like Jax Teller's—and he did. Situational ethics at its best.

I'd just turned on the episode and grabbed my first gooey breadstick when my phone started playing "Forever in Blue Jeans." It wasn't my night to be on call for breaking news—which rarely happened unless it involved my mom—so whatever reason Spence was calling for must be important. I muttered a string of swear words—not the imitation kind—and answered. "Hey, Spence."

"I'm sorry to bug you, but there's a pile up on Main Street."

I took my phone from my ear and stared at it, sure I hadn't heard him right. "Do you mean a pile up on the freeway? Because that would actually make sense."

"Nope. Main Street. Can you cover it?"

My eyes went from my breadsticks to the TV longingly, and I sighed. "Yeah, I can. You okay?" Spence was the person on call tonight.

"Yeah," he said, the hint of a smile in his tone. "I'm just busy at the moment."

That got my attention. "Busy with what?" I asked, genuinely curious. Spence didn't have a lot of friends in town. I think it was partly because he was nervous to let his guard down. He wouldn't be looked on kindly if anyone else found out he was gay.

"Nothing you need to know about right now."

The Devil Wears Tank Tops

I heard a low laugh in the background and narrowed my eyes. I'd be interrogating him more about that later. "Fine. Where on Main Street?" Main Street ran the entire length of town and encompassed everything from businesses to farms.

"By the four-way stop. It will be hard to miss."

That sounded promising. "Okay. I'll take care of it." I swiped my phone off and gave one last yearning look at Jax before hitting the power button on the TV, putting my remaining breadsticks in the fridge, and leaving for the four-way stop.

Chapter Four

Spence was right. I couldn't have missed it if I'd tried. A giant piece of brightly colored fabric was draped across both lanes of traffic, and over the field next to it. Based on the fire trucks spraying it down, and the smoke coming off of it, the fabric had recently been on fire. In the midst of that, four cars were piled up on one side of the fabric, crushed together like a demolition derby, and three more cars were smashed in a similar manner on the other side.

I stared at the scene, trying to piece it together. It looked like a circus tent had spontaneously combusted on the road. I checked the cars for my mom's make and model. This looked like something she could have caused if she'd escaped my dad's watch. Luckily, I didn't see her truck. I finally gave up trying to deconstruct the scene, and went to find Officer Bob. I was sure he'd be there, he always was. I was right.

"What in the world happened, Bobby?" I asked, walking up to him and snapping some pictures.

"Chaos," he answered, looking over the scene. "As usual."

I gave another wary look around as I kept taking photos. "My mom's not here, is she?" My mom had a reputation for getting in the strangest predicaments and causing all kinds of trouble. People in town even had a nickname for her: Catasophie, a combination of "Catastrophe" and "Sophie."

"Nope. Not this time. Too bad, though. She usually has treats for us. And I could really use a treat."

I heard a noise that sounded like a cross between a hyena and a bird, and looked around trying to identify it. I saw plenty of people, but no species hybrids. I turned my attention back to Bobby. "What's the fabric doing on the ground?"

"Not flyin', that's for sure."

I looked at it again. In front of one of the cars, I saw a large lump under the fabric and realized what I was seeing. My eyes widened with the knowledge. "A hot air balloon crashed?"

"And burned."

I didn't even think we had hot air balloons in Branson. "Where did it come from?"

"The fair."

That made a little more sense. "Why did it crash?"

He made a hmmph noise like he was utterly disgusted. "Because the darn pilot didn't know diddly-squat about flyin' a hot air balloon."

Bob's answer implied he *did* know diddly about flying a hot air balloon. I questioned whether or not that was actually the case. "So what went wrong?"

He hitched up his pants before crossing his arms over his chest. "We got a call that one of the hot air balloons at the fair had been stolen. Bunch a nutballs think watchin' a couple episodes about balloon flyin' on TV gives them enough knowledge to pilot a balloon." I suspected that's exactly where Bob's balloon knowledge had come from, but didn't say so. "The thief learned quick that it's not as easy as it seems. We got calls about a balloon flyin' real low. Near as we can tell, he must've released the hot air too fast from the parachute valve and came down like a sack of flour."

I widened my eyes. "Was anyone hurt?"

"The balloon was flyin' low enough that it wasn't a huge drop. And crops in the field helped cushion the fall. The people in cars that had to swerve to miss the balloon were worse-off than the balloon thief, but no one's seriously hurt."

That was a relief. And I already had a working headline: Balloon Bandit. I heard the hyena noise again and wondered if I was hearing things. Last I checked, we didn't have hyenas in rural Utah. I shook my head and turned back to Bob. "Who stole the balloon?"

"Well," Bob said, his jaw shifting to the side as he bit his lip, looking confused, "that's the funny thing. It was Fred Young."

The Devil Wears Tank Tops

My eyes went as wide as saucers. "The Third Ward bishop?" Members of the Mormon Church are divided into wards based on where their homes are located, and every ward is presided over by a male bishop—the man who's supposed to be a shining example of righteousness to all other ward members. Fred Young was one of them. And he was one of the most serious, soft-spoken men I'd ever met. He definitely didn't seem like the Balloon Bandit type.

Bob nodded. "And he sure as heck seems to think it was hilarious."

Several things clicked together in my head at once. The high pitched noise wasn't the result of a sudden hyena hybrid infestation. It was Fred Young laughing. And it was terrifying. "Where is he?"

Bob pointed to the ambulance and I went over. Annie was there, trying to get Fred to calm down. "Hey! It's been a busy day for you," I said loudly, so she could hear me over Fred's laughter. Between this and Opie at the parade, she was probably exhausted.

My eyes moved to Fred, who was dressed in a white button-down shirt and tan khaki pants held up by a Mormon male wardrobe staple: a braided brown belt. I couldn't believe he was wearing a long-sleeved shirt when it was over a hundred degrees out. Maybe his problem was heat exhaustion that had morphed into hysteria.

Annie nodded between Fred's fits of giggling frenzy. "We always expect more incidents when the fair comes to town, but they're usually confined to the rodeo." Fred rolled to his side, laughing so hard he was starting to turn red. Annie sat back, but kept one eye on Fred as the other EMT gave him some oxygen. After about thirty seconds, his face started to recede from tomato to normal color. "This is definitely…different."

"How's Opie doing?" I asked, thinking of the CTR clown.

"He's stabilized, but they're not sure what caused his heart attack. They're running some tests."

"When will the results be back?"

She shrugged. "With the fair going on? Who knows." She applied some disinfectant to the scratches on Fred's arm. "Hey!" he said between laughs. "That's not nice!"

Fred Young was an executive at the town paper company where many Branson residents were employed. I'd rarely heard him laugh, let alone do a wild animal impression. "Has he been acting this way long?"

She looked up at me, a combination of amusement and annoyance. "Yeah."

"Did you give him something to make him giggle like a five-year old?"

"Yes, but he was laughing before we gave it to him, too. I'm not sure what's wrong with him."

"Mr. Young," I said, trying to get his attention.

He turned an unfocused gaze in my direction. I doubted I'd get much information from him at the moment.

"Can you tell me why you stole the hot air balloon?"

He answered between more giggles, "Because he told me to."

42

"Who?" I asked, not understanding.

Taking great effort, he sat up, scooted to the edge of the bed, and then leaned into me and whispered in a conspiratorial tone, "The minotaur!"

Annie snorted.

"Great." I folded my notebook back over and capped my pen. "Thanks a lot, Fred. I'll be sure to quote you on that."

I gave up and decided I'd have better luck talking to witnesses of the crash. I waved to Annie and went over to where a group was gathered by Officer Bob. I asked them what they'd seen and they told me the same thing as Bob. A balloon was flying low and suddenly fell from the sky. Cars swerved to miss the balloon and crashed. Then Fred Young popped out of the corn field and started dancing on the balloon. "He was dancing?" I asked, completely baffled.

Jane Carter nodded. "Like a fairy in heat."

Also a great quote for my story. I wanted to ask if she'd actually seen a fairy in heat, or if she was going completely off assumptions. Because if she'd seen one, I wanted to see it too, and write the article about it. If that didn't win me top prize with the Utah Press Association, nothing would.

I was taking more notes when a deep, sexy voice whispered in my ear. "Hey, Kitty Kate." Every part of me was instantly aware of his presence. Even the hair on my arms paid attention. I was surprised I hadn't smelled his Swagger body wash before I heard him. I turned around and my breath hitched. I took him in from head to toe. His sandy brown hair was short and messy, like he'd styled it with just his hands, and his light green eyes were even more piercing in the sun. His faded jeans fit his ass perfectly, and hung looser around his thighs. His tight, teal t-shirt clung to his hard abs and biceps with a tattoo that peeked out from under his sleeves. I was determined to find out what it was a tattoo of—and if he had any more. But, it hadn't happened—yet.

"Hey," I said back, my voice breathy. "What are you doing here?"

"I was a witness," Hawke answered. "I just gave my statement."

I looked around. I hadn't seen his super sexy blue 1967 GT Shelby Mustang with white racing stripes. My eyes were trained to notice it. I would have found it immediately.

"I don't have it today," Hawke said, reading my mind—no doubt one of his *many* talents.

Hawke had two giant red brick buildings on his property that matched his giant red brick house. One was a gym. The other was a garage. Though I'd wanted to go in the garage, so far I'd only been invited to Pain—my nickname for his gym. I'd been looking forward to checking out Hawke's car collection, and wondered what he could possibly be driving today. I looked around. I didn't see a Lamborghini, and I was a little disappointed. "What are you driving, then?"

He nodded in the direction of a glossy black Harley with some sort of tribal design in matte black that stood out against the gloss. A black matte helmet hung from one of the handlebars. Everything about it said smooth, sexy, and dangerous. I sucked in a breath. I'd already been in lust; Hawke on a bike catapulted my emotions straight to I'll-do-anything-you-want-just-say-the-word territory. A vision of Jax Teller merged with Hawke in my head. My face got hot at the thought.

Hawke's lips slid into a slow smile. "Want a ride?"

Did I ever. And not just on the bike. I swallowed hard and glanced up at him. One corner of his lips tilted up in a knowing grin.

"You know," he said, licking his lips, "I'm still pretty upset that I didn't get what I wanted."

After my last adventure involving a crazy teenager and a gun, Hawke had told me he was giving me shooting lessons. He'd inferred that he'd planned to teach me some other, less violent, things as well. That situation had been interrupted by some kids who seemed to think Animal Planet was some sort of instructional guide and they were using their knowledge base to "capture critters" and build a skunk pit. I'd used that quote in the story headline. Believe me, I wasn't happy about leaving a hard-bodied, ready and willing Hawke to go cover some kids being rescued from their skunk pit. "Yeah. Me either. So we can be unsatisfied together."

He raised one eyebrow. "We don't have to be. In fact, we could solve the problem right now."

I looked around, widening my eyes. Our options were kind of limited. "In a field?"

His lips slid into a grin. "Bet you've never done it there."

Nope. I hadn't. The closest I'd come to a corn field at all was during a high school double date when we'd watched *Children of the Corn*—in the field. It had made me terrified of agriculture and blonde children…a problem when Branson is full of both. I cursed Jimmy Sall to this day for taking me on that dumb date. "I had a traumatic experience with corn." Plus, I wasn't interested in sex being interrupted by field mice and snakes. An involuntary shudder rippled through me at the thought.

Hawke's eyes lowered, raking over my blue and white striped tank top and coming to rest on my lips. His eyes darkened and he pulled me into the field anyway. "Then I guess this will have to do for now."

He pushed into me, his lips hot on mine, full body pressing deliciously—and indecently—into my own. It was already scorching outside, but Hawke managed to make it hotter. I felt every plane of his abs against my stomach and chest as his hands moved down my back and over my butt. He grabbed me. Hard. And bent his knees as he lifted me off the ground. I gasped and wrapped my legs around his waist. He took my mouth deeper. But almost as fast as it started, it was suddenly over. He put me down gently. I staggered back, grabbing an ear of corn for balance. It broke off in my hand. Hawke was lucky I'd grabbed the corn instead of something else. Hawke held back a laugh as he steadied me. "That should help you remember me."

It took me a moment to process since all of my blood was currently located in places that had nothing to do with brain cells. "Are you going somewhere?"

"Work."

I eyed him suspiciously. Hawke had an interesting job, and one that was rather undefined. He kept it that way on purpose. If rumors were to be believed, he'd been everything from a member of the Secret Service to a contract killer. Oh, and he also rescued kittens. "Off to kill some people, huh?"

He grinned. "You never know."

"I'm aware. And it scares me."

He lifted a hand to my cheek and held my eyes. "It shouldn't. You're one of the few people I care enough about to keep in my life. It's a very short list. I'll be back soon, Kitty Kate. We'll finish this then, I promise." He kissed me one last time, slow and soft, as his hands moved up from my waist and cupped my breasts, the cleavage even more visible from my current agitated state. "I like this shirt," he said, voice rough.

My breath was ragged as I answered, "You're the only one."

His head canted slightly and his lips lifted. "I doubt that." He waved as he walked away.

I looked down and smoothed my striped tank top and grey shorts, checking for items that screamed I've-been-almost-sexing-in-a-corn-field. Luckily, I didn't find anything. I peeked through some corn leaves to see if anyone was paying attention before I walked out of the field. I was fine . . . until I was accosted by Mrs. Olsen, the town busybody who liked to tell everyone else exactly what they were doing wrong and which level of the afterlife they'd be relegated to because of it—

Mormons had three levels, and only one was an acceptable placement for the faithful.

She pointed at my hand. "You're carrying a cob of corn."

I grimaced inwardly. So I was. Clearly, my senses were still back in the field with Hawke and I'd forgotten to drop my balancing cob on my way out. Now I had to go with it. "Yep," I answered, throwing the cob back in the field behind me.

"Why?" She slitted her eyes. "What were you doin' in there?"

The lie came swiftly. "I dropped my earring and was looking for it."

She looked from one lobe to the other. "No you didn't. You're wearin' one in both ears."

I could have told her I'd already found and reattached it, but I was hoping to distract her. I made a show of reaching up to my ear, and hoped her memory was lagging so she'd forget about the corn. "Oh my gosh! Look at that! You found it! Thanks, Mrs. Olsen!" I quickly changed the subject. "Did you enjoy the parade today?"

She wrinkled her nose in disgust. "Can't believe the clothes they're lettin' some of these girls wear. Downright immodest." She glanced over me, assessing with an eye honed for judgment. "And you're no better with that shirt. Showin' off your shoulders and chest like that is somethin' only a hussy would do! You might as well not wear anythin' at all."

I looked down at my tank top and suddenly the strange stares and finger pointing / name calling from small children all made sense. Tank tops were considered immodest by most residents of Branson Falls. Anyone caught wearing one was either not a member of the church, or in serious trouble. Personally, I wore them because it was hotter than the seventh circle of hell outside. "It makes the heat bearable."

She scowled, her face scrunched up in a way that made me concerned she might be having a stroke. She wasn't. "I hope that's what you think when you're livin' in the horrors of Outer Darkness."

I gave her a sweet smile. "I've always preferred the dark."

Her jaw dropped.

I smiled wider, and walked away.

Chapter Five

I spent the next day at the fair covering the animal judging and auction. I'd had pets growing up, but I could never bring myself to raise one with the knowledge that it would be sent off to slaughter. I had a hard time even covering the story. I kept having to repeat: food, not friends. It was enough to make me a vegetarian for a couple of days at least.

After the auctions, I wandered over to get some photos of one of the most popular fair events: the poop drop. Areas of a field were separated into a numbered grid like a checkerboard. People could choose a number, and place their bet. Then, a cow was let loose in the field. Whichever square he chose to poop in was the winner, and the person who had bet on that square got all the money from bets placed. In the past, there had been some debate over whether or not it constituted gambling—a no- no in the Mormon Church. But most people just considered it good fun, and many winners donated the money to charity. That was one thing I really liked about Utah and Mormons: their willingness to help those who were less fortunate.

The air was sticky and stifling outside, so I took a break to get a tart, frozen strawberry lemonade, and sought refuge in the air conditioned buildings. As I went from booth to booth, I couldn't help but notice the sheer lack of people visiting most of the vendors. The buildings were usually packed.

When I got to the animal rescue booth, I smiled as I watched a couple of puppies jump and play tug of war with a blue and white braided rope. One was a golden lab, another was a small black and gray mix of something that looked a bit like a terrier. His gray beard around his mouth reminded me of Gandalf from *The Lord of the Rings*. "They're so playful," I said to Michelle James, the shelter owner. She had eight kids and ran the shelter. I was pretty sure she also moonlighted as Wonder Woman. I bent down to scratch the puppies behind their ears. Gandalf flipped right over and demanded a tummy rub. I smiled at the little guy, and happily obliged.

"They have a lot of energy today," Michelle said, cocking her hip out and leaning against the table as she watched me.

"Because of all the people?" I asked.

She shook her head. "Because of the lack of people. Usually the animals I bring get adopted pretty fast at the fair, and they get tired from everyone playing with them. We just haven't had a lot of people stop by this year."

I furrowed my brow and glanced up at her. "That's weird. Why do you think attendance has been low?"

She tilted her head to the right. "Because everyone's over in the baked goods building."

"Ah," I said, watching as the puppy pawed my hand, annoyed I'd stopped his tummy massage. I gave him an extra scratch in apology as I answered, "The cookies."

She gave a sigh. "Yep. The cookies."

"I've never seen so much fervor over sugar and flour."

"Me either," she said. "But they're yummy. One of our German Shepherds hates them, though. As soon as I brought the bag in the house, he sniffed it, then grabbed the bag and destroyed it, and the cookies. He didn't even try to eat them. I had to buy another bag."

I laughed, thinking he'd get along well with my mom. "He must have a cookie vendetta."

She smiled as she watched me with Gandalf, nodding her head toward us both. "He really likes you."

I grinned down at the cute puppy, still getting petted. I couldn't stop. "I like him too."

"You should take him," she said.

I froze and stared at her. "Take him? Like adopt him?" Another living thing was a big responsibility. I'd had to plant a seed and grow it for a class in elementary school. I'd overwatered it and killed within days. If I couldn't keep a plant alive, how in the world could I take care of a dog? Then again, the plant situation had happened years ago. I probably had more sense now…probably.

"Yeah! He'd be good for you, and you'd be great for him. You'll never have anyone in your life who will be as loyal, or love you as much as a dog." She watched him squirm under me to get a better position, his tongue lagging to the side, a happy smile on his face. "The fact that he flipped on his back and gave you his tummy means he trusts you. He already thinks you're best friends."

I thought Michelle was overstating that by a lot. Gandalf would have been best friends with a bear as long as it scratched his tummy. "I don't know. I've never owned a pet of my own before."

I stood up and the puppy immediately rolled over and sat, staring up at me, waiting for a command—or a treat.

"I can help you with whatever you need," Michelle said. "It's really important to me that the animals I place go to good homes. You're a compassionate person, and would make a great pet parent. I know he'd be taken care of if he was with you."

"How old is he?" I asked, throwing his tiny tennis ball. He bounced after it with a playful growl.

"About a year, we think. He was found abandoned on the side of the road a couple of months ago."

My chest constricted at the thought of someone leaving a helpless little dog like that. I bent down to rub the top of his head and behind his little ears, like somehow, that small bit of attention might help erase some of the abuse he'd been through. I knew it wouldn't, but it made me feel better, and I hoped it made him feel better too.

"He's already house trained, and is really good with people," Michelle said, handing me a treat to feed him. I laughed as he smelled my hand, looked up at me for permission and then immediately ate the treat, his little tongue rough against my palm. "You could take him with you when you need to cover a story, or he'd also be fine at home as long as he had toys to keep him company. He'd make a great watchdog, too." She eyed me, assessing. "I really think he'd be a good fit for you and your lifestyle."

I looked at him, trying to envision myself as a dog owner. "My life is so hectic, though. I don't know if I could give him the time he needs. I'm always running somewhere."

"Dogs are pretty resilient," Michelle said. "It's not like he needs a babysitter. You can leave him home when you need to."

I considered Michelle's words. I could definitely use a watchdog. And it would be nice to come home to something other than just my TV. The thought of getting a dog was simultaneously terrifying and exciting—kind of like how I felt around Hawke and Drake. I wasn't sure I was ready for the commitment, but as the little guy bumped his head into my hand again for another pet, asking me to accept him, it made it really hard to say no. Still, I wasn't sure if I could do it.

"I don't know…" I said, hedging.

"Tell you what," Michelle said, picking Gandalf up. "I'll keep him at the shelter until you decide. That gives you some time to think about it, and figure out if you think it will be a good fit. If not, you can tell me and I'll adopt him out to someone else."

My stomach clenched at the thought of little Gandalf going to anyone but me, but getting a dog and caring for it was a huge decision. It wasn't something I wanted to decide lightly. "Okay," I said to Michelle. I reached down to pet Gandalf one more time. "But if anyone comes in and tries to adopt him, let me know first."

She nodded, and I walked away thinking of little Gandalf and wondering if I was really old enough, and prepared enough, to be responsible for another living thing. I wasn't sure, but I couldn't stop thinking of that cute, furry little black and gray face.

I passed by the booth with the cookies, and Michelle was right. Everyone in the entire county seemed to be crammed into it. Clearly, these cookies were a big deal, and a story the *Tribune* should be covering. There was no way I'd get through the throngs of people to talk to them now, though, and last time I was there with my mom, it was just a bunch of teenage employees working, not the actual cookie business owners. I wrote down the company name—not that I could forget something like Saints and Sinners Cookies—and made a note to call them for an interview.

I was on my way to get some pictures of cute kids winning stuffed animals and eating ridiculous food like fried Oreos, when my phone started playing "Sweet Caroline." I looked at the number, but I didn't know the caller. I answered, "Hello?"

"Kate, this is Jay Peri." I took a few seconds, trying to place him. "With Peri towing."

Oh, right. "Hi, Jay. What can I do for you?"

"Well, I was hoping you could come to Miller's pond."

I wrinkled my brow. "Is there a news event happening that I didn't get word about?" Spence monitored the police scanner almost as well as the Ladies and other town busybodies. If he didn't know about it, then it was a situation that was still happening, or one that the police didn't have word of yet.

Jay gave a strained laugh. "Oh, it'll be news all right. Get here as soon as you can."

He clicked off the phone.

I frowned, thinking that was a really weird conversation. I rummaged through my bag for my keys and called Spence to let him know he needed to send someone else to get photos of cute fair kids before they made themselves sick from all the crap they were eating, and wouldn't be cute anymore. "Where are you off to?" Spence asked after I told him I had to leave.

"I'm not quite sure," I said, arriving at my Jeep. "I got a tip that something's going on at Miller's pond."

"Hmm, sounds interesting."

The Devil Wears Tank Tops

"I'll let you know."

I hung up, and drove five miles across town. Miller's pond runs next to the road on the Miller's farm property. It's about twenty feet wide, forty feet long, and between three and five feet deep depending on how much irrigating the Millers are doing at the time. By those measurements, I felt like it was better classified as a ditch.

I pulled up next to the tow truck, and pond-ditch, and noticed something in it. I got out of my Jeep, my eyes squinting in the bright light from the late afternoon sun. All at once, the scene came into focus and I stopped dead in my tracks, my heart shooting into uneven palpitations. My dad's 1966 silver Mustang, the one he'd been meticulously working on for more than a year in an effort to combat the stress from my mom's Catasophies, was angled in, and partially submerged in the water. Apparently it wasn't an irrigating day.

Jay had just started pulling the car out of the water. I stood by and watched as one of my dad's favorite things in the world was birthed from the pond, covered in mud and dripping. Jay hopped out of the truck and said something to another guy standing by a bright orange car that looked like it had ears on top of it. I was trying to calm down by attempting to decipher the car's costume when I heard Jay's voice, "Hey, Kate."

I closed my eyes and shook my head. "Please, please, tell me that's not my dad's Mustang."

He winced. "Wish I could."

The profanity running through my head was epic. And it would be nothing compared to what my dad would actually verbalize when he heard about this. "How did it end up in the ditch?" I already had an excellent theory about *who* had deposited it there, and it said something that the thought of my dad driving it into the pond didn't cross my mind even once.

I looked around and saw two wide eyes peeking above the hood of the tow truck and recognized them as being attached to the means of Mustang destruction. Her hair was sticking out in every possible direction, and her gaze went back and forth in a jittery motion. She looked like me the time I'd accidentally ordered a drink with six shots of espresso in my morning coffee instead of two. I stared at her, wondering what in the world was going on. She looked really strange. "Mom!"

She jumped up immediately, spryer than I'd seen her in a long time. "I'm fine!" she yelled, like I was suddenly hard of hearing. "Don't worry about me one little bit. And Jay says the car will dry right out." She punctuated the statement with a decisive nod, her lightning strike-like hair bouncing with the movement.

I stared at her face, really taking her in. I realized my first impression of 'strange' was an enormous understatement. Aside from the hair that looked like it had been styled by a tornado, she was wearing some weird thing tied around her head...a scarf, maybe? "Jay might be able to save the car, but I'm not sure he'll be able to save you from Dad," I answered.

She blew out a laugh through her mouth, her lips vibrating like she was blowing on a baby's stomach. "Don't be silly," she said, waving a hand in front of her face like it was completely normal to drive rare, classic cars in ditches and be forgiven for it, "I'll make him a pecan pie."

She came out from behind the truck and I froze. My eyes went over her in complete disbelief. I didn't know who had chosen her outfit, but I was fairly certain it hadn't been her. She looked like a Teenage Mutant Ninja Turtle. Her black Capri pants were tied at the bottom with some sort of material—the same material that seemed to be wrapped around her head—and she had it tied around the short sleeves of her billowy lavender top. She looked like she'd been getting fashion tips from an 80s boy band.

I was stunned speechless for a good thirty seconds. "What in the world are you wearing?" I finally asked.

Jay leaned over, his head close to mine. "I wondered about that, too," he said in a low tone, "but thought it best not to ask."

She reached down and pulled at each of the strips, tightening the material. I wasn't close enough to be sure, but it looked like the fabric might have cowboy hats on it. "Protection! That's what!"

When I thought of protection, I thought of it in two forms: self-defense, and birth control. The knotted material didn't look like it would be helpful in either case. "Protection? How is that protecting you? And from what?"

"From the mice!"

Jay nodded. "She told me about the mice. I thought she might be having some sort of breakdown, that's why I called you."

"Mice?" I asked.

"In the car!" she answered, exasperated. Jay and I stared at her in response, so she continued her explanation. "I was taking some warm brownies to the Brody family—they just had a baby, you know. My car is in the shop, so I took the Mustang instead." I was one-hundred percent certain she didn't have the authority to take the Mustang. Frankly, I was surprised my dad had given her the location of the keys. "It took a while to find the keys." There you go. "But once I did, I was ready! I walked out to the garage and saw one of the nasty little buggers run across Xena's seat. Scared the bejeebers out of me, I tell ya!" She shuddered at the memory.

"Xena?"

"The Mustang's name! Keep up, Kate!" She huffed as she put her hands on her hips. I had no idea the Mustang had a name, let alone that it had been christened after one of my teenage heroes. I wondered when that had happened. "I couldn't let it run around in there willy-nilly. I had brownies to deliver! I had to take action!"

Of course she did. Because going back inside and calling for help just wasn't her style. "So you thought it would be a good idea to drive Dad's *classic* Mustang into Miller's pond?"

She pressed her lips together, a sign that she was irritated. "No, that was Arnold's fault."

I blinked. "Arnold?"

"Yes!" she said, her voice going higher on the 's'. "Arnold the mouse. And all of his furry siblings. There were a herd of them."

The Devil Wears Tank Tops

My eyes went wide. "A herd, huh?" I waved my hand, encouraging her to go on and tell me the captivating story of Arnold and his mice herd.

She brought her index finger to her lips and gazed at the Mustang thoughtfully. "They might have been building a colony and preparing for a hostile takeover. Who knows? I can't believe your dad has never seen them. It's not like they were trying to hide. And a few of them are downright evil. Not Arnold, but some of his family members are little delinquents."

With a lot of my mom's "adventures," there's often too much information to digest all at once. You have to break it down and take it a bit at a time or you get completely overwhelmed and don't even know where to start. It's a good thing being a reporter had trained me for these situations, and growing up with my mom had probably trained me to be a reporter. "Okay, so you had your *warm* brownies, and the car was being taken over by tiny mice tyrants. How did Dad's car—I'm sorry, *Xena*—make it into the lake?"

She pressed her lips together and gave me a solid glare. If I'd been thirteen instead of twenty-five, it would have terrified me. "Well, first things first, I marched right back into the house and grabbed some quilt strips from the baby quilt I've been working on. Then I tied them around my pant legs and arms. And my head. I put that one on because it made the outfit really come together."

I stared, completely confounded. I looked to Jay for help, but he held his hands palms up and shook his head. His expression indicated he didn't know what to do with her, and really hoped I did. Unfortunately, my training—both as a reporter and as Sophie Saxee's daughter—hadn't included mice herds and fabric strips. That certainly explained her current attire, though. I had the thought that if Rambo was a quilter, he'd look a lot like my mom. "Okay, so tell me why you tied quilt strips around your legs and arms?"

"To block off access, silly! They're mouse-ties!" She said this like *I* was the crazy person. "I couldn't have Arnold and his buddies running up my pant legs or into my arm holes while I was driving! That would be dangerous!"

I gave a pointed look at the Mustang hanging from the tow truck and still dripping water onto the ground in streams. "Yes, I can see how you'd be worried about that." Her eyes narrowed and I quickly pressed on before she could remark on my level of sarcasm. "Even after seeing the mouse herd in the car, you still decided to take it to the Brodys' house?"

Her brows pushed together and her mouth fell open a bit, incensed. "Of course I did! The brownies were warm! Priorities, Kate!"

I shook my head, astounded. Only my mother would risk a mouse attack and car accident to get warm brownies delivered before they cooled. The postal service had nothing on my mom.

She kept talking, "Luckily, I had one of those spider trapping sticky pads in the garage by the door. Those pads are so helpful!" She paused, her face wrinkling in thought. "It already had some dead spiders on it, but…"

"Warm brownies," I offered by way of explanation.

"Exactly!" she said with wide smile, happy that I finally understood.

"So you were on your way to the Brodys'. Then what?"

"Well, I'd only seen one mouse running around when I was in the garage. Little did I know there were actually hundreds!"

My eyebrows shot up. "Hundreds?" I looked to Jay. He lifted his shoulders and hands in an "I don't know" gesture.

"Yes!" She exclaimed. "I knew they were all hiding out under my seat, so I stomped my feet on the floor while I was driving, alternating feet to be safe, you know. I figured my feet probably looked like giant killers to them, and the tiny mice wouldn't want to be where my killer feet were stomping, so they'd run the other way. That's when I captured some of them on the sticky sheet. Darn convenient those sheets. I wish entire floors could be made of them. But then I'd get stuck too…and I'd always have to replace them. Probably best I just keep them in corners and wait for bugs to land there."

She was rambling, and I had so many questions, I could barely think straight. I was seriously questioning her mental state, and wondering if I should call for help, but what would I even say? It's not like they have protocol for mice herds and Rambo quilters. Annie would probably understand, though. My mom broke my thought process as she continued. "The mice were running around the car, and then they started to gather on the floor of the passenger side next to their stuck comrades. They were tittering away, making the most horrible noises! I knew I'd be fine if I could just get to the Brodys' house. I was almost there when one of the mice, the biggest brown one—he's their king—jumped up on the passenger seat, mad as all heck! His red eyes gleamed, and I knew I was about to be attacked. He lunged, and I swerved." She lifted her arms like she was holding a pretend steering wheel, and reenacted her jerk to the side. "Reflexes like a fox, I tell ya. That's what I've got. But Xena's reflexes aren't nearly as quick as mine," she gave a forlorn look at the car. "And that's how I ended up in the ditch. I got right out and called Ned's Exterminating."

Ned held back a snicker as he waved. So that's why the other car looked like it had ears. I glanced at it again, this time noticing it also had a little black tail. "You called the exterminator before the tow truck, or anyone else?"

"Of course I called the exterminator first! There were vermin that needed to be eradicated!"

I closed my eyes and pinched the bridge of my nose. "I'd like to be there when you explain that getting warm brownies to acquaintances was more of a priority than Dad's prized car."

She wrinkled her nose. "Oh, fooey," she said, her tone dismissive. "You worry too much. It's not his Fastback. This is just the one he tinkers with."

She was lucky it wasn't his Fastback, or I'd have to help him hide her body. And I wouldn't do well in prison. "How many mice are now stuck to the pad?" I asked, wondering if Ned could help liberate any of them.

"At least two." Her lips pulled down as she thought about it. "I think they died from the water."

"Oh my gosh!" I yelled, horrified. "You're a mouse murderer!"

"I am not!" Her tone took on an air of defense. "I saved myself, and Xena, from a mouse herd attack. I'm sorry I couldn't save the mice, but they shouldn't have broken into and entered the car, the little B & E bandits. If they hadn't, they'd all still be perfectly alive, running around in a nice field and they would have never even met me."

Given her current mental state, I decided it best not to say that I was sure there were a lot of people who had similar sentiments about her impact on their lives—my dad included. People frequently called him a saint.

"Any who, I feel really bad about the little furry fiends dying. I didn't want them in the car, but I didn't want to kill them either…just relocate them. I didn't really have enough people for a funeral, but I did say a prayer that they enjoyed their lives, and judging by all the mouse tracks, they had a fantastic time on their last day in your dad's car!" Her lips lifted in a wide smile. She seemed genuinely happy the mice had had a chance for frolicking before she killed them all. Her justification methods were astounding. She could be a politician.

I put a hand to my temple and closed my eyes before turning to the exterminator. "Where are all the mice now?"

"Well, Kate, that's the thing," Ned the exterminator shifted from foot to foot, biting the side of his lip like he was delaying his answer. Finally he looked up at me with sincere eyes. "We didn't find any mice."

My mom's eyes bulged. Mine were pretty big as well. "What do you mean you didn't find any?" I asked.

He looped his thumbs in his pockets and shook his head. "I searched the whole car once we pulled it out of the lake. There's no trace of a mouse in the space."

"Liar!" My mom yelled, pointing. Her demeanor, frizzy hair, and wild eyes reminded me of the woman in the cottage from *The Princess Bride*. "You can see tracks all over the seats and floor!"

The exterminator raised a brow. "Actually, Mrs. Saxee, I couldn't. Do you want to show me where you found them?"

My mom's mouth fell open at the insinuation that she might be wrong, and heat started rising in her face. I knew this look. I'd been the recipient of it many times as a child, and nothing good had followed. "Do I want to show you? Do I want to *show* you?" Her voice was getting higher with each word. "Oh, you bet your pretty pants I'll show you." She marched past me, grumbling about having to do someone else's job for them. She swung the door open and started pointing to the tracks. We'd all followed her to witness the tracks ourselves, but I couldn't see anything either. She opened the door and pointed at the passenger seat, which was still slightly damp. "See! Right there! The prints are everywhere!" Her hand went over the area in a wide sweep.

Jay, Ned, and I all looked at where she was pointing, and then exchanged a worried glance. There was nothing there. No trace of mice, or their tiny little footprints. But my mom was agitated enough that I knew better than to disagree with her. I looked at Jay and Ned, giving them a nod to indicate they should just play along. "Right. They're right there." I took my mom by the shoulders. "Why don't we let Jay tow Xena back to the house, and I'll take you home."

My mom, feeling sufficiently vindicated, nodded in agreement, and went to get in my Jeep. I gave Jay instructions on towing the car, and paid both him and Ned. I didn't think there was much in my account to pay them with, but the card cleared, so I took it as a win.

As I started to leave, Ned said, "I can't wait to tell people I was a Catasophie witness!"

I winced, thinking this little adventure was bound to start the Ladies' gossip phone tree and answered, "It's not really a distinguished list."

After a discussion with my dad about less than stellar prison food and beatings, he agreed not to murder my mom. We were both concerned about her stranger-than-usual behavior, though, and my dad set up an appointment to take her to the doctor.

I made it home and had just crashed on the couch when my phone buzzed with a reminder text from Annie about dinner tomorrow night. I smiled, thinking of hanging out with friends like a normal twenty-something instead of my usual schedule, which involved things like skunk pits, hot air balloon crashes, crazy teenagers with guns, cow suicides, and now fake mice herds.

Chapter Six

I spent the afternoon at the *Tribune* office catching up on some things. It was pretty quiet because most people were still at the fair. I'd already written the story about Opie's lemonade stand crash, and tried to call the hospital for more information about his condition. They'd been less than helpful, which was pretty typical. I'd also called the Saints and Sinners cookie company for an interview, but got a voice mail. I left my name and number. I was in the middle of finishing an article about the fair auctions—with lots of photos of kids and the animals they'd sold—when Spence came in.

"Hey," I said, leaning back in my seat and raising my hands above my head to stretch.

"Hi," he said, his lips lifting slightly. He was wearing a nice pair of black slacks that hugged his lean muscled frame, and a button down emerald shirt with sharp lime pinstripes. It looked fantastic against his mocha skin. He was hot as hell, and had a lot less baggage than the other men in my life—unfortunately, I wasn't his type. I whistled at his clothes choice. "Lookin' good! Where are you off to?"

He glanced down at his clothes, a slow smile stretching over his face. "The fair." His voice held a bit of hesitance, and was not at all convincing.

"Yeah, right," I said, my tone disbelieving. "That outfit doesn't exactly scream cattle, pigs, and deep fried Twinkies. Plus, the other night I had to cover for you on the hot air balloon crash, and I heard a rather masculine laugh in the background when you called. What gives. Who have you been hanging out with?"

His smile widened, a secret clearly hidden behind his lips. "A friend."

A quirked a brow. "A friend? Or a *friend?*"

He thought about it before committing to an answer. "A friend I'm hoping is on the way to becoming a *friend.*"

My eyes lit up. I wanted Spence to be happy, and knew that was a hard request in a place like Branson Falls where gay people were still often ostracized. I was worried about what would happen when he finally came out of the closet to someone other than me. Apparently he was, too, because the minute the door chime went off, indicating someone had just walked in the back door of the building, he stopped talking.

"Hey ya, Katie!" Ella said, wandering in with her giant purse slung over her shoulder. The purse was bigger than she was, and could easily be used as a weapon.

I took a deep breath. "I'm never going to be able to get you to stop calling me Katie, am I?" Drake had started it, and I kind of hated him for it.

"Nope," she said, leaning against my desk. "And speakin' of Drake, he was seen buyin' condoms at the convenience store the other day. Word is you're the lucky gal. How was it?"

My jaw dropped and I couldn't speak for at least thirty seconds. "Are you kidding me?"

She shook her head rapidly.

"So just because one of the men everyone thinks I'm having an affair with—even though I'm not—buys condoms, we're having wild monkey sex?"

Ella's eyes went wide. "Who said anythin' about monkeys?" She paused and seemed to be thinking. "Is that even possible?"

I rolled my eyes. "I don't know who he was buying condoms for, but it certainly wasn't me. I've had a *long* dry spell." One I wasn't happy about.

Ella nodded and gave me a sympathetic look. "Me, too." But her dry spell was for religious reasons and the fact that most men her age were dead. Mine because I was slightly terrified of my sex partner options.

"I assume the Ladies told you about this?"

"Yep."

"Speaking of that, I have a bone to pick with you," I said, pointing at her. "Why didn't you tell me about the Facebook page?"

Ella toed the sage colored high-traffic carpet with her shoe and looked in every direction but at me. "What page?"

I shook my head and winged a brow. "Don't try to pretend like you don't know what I'm talking about. When was it started?"

She plopped down in a seat at an empty desk across from me. "The Ladies started it a couple of weeks ago. Thought it would be easier to keep track of you that way."

I took a few deep, calming breaths so I wouldn't try to kill someone. I needed to turn on Neil Diamond. His soothing songs had stopped me from committing murder on several occasions. I put my hands on my hips. "You need to get me in that group," I said to Ella.

Her mouth opened in a surprised "O" as she gestured to herself. "Me? Why me?"

"Because you're the only one I know who can."

She shook her head over and over again. "I don't think I could do it. They don't want you seein' what they're sayin'."

"I know. That's exactly why I want to be in the group."

She looked at me thoughtfully. "Let me think about it and see if I can figure out a way."

"Thanks, Ella," I said, meaning it. "Hey, have you heard any more on Opie's condition?" I asked her. As one of the Ladies—one of the non-crazy ones, at least, most of the time—I thought she might have more information than I'd been able to gather from Annie and my subsequent check in at the hospital—which had gotten me nowhere.

Ella didn't answer and looked like she was staring off into space. "Ella!"

She jumped. "Sorry, I was still thinkin' about the monkeys."

I was working on the newspaper layout when my phone started playing "Sweet Caroline." This time, I recognized the number, and thought I should probably assign him his own song considering how often he was calling me lately. "Hey, Bobby."

"Hi, Kate. I have some news about the body we found in the sugar factory."

"What did you find out?" I'd been waiting for the info from Bobby before calling Kory Greer, the sugar factory owner.

"We're still tryin' to identify the body…it's hard in a fire situation. But we know it wasn't any of the factory workers, and we don't believe the person was from around here."

"Do you know what they were doing at the factory?"

"Not yet. We're lookin' into it." He paused. "The body was a bit mangled thanks to the explosion."

I wrinkled my brow, unsure whether I really wanted to ask my next question, but going for it anyway. "What do you mean 'mangled'?"

"Well…" he hedged and seemed like he really didn't want to go on before saying, "the body was missin' arms and legs."

I blinked and it took me several seconds to recover. "Arms and legs?" I muttered.

"It probably happened during the explosion. It was a lot of force."

The image made me recoil. "That's horrifying."

"It wasn't pretty to see in person, either."

I couldn't imagine it was. "Anything else you can tell me about it?"

"Not right now."

"Okay. Thanks, Bobby." I hung up.

I took a few deep breaths to try to get the thought of mutilated bodies out of my head, then dialed the number for Kory Greer, the sugar factory owner. I got his assistant and told her my name. She put me through to Kory.

"This is Kory."

"Hi, Kory. This is Kate Saxee with the *Branson Tribune*. I'm covering the story on your sugar factory fire, and I have a couple of questions if you have time."

"Sure, Kate," he said, his voice a rich baritone. "What can I do for you?"

"Do you know what caused the fire?" The theory was sugar dust, but I thought Kory might have more information.

"The firefighters are still investigating, but we think it might have been a spark from an old machine. We've been having problems with one of our mills lately, and we were going to have a new machine installed this week. The machine could have sparked and caused a fire at any time; we were just lucky it happened on a night no one was working."

That was pretty lucky...and convenient. "Do you plan to reopen the factory in the future?"

"We've moved production off-site for now. The location is smaller, but everyone should be able to keep their jobs. We'll rebuild the main factory as soon as the insurance money comes through."

"That's good. I'm sure your employees appreciate that. Jobs are hard to come by in small communities."

"I agree."

I knew the police had talked to Kory about the body, and I needed to ask him about it too. There was no real way to ease into a question involving charred, mutilated remains. I just decided to go for it. "One more question. The police said a body was found in your building. Do you have any idea what the person was doing there?"

His tone became morose. "I wish I did. I'm sad someone lost their life."

"So you don't think you knew the person?"

"Not that I'm aware of. But they're still trying to identify the body. If I had to guess, I'd say it was probably someone who got caught in the fire during a robbery. The person could have been anyone, though."

"They picked a bad night to break into your building if that's the case."

"Yes. I hope the person's family will be okay."

A thought struck me. "Do you think the person had something to do with starting the fire?"

"That's one of the things the firefighters and police are investigating."

"Okay. Thanks for your time, Kory. I appreciate it."

"Anything to help. Have a nice day, Kate."

I thought it was pretty coincidental that the fire had started the same time someone broke into the building. I had a feeling the two were connected, I just didn't know how. I'd wait until I had an identity for the body, and go from there.

Chapter Seven

I stopped by the store to get some sparkling cider for Annie and her husband, Rich. Sparkling cider was the equivalent of wine in Utah, and I tried to keep it on hand for social gatherings—though, I rarely attended any. Really, I should have brought Jell-O or a casserole like most people in Branson, but it had been a long week and I didn't have it in me to cook anything. My recent war with my bread maker helped solidify the fact that I wasn't a capable cook—even if a machine was doing the work for me—and shouldn't be making food for myself, let alone other people. I had no interest in being the cause of someone's food poisoning. Sparkling cider was a much safer option.

I didn't even have to knock before Annie was opening the door of their recently built, two-story home. The upper story of the house was a latte colored stucco, and the lower half was a red and beige brick that complimented the stucco. The fact that Annie was so Johnny-on-the-spot made me think she'd been watching for me.

"I heard there was a situation with your mom yesterday," Annie said as I stepped into the house. She was wearing a long black skirt and teal shirt with cap sleeves. It complimented my own outfit—a white skirt with big black flowers, long white tank top, and sea green beaded bracelet and necklace—well.

My mom's mouse adventure was probably the reason Annie had been watching for me. I'd have wanted to know about it too if I hadn't seen it firsthand. I snorted a laugh. "'Situation' describes it mildly."

Her eyes got bigger with intrigue. "Apparently there was a tow truck and an exterminator present?"

I sighed and followed Annie through her house—decorated in relaxing, cool tones of blues and whites—to the backyard. They had a wood pergola, stained a deep shade of brown, and a misting system to keep it cool in the hot summer months. I loved her for that alone. It was like having air conditioning outside, and I decided I might never leave.

I handed her the bottle of cider. She opened it and poured us each a glass before we both settled into the comfortable patio chairs with thick cushions. "Yeah, she thought she saw a bunch of mice running around inside my dad's Mustang while she was delivering some brownies and crashed into Miller's pond. The exterminator couldn't find any evidence of mice, though." I took a sip. It was very sweet, and tasted just like carbonated apple cider. "My dad didn't kill her when he heard about the submerged car—that was a surprise."

Annie laughed and laughed. "Her brownies are pretty amazing. I bet the recipients were glad she tried to get them there."

I shook my head. "She didn't even get to deliver them. The brownies got wet with everything else." A fact she'd been rather upset about. Even more upset than the knowledge that she'd crashed my dad's car after a probably fake mice herd had staged a revolution. "I took her home for my dad to deal with. I could see him sprouting new gray hairs with each new piece of information I explained."

"But you said there were no mice?"

"Nope. It was strange—even for her. My dad made her an appointment with the doctor."

"A lot of strange things have been happening lately," Annie said. "I mean, we get our share of weird—mostly from your mom—but we've had a lot of odd stuff happening the last few weeks. And the hospital has been pretty busy."

That piqued my interest. "Weird things like what?"

Annie shrugged. "A lot of car accidents—mostly fender benders, but more than usual. Barney Jacobs had a full-on conversation with his farm animals, and was convinced one of them was planning a hostile takeover of his barn."

I suppressed a laugh at the image that conjured up. I wondered if he'd been reading *Animal Farm*.

"And we've had some calls about heart palpitations and fatigue. I mean, it's not stuff that would normally stand out, but it's just happening a lot. Must be something in the water."

I snorted at the hypothesis. "Like pregnancy." It seemed like everyone I knew always got pregnant at once.

Annie laughed.

"Then again, this is Utah where everyone is always pregnant anyway."

Annie nodded, picking up a handful of crackers she'd brought out earlier with hummus as an appetizer. "Rich and I haven't had kids yet. The whole church congregation seems rather concerned about it."

I rolled my eyes. "Of course they are. Because people's procreation choices are *everyone's* business."

"Around here…" she trailed off as she tilted her head to the side in annoyed acceptance.

"How long have you been married?"

"Three years."

"They probably think you're barren," I said, totally serious. A couple without kids in Mormon-heavy Branson was rarer than a Bigfoot sighting.

She nodded. "And they're not afraid to ask about it, either."

I could tell Annie was frustrated by it. I would be too. I hated having my own choices questioned, and Annie and Rich's membership in the church meant they had to justify their decisions to the masses constantly. I didn't know what their reasons for staying childless were, but it was none of my damn business. "It's so ridiculous," I said, getting more annoyed as I thought about it. "And it really pisses me off. I've had friends who want kids and can't have them, but they're constantly being asked about it anyway. It makes them feel horrible. And I've had other friends who just don't want kids, but they get harassed about that and called selfish. It's such a personal decision. People who can't be parents, or don't want to be parents, shouldn't have to explain their choices to anyone else."

Annie smiled as she finished eating a cracker. "I think we're kindred spirits."

I smiled back as I leaned forward to reach the appetizer tray. "I agree," I said, dipping my own cracker in hummus as Rich, came out of the house holding a pitcher of mixed drinks. And by 'mixed drinks,' I mean Sprite-spiked fruit punch—a Branson staple. "Hey Rich!" I said. We'd been introduced earlier this summer when I ran into Rich and Annie at a town party.

"Hey, Kate," he said, nodding in my direction.

I noticed someone was following behind him. Huge shoulders with a muscular build framed the body in the doorway.

"Look who I found at the grocery store," Rich said.

I swore under my breath as every last, large, looming part of him came into focus.

"We were talking in the produce section and he didn't have plans," Rich, a business analyst for a healthcare company, explained, "so I invited him along."

Of course Rich did. Because apparently, one night of relaxing with normal people I liked spending time with was something completely out of the realm of possibility for me.

Annie glared at Rich before giving me a consoling smile. I knew she was remembering my experience earlier this week that had sent me to the grocery store for coping treats. "Hi, Drake," Annie said.

Drake's mouth slid into a smile as he met my eyes and held them for several seconds before turning his attention to Annie. "Thanks for having me, Annie." He held up a bag. "I brought cookies."

Annie's eyes widened as she recognized the bag. "Saints and Sinners Cookies? How did you get those? I thought they sold out at the fair."

Drake grinned. "They did."

Great. Now he was going to be revered not only as Branson's most eligible bachelor, but also the freaking cookie wizard. He could conjure up treats by sheer willpower alone. I frowned as I thought about it. He probably made a deal with the devil to get them. I took a deep breath and fought to come up with something that wouldn't be antagonistic. "Drake. Shouldn't you be off somewhere hitting on teenagers?" I failed.

His eyes raked over me as his expression darkened. If I didn't know better, I'd say he was turned on. But men like Drake were always turned on, so I didn't take it personally. "They're not who I want to be hitting on."

My eyes widened at the same time I noticed Annie quirk her brow and stare at us thoughtfully. I gave her a look back that said, *don't read into it. He's paid to lie and charm people.*

The Devil Wears Tank Tops

However, I didn't like the insinuation in Drake's statement. Okay, so that was a lie. I *did* like it, but I didn't want to deal with what my liking it might mean. And Annie noticing Drake's interest didn't help anything either. I needed a subject change. Immediately. "I don't know why everyone's making such a big deal over these cookies," I said, pointing to the bag of chocolaty sweets. "They look pretty normal to me."

Annie's eyes widened like I'd said something sacrilegious. "Have you tried them?"

No, in fact, I hadn't. Probably because I thought my mom would murder me if I did. She still wasn't over her cookie slight at the fair. She'd even mumbled about it on the way home after the mouse-tie incident, saying something about how she'd been trying to replicate the recipe for two days, but couldn't figure out what was in "those gosh darn cookies."

"Not yet," I answered.

Annie grabbed the bag off the table, her face a study in disbelief. "You have to try one *right* now! I can't get enough!"

"In the grocery store, you said they weren't as good as my mom's."

"Oh," she said, pausing to think about it. "Well, they're close, and they're available at the store. Your mom's aren't."

I took the cookie, examining it. It looked like every other cookie on the planet, and I couldn't figure out why everyone seemed to be in treat tizzy. "Have you had them yet, Drake?" Annie asked.

"I tried one a couple of days ago. They were really good."

She offered the plate to him, but he shook his head, putting his hand up. "Not tonight."

Annie looked taken aback. "But you bought them!"

"I haven't been to the gym in a couple of days."

I snorted, and Drake sent me a mildly amused glance. I rolled my eyes. I mean, I appreciated the fact that he cared about his body and went to the gym—every woman who set eyes on him did—but treat deprivation seemed extreme. He and I would never work for that reason alone. I paused, totally stunned that I'd been thinking of us working in any capacity. What in the hell was wrong with me? Unwilling to deal with this newest revelation about myself in regard to Drake, I blurted, "There's not much point to living if you can't enjoy it." I immediately took my first Saints and Sinners bite in an attempt to give myself something to do other than think or speak. The cookies were delicious: peanut butter dipped in thick milk chocolate, but frankly, I thought my mom's were far better. I wasn't sure why everyone was in such a fit over these.

"I agree," Drake said. "And I do. In moderation."

I snorted again at that and almost spewed cookie crumbs. Moderation my ass. "I've heard about your moderation."

Annie excused herself to go help Rich in the kitchen. Alone with Drake was not something I was comfortable with. Ever. I could never decide if I wanted to punch him, or kiss him. It was a problem. One that was clearly getting bigger each time I saw him.

The Devil Wears Tank Tops

"I've told you not to believe everything you hear," he said, pointedly.

I shrugged. "When you hear something repeatedly, it's hard to ignore."

His lips flattened like he was frustrated. He took a breath and said, "Speaking of rumors, I hear you're still dating that idiot, Hawke."

I gave him a condescending smile. "I heard you were buying condoms recently. I'd think someone with your experience would know better than to get them in town. Must have been an emergency. So, who's the lucky Barbie Bimbo you're screwing this week?"

His hands tightened slightly where they were resting on his legs. "I wasn't buying condoms. I had a stomach bug and needed something to stop me from dying. The grocery store was already closed, so I had to go to the convenience store."

I ran my tongue over the inside of my cheek. "Uh huh. Pepto and Trojans are *so* easily confused." Truly, it was entirely possible. If Drake showed up at the convenience store in the middle of the night, people would automatically assume he was there for booty call accessories, not medicine.

"Believe me or don't. It's still the truth." He paused. "And you should be careful calling the women I date names—considering you're one of them."

I gave a disbelieving laugh. "We've never dated. And you know it."

Drake lifted his hand and started ticking off points. "You went to the party at the legislature with me, we went to dinner at the Mexican restaurant together, my car has been seen at your house on multiple occasions, and you sat with me on my blanket to watch the fireworks in the park," he said. "In the eyes of Branson residents, not only are we dating, we have a serious relationship."

I rolled my eyes. "We've never dated. That's that."

He steepled his fingers as he studied me. "Why does it bother you so much that people think we're together?"

"Because of your reputation."

He blew out a long-suffering sigh. "Come on, Katie. Ryker Hawkins? It doesn't even sound like a real name. Hawke's reputation is much worse than mine. You date him openly, and don't care what people say. What's different about me?"

I leaned back in my chair and crossed my legs, resting my hands in my lap. "Because to me, your womanizing reputation is much worse than anything Hawke's done. Men who wish they hadn't gotten married within six months of ending their Mormon missions are living through your conquests. Your love life is legendary. And somehow, you get away with it without the guilt and judgment every other Mormon in town gets—especially women. It's an absurd double standard—"

"I agree."

I stopped mid-soap box. "I'm sorry, you what?"

"I agree. With everything you said." His eyes and tone were completely sincere, and I was stunned at his opinion, and that he wasn't afraid to share it. He elaborated further, "Men are judged much less harshly in our community than women. I don't like it, and I don't agree with it. But I'd also like to remind you that rumors are rumors regardless of gender. I've told you before that you shouldn't believe everything you hear. Those same men who are telling stories about my conquests and trying to live through me are embellishing stories just as much as the Ladies. Half of the things they say I've done haven't happened at all, and the other half are exaggerated beyond recognition."

It was hard to believe Drake was telling the truth, but having been the victim of Branson's rumor mill myself, I couldn't write off his explanation completely. "It makes it hard to figure out who you really are, Drake. I can't trust what people say about you, and I can't trust you, either. I don't know you well enough."

A muscle worked at his jaw. "But you think you can trust Hawke? You've known him less time than you've known me. And Hawke is one of the most dangerous men you've ever met."

I shook my head, taking a drink of my cider. "You keep saying that about him, but he's never been threatening around me."

"Every time he's even in your vicinity he's a threat to you. He's not the type of person you want to be connected to, Katie."

Drake had serious issues with Hawke, and Hawke didn't seem particularly fond of Drake either. I wanted to know why. "What's the problem between you two? Why do you hate each other?"

Drake shrugged. "Ask him."

"I have," I answered. "Now I'm asking you."

He looked at me, eyes narrowing. "It's between me and Hawke."

I rolled my eyes again and caught Annie's gaze. I didn't realize she'd come back outside, and wondered how long she'd been there, and what she'd heard. She seemed to be completely riveted by my interaction with Drake. Luckily, Annie was my friend, and Annie and Rich weren't the gossiping type. But I figured I better tone it down for the rest of the night. The best way to do that would be to not really interact with Drake. So that's exactly what I did for the next two hours—avoid, avoid, avoid.

Eat a cookie. Ignore Drake.

Eat my hamburger. Ignore Drake.

Drink my Sprite-spiked fruit punch. Ignore Drake.

More cookies. More ignoring. I wasn't sure, but it seemed like the cookies were getting better the more I ate. Or maybe I was just happy to have something keeping my mouth full.

I could only avoid Drake for so long, however. And when it was time for me to leave, Annie handed me the remaining Saints and Sinners cookies—a hostess concession I was sure she'd regret making since she liked them so much—and Drake decided he would leave at the same time as me.

He followed me to my Jeep. His ginormous, ridiculous, planet-hating bright yellow Hummer was blocking my way. I wasn't surprised. Drake liked to take over things, driveways included. I'd been hopelessly in love with him as a teenager, but I'd learned my lesson. While I'd grown up looking at him with awe and unrealistic hopefulness, my college women's studies class had made me see him for what he was: a raging egotistical womanizer who reminded me far too much of my old boyfriend—a man who wanted a Stepford Wife, not a woman with a brain. Now I just needed to remind my conflicting hormones of that.

Drake opened my Jeep door for me and I got in, hoping that meant our discussion was over. I hoped too soon. "Why do you dislike me, Katie?"

I took a deep breath, not wanting to have this conversation. At all. "I dislike what you represent. We've talked about this before. We even talked about it earlier tonight."

"Because you think I represent jerks who treat women poorly?"

I hedged. Well, he hadn't done anything that I'd *seen*...but still. I'd heard enough to warn me off.

"Have I done something to make you think I'm a womanizer, Katie?"

I stared at him. Of course he had. He was born. You couldn't look like that and not be a womanizer. "I saw the girls you dated in high school, Drake. And I've heard enough about the women you've dated since to know you're not looking to settle down. You just get away with sleeping around because all the men you socialize with are living through you, and the women hope they'll be your next conquest."

A muscle worked at his jaw. "So everything you've heard is based on rumor. You have no facts that I'm this jerk who's just looking for the next woman with big boobs who will take her clothes off."

I used a line that had been used on me recently. "When you hear a rumor enough, there's usually some grain of truth it started from."

"If you really believed that, you wouldn't be happy with what's being said about you right now. It involves a corn field."

I was able to refrain from stomping my foot and shouting. Barely. I really thought I'd gotten away with that one. "Sheesh! I wish people would stay out of my personal life!"

Drake arched a brow. "Exactly."

"You're a public figure. It's different," I said, shutting my door. The window was already down—small town and all.

"It's really not. I'm being gossiped about because I live in a small town, just like you. I told you: don't believe everything you hear."

I stared at him. He had a point, but still. He hadn't given me anything solid to refute the gossip I'd heard. I was a reporter and worked in facts. Facts I could understand and move forward with. Blind faith was significantly harder.

"Have you investigated any of the stories you've heard about me to see if they're true?" he asked.

Uh…no. I hadn't. And I wasn't sure why. When everyone had warned me to stay away from Hawke, I'd defended him tirelessly, and then went to Google and the *Tribune's* background check software to get facts to back him up. I had no idea why I'd been so quick to defend Hawke, and even quicker to believe the horrible gossip about Drake.

Drake must have read the answer in my expression. His lips tightened as he nodded once. He turned to leave, but stopped abruptly and walked back over to me. Good grief, he took up a lot of space. Cavegirl Kate liked that. Cavegirl Kate was a traitor.

Drake put his hand on my windowsill and leaned down, his face inches from mine. "And for the record, I've been hung up on one particularly infuriating woman for years. Then I heard she was moving back to town and becoming the editor of the *Branson Tribune*. I haven't dated anyone since."

My mouth dropped. I couldn't have been more shocked if Neil himself had just shown up and started singing "Cracklin' Rosie."

"I might not be able to change everyone's mind about me, Katie. But I'll prove I'm not the person you think I am."

My mouth was still hanging open as he walked away.

Chapter Eight

I stretched as I woke up and smiled. I'd slept like a log, and it was the best night of sleep I'd had in years. Still groggy, I wet my lips and rolled over, hitting the alarm clock. That's when I noticed something strange. My black silk robe was covering my arm. I rubbed my eyes, sure I was still dreaming. When I opened them again, the silk robe was covering my other arm as well, and tied in a haphazard bow around my waist. This was the robe I wore to make toast in the morning after my shower, not one I wore to bed—especially when it was as hot as the inside of a volcano outside.

I threw my legs over the side of my bed, trying to remember the previous night, but my memory was fuzzy. I'd gone to Annie's for dinner, then I'd come home. I'd sat down on the couch to watch TV with my bag of cookies and some milk, and I thought I'd fallen asleep there. So how did I get to my bed?

To say I was disturbed by my lack of memory was an understatement. I was in the beginning stages of a freak out. One that escalated to full-on meltdown when I untied my robe and found I was wearing my sexiest, see-through except for a few strategically placed pieces of lace, black and hot pink lingerie.

I had no recollection of how it got on my body. My heart was racing as I walked through the house, hoping that something would trigger my memory—and hoping also that the something wouldn't be a strange man. I paused and frowned—or a familiar one.

The house was empty as I padded down the hallways on my hardwood floors. I went in the kitchen and noted that the back door was locked and secure. Every room I'd checked so far didn't include my secret, stray lover. When I got to the front room, I noticed the bottom door handle lock was secure, but the deadbolt hadn't been engaged. I locked the deadbolt every night without fail so that seemed fishy.

I looked around my living room and noticed my cell on the coffee table. I rushed to the table and sat down to look through my messages, hoping there would be a clue as to what had happened the night before. I looked through all of my social media accounts; no information there. I scrolled through phone calls, nothing strange. No text messages either.

I furrowed my brows in total confusion. Why couldn't I remember what had happened? And why was

I wearing my throw-me-against-a-wall-and-screw-me uniform?

The only concession I had to my night of unremembered passion was the fact that I was still wearing the lingerie. If I'd done anything scandalous, my clothes would have been missing—in theory.

The questions continued to plague me all through my shower. I hated not knowing things, and not knowing something that might have involved my girl parts was upsetting, for multiple reasons, including the fact that I hadn't been laid in over a year, and really wanted it to be memorable, and preferably with a hot private investigator named Hawke. Was he even back in town?

I stretched my legs and arms a bit as I got out of the shower, testing my muscles. Considering my dry spell, if I'd done any sort of sheet gymnastics, I was sure something would have hurt. Nothing did. That made me feel better. I was relatively confidant nothing had happened other than a costume change, but I still wished I knew the exact series of events.

I thought about it on my way to work, and screwed my face up into a determined expression as I walked in the back door of the *Tribune* office. I'd figure out the lingerie mystery if it was the last thing I did. I made a pit-stop by the treat table. Spence had brought doughnuts from Frosted Paradise and considering the morning I'd already had, nothing could make me happier than carbs. I took a bite, and almost choked as I turned around, noticing my desk. There was a humongous bouquet of brightly colored flowers in the middle of it. I looked across the room at Spence's office where he was working on his laptop. "Hey," I said, my voice hesitant.

Spence glanced up from his work. "Hey, yourself. Nice flowers."

"Yeah…about that…do you know who delivered them?" I was hoping the mystery flower giver had dropped them off himself.

Spence shook his head. "They were delivered by Beautiful Bouquets this morning."

I wrinkled my nose as I stared at the appropriately named beautiful bouquet like it was a ticking time bomb. For all I knew, it could be. After several seconds of debate about whether to extract the card or call the police, I finally decided to read the note. I gingerly pulled the card out of its envelope, and exhaled a deep breath when nothing exploded. Sheesh. I was spending too much time with my mother.

The card had a border of frilly pink loops, and a message written on the inside in strong, angular letters. It said: *I hope I get to see your wild side again soon.*

My mouth fell open. And stayed there. I knew two men with handwriting similar to that. One I'd be happier about witnessing me in my screw-me clothes than the other. Regardless, though. It was humiliating. And the fact that I couldn't remember any details at all made it even worse. My number one goal was to avoid both Hawke and Drake until my memory decided to return, and I knew whether I should be grateful to them for not taking advantage of me, or if I should hire a hit man.

I sat back, thinking through everything all over again. I'd gone to Annie's, antagonized Drake, argued with him while checking out his great ass, and then I'd gone home and eaten myself into a cookie coma.

I picked up the phone and called Annie. "Hey," I said when she answered. "Did you or Rich have any strange reactions to our food last night?"

"No," Annie answered, confusion in her tone. "Is something wrong? Are you sick?"

I shook my head even though she couldn't see me. "No, I'm fine. I just had some memory issues this morning."

"Too much sparkling cider," Annie said, her voice teasing.

"Something like that."

"Well, let me know if you want me to take a look at you. Or if you're feeling strange, go to the hospital."

"Thanks," I said, and hung up.

I probably should have called Drake to ask him about his health situation too, but I wasn't ready to deal with that conversation if he'd been the one to see me in nothing but lace.

The thought of Drake made me remember his challenge to investigate him like I'd investigated—and defended—Hawke. I pulled up the *Tribune's* background search software and typed in his name. I got a list of all of his properties—which were substantial—bank accounts—also substantial—and found out he'd never been married. Surprise, surprise. I snorted, thinking the background check service would be envied by many women in Branson. If the Ladies knew about his financial state, they'd be trying even harder to wrangle him. Money didn't impress me; however, character did.

The background check was helpful, but not exactly what I needed for information about who Drake really was. I did a search for Dylan Drake's personal life. I found several articles about the charities he was involved in, including the children's hospital in Salt Lake. He was also a huge fundraiser for one of my favorite animal shelters. No wonder he spent so much time in Salt Lake instead of Branson. Aside from his duties with the legislature, he was on the board of trustees for so many non-profits that he'd have to live there just to make it to all the meetings.

Reading about his philanthropic efforts made my stomach flip, and I thought I might be having a change of heart about him until I clicked on images, and saw all of the women he'd been photographed with. They were all stunning with bodies that would make a goddess jealous, and ginormous boobs. I hated every single one of them. My eyes narrowed as I realized I was feeling envy for the women on Drake's arm. I didn't want to be one of them…did I? I was contemplating this unwelcome question when Spence called to me from his office. "There's a story at the high school you need to get to."

I lifted my eyes to meet his. "About what?"

"Immodest clothes. The TV news stations are on their way, and I'm sure it will go national."

I took a deep breath and rolled my eyes. Someone had probably been sent home for wearing shorts that were shorter than three inches above their knees. Legs are scary. "Okay, I'll take care of it."

I grabbed another doughnut on my way out the door. If anything could make me feel better at this point, it was copious amounts of chocolate frosting and sugar.

All high school seniors in Branson Falls had senior portraits done every summer. The photos usually had several different shots, and each student could choose which photo they wanted to use for their senior picture in the yearbook. They were supposed to pick the finished photos up on the first day of school.

Some seniors—all girls—had gone in to get their pictures and realized that their photos had been altered. Some of them were wearing a lot more clothes than they had been during their photo shoots. One girl's neckline had been altered to be higher, even though the shirt she originally wore showed no cleavage; another girl's tattoo had been removed; and three girls' tank tops now had sleeves. In every instance, the photos had been changed to correspond with Mormon Church modesty standards. I was annoyed. I thought I'd eventually get used to crazy stories relating to the church governing everything in the state, but this was ridiculous.

The Devil Wears Tank Tops

By the time I arrived, there was already a group of angry parents and students arguing in the main office. The sides were clearly divided into Team Tank Top, and Team Modesty. The arguing was impressive.

"You don't get to decide what's okay for my kids to wear," one angry mother pointed out to a mom on Team Modesty.

"Well someone has to," another angry mother shot back, "because you're not doing your job."

Blood rose in the first woman's cheeks, her anger visible. "You have no right to judge me—or my daughter."

"Your daughter's clothes are temptin' my son!" A Team Modesty mom shot back. "When he does something he shouldn't, it'll be the fault of girls like your daughter!"

I was furious at the opinion, and I wasn't the only one. Blood started to rise in Team Tank Top's face, and I could see her pulse beating furiously at her neck, adrenaline and anger coursing through her. "It's not a woman's job to regulate what someone else feels. If showing shoulders in a tank top is too tempting, someone needs to teach your son self-control. And it doesn't say much for what you think of your son if you believe seeing a girl in a tank top is going to make him an uncontrollable sex fiend."

One person on the Team Modesty turned to me and hissed, "This is all your fault. You're the one who started wearin' tank tops. You made girls think that was normal and tempted them into bein' Jezebels. You need to realize what your immodest clothes are doin' to people."

My mouth fell open. I'd been blamed for a lot of things since moving back to Branson Falls, but corrupting people as a result of my clothing choices was a new sin. I'd have to write it down so I'd make sure to remember it—and do it again. When someone tried to tell me what to do, I made it a point to do the exact opposite.

I really shouldn't have said anything, but passive-aggressive was not something I'd ever been, or ever would be. I'd rather get my feelings out on the table, deal with them, and move on instead of harboring resentment and trying to get my point across in a sneaky way that would most likely be lost on the individual anyhow. So, I spoke up, like usual. And would probably pay for it later. At least I'd been true to myself. "I believe Mormons are taught that they have the free agency to make choices, and they're not supposed to judge people for their decisions. How is your reaction to these girls' clothing choices honoring either of those things?" I asked.

The Team Modesty woman's face went fire engine red, and I could practically see the steam coming out of her ears. I could tell she wanted desperately to launch into an argument with me. The problem was, she didn't have one. No counterpoint. At all. I was certain she was about to attack something completely unrelated to my question when the principal stepped into the room. "Everyone," his voice was deep, and louder than the fervor. "Let's try to discuss this in a civilized manner," he said, attempting to calm everyone down.

Aside from my argument with Team Modesty, there were a lot of smaller arguments happening all around me. The situation was only escalating as the principal kept talking. He eventually got the two sides separated in different rooms, and that's when I was allowed to talk to them in my capacity as reporter.

I had empathy for the girls. They were sitting with their parents, and someone had procured Saints and Sinners Cookies and put them on a plate in the middle of the table. I thought that was smart; I knew from first-hand experience that desserts were a good way to diffuse emotions. The cookies looked tasty, and I wondered where they'd come from since Drake and Annie said the cookies had sold out at the fair.

"You have Saints and Sinners Cookies?" I asked one of the office assistants who had just come in with some bottled water for everyone.

She nodded. "They're selling them in a kiosk in the cafeteria before school and during lunch."

Interesting. I knew what my next stop would be. Not only did a cookie sound good, but I still hadn't been able to get the cookie company to call me back. I was hoping I'd have more luck at the kiosk.

The meeting went on, and I talked to the Team Tank Top girls and let them know I was on their side personally, even if I did have to tell Team Modesty's story in the *Tribune*. "I understand. Every time I wear a tank top in town, I get glared at."

"It's too hot!" one of the girls said, throwing her hands in the air. "And why are tank tops bad, but swimsuits are okay? The cheerleaders and dance team are allowed to break clothes rules, so why can't everyone else?"

I shook my head in disgust for the silly policies. "I never understood that either."

I went to the Team Modesty room next, and got glared at while I asked questions. I got the quotes I needed for the story, said hi to some of the TV reporters I knew who were now on the scene and getting ready to do their stand-ups for the noon news, then quietly excused myself.

Since it was just before lunch, the cafeteria was open. I looked around the room at the various kiosks. Branson students were allowed to leave campus for lunch, but with only a thirty minute meal period, it was hard to leave, eat, and get back before classes started again. Because of that, the school allowed a few restaurants around town to serve their food in the cafeteria. I saw the bright blue Saints and Sinners Cookies sign and headed in that direction. Then almost tripped when I realized who was manning the booth.

Amber Kane.

Amber was one of The Ladies, and an evil one at that—more evil than most. We'd had many run-ins, both before I left Branson Falls for college, and especially since I got back. She seemed to be under the impression that I was diddling every eligible bachelor in town. Before last night, I could have called her a complete liar. Now, I wasn't so sure.

The Devil Wears Tank Tops

Her harassment had resulted in threats from Spence, Drake, and Hawke to leave me alone. She hadn't been happy about those, either.

She looked up and saw me, her frizzy, permed hair becoming even more electric before my eyes. Her face screwed up into a look that said she might try to kill me with one of her cookies. Her hands showed white knuckles as I approached.

"Hi, Amber," I said with a too-sweet smile. "I didn't know you worked here."

Her nostrils were flaring so hard I thought they might shoot fire. "I just started."

I nodded. "How do you like the company?"

"Why," she said with a sneer, "you lookin' for a job? I bet you're great at sellin' things—like your soul."

I gave her a smile meant to be unpleasant, and asked another question instead of responding to her provocations. "Do you know the people who run the company?" I'd left two messages, but still hadn't received a phone call back. I wanted to interview them and find out more about their treats, and why they thought everyone was obsessed with their cookies.

"Selma saw you talkin' to Drake at Annie and Rich's house yesterday," Amber said.

I held back a sigh. Amber had a bee in her bonnet—as usual when it came to dealing with me. I knew I wouldn't get any other answers out of her. "Selma is almost ninety. I don't think I'd use her as one of your watchdogs." She'd probably confuse Drake and a bear.

103

"His truck was there. She's not the only one who saw it. Then, his truck was at your house for over two hours last night."

My eyes widened and I fought to keep my expression under control. Now I knew the identity of the flower sender—and the person who had gotten me to bed…at least, I hoped I knew, and that he just put me to bed, and didn't crawl in too.

My face immediately got hot as the humiliation sunk in. A humiliation I still couldn't fully remember. It wasn't like I could *ask* him what had happened. He'd think I was insane. Ugh. This would have been so much easier if my mystery lover had been Hawke. Still embarrassing, but he knew about my quirks and had his own issues. He wouldn't judge me.

I took a deep breath and put everything to the back of my mind so I could answer Amber's accusations. "Drake was at a dinner at Annie and Rich's. So was I. And it's really none of your business."

She tsked, and her lips formed an annoyed sneer. Drake had been at the top of Amber Kane and Jackie Wall's—the Ladies' leader—list of replacement husbands after they'd both gotten divorced. Drake didn't seem interested in either one of them, and for some ridiculous reason, actually seemed to be paying attention to me instead. The Ladies had made me pay for Drake's attentiveness ever since I moved back to Branson earlier this year. "You live in Branson, Kate. *Everything* is our business."

I rolled my eyes. I wasn't going to get into this with her. It wasn't worth it. I had work to do. And now I couldn't get a cookie either because Amber was serving them. She'd probably poison mine.

"Thanks, Amber. You're always such a pleasure to talk to," I said in a sarcastic tone before walking away.

I was still irritated at the photo altering, and that combined with the Amber altercation made me feel like eating all the sugar. In the world. I left to go back to the office and work on the Show a Little Shoulder story—including a comparison photo of the digitally altered pictures, and what the girls actually wore.

Chapter Nine

I got back to the office and was immediately distracted by the pretty flowers on my desk, which I now knew were from Drake. I spent a good five minutes reorganizing my space and trying to pretend they—and the implications of the message attached to them—didn't exist. I was baffled by the fact that I couldn't remember what had happened the night before. What caused selective memory loss? Ruffies? I was pretty sure I hadn't been slipped one of those. I was at a dinner with friends, not jerks who wanted to cause me harm. I lost track of time as I stared at the wall, obsessing about my memory loss, and trying to figure out what had happened to me. I finally moved the flowers to the shelf behind me so I could concentrate.

The Devil Wears Tank Tops

I decided to actually do some work and checked my email. There were several community news articles in my inbox.

If you can believe it, there are even smaller towns that surround Branson Falls. The *Branson Tribune* serves each town, and each town has a community reporter with a column to report on what has happened during the previous week. Some of the town populations are between twenty and eighty people, so that means a lot of columns are about what movies the Winns watched on Netflix that week, and the exact contents of the Jorgensens' dinner, as well as their bedtimes.

Spence came out of his office and sat on the edge of my desk. "What are you working on?"

I glanced up at him. "Editing the community news."

Spence picked up the stress ball by my stapler, and started throwing it in the air and catching it. "That's why I hired you," he said with a grin, "so you'd have to edit it instead of me."

I narrowed my eyes at him. "Why don't we get rid of the columns? There's never real news to report, and if anything important ever does happen in one of the towns, I'd be the one to write the article."

"We tried to get rid of that section," he said as the stress ball hit a stack of papers on the table behind me and knocked them to the ground.

"When?" I couldn't remember a time *The Branson Tribune* didn't have the community news.

"About a year ago. The uproar over the missing columns was legendary. There were more letters to the editor about it than there were when the Democrats got control of the House and Senate and won the presidency."

I rolled my eyes and shook my head at the ridiculousness of the situation. "I guess we'll have to keep the columns, then."

Spence nodded, and kept throwing the stress ball. I watched him for a minute, the ball going up and down, narrowly missing light bulbs and the flat screen TV on the wall behind me, before changing the subject. "How well do you know Drake?" I asked.

Spence pushed his bottom lip out. "Well enough, I guess, why?"

I lifted a shoulder slightly and tilted my head. "I'm just trying to figure out if he's the person everyone says he is."

Spence eyed me like he was dissecting my question. He opened his mouth to say something, shut it, then opened it again. "I met Drake when I first bought the *Tribune*. He was one of the nicest, most *accepting* people in town." Spence emphasized "accepting," making me think Drake might also know, or at least have suspicions, about Spence being gay. "I think he has a bad reputation, by no fault of his own. He lives in a small town. You know what that's like." I did, and that's what scared me. What if Drake really was the person I'd always dreamed he'd be. How would I handle that? "I've never seen Drake do anything to deserve the reputation he has."

"Yeah, but he's smart enough that he'd know how to cover it up, too."

Spence shook his head. "I don't think he's like that, Kate."

"His dating history alone is terrifying."

"Whose dating history? Are we talkin' about Hawke? Because I really hope we're talkin' about him. Where is he anyway? I haven't seen him for a while," Ella said, sauntering in from the archive room. She must have come in while I was at the school covering the I'm-too-sexy-for-my-shoulders story.

"Hawke's out of town on business," I answered. "I'm not sure when he'll be back."

"That's a pity," Ella frowned. "Who were you talkin' about, then?"

"Drake," Spence answered.

Ella nodded. "He does have quite the reputation with the Ladies," she paused, thinking, "but to tell ya the truth, I don't know how much of it is true, and how much of it is people blowin' smoke up other people's bums."

I raised my brows at that. "Why do you say that?"

She leaned against my desk. "I've never seen him on a date. He always seems to be workin'. Some of the Ladies have tried askin' him out, but they say he keeps turnin' them down. He hasn't been on a date in months."

I managed to keep my mouth in place. Ella has just confirmed Drake's story about not dating anyone since I came back to town. My stomach did a little flip, and my heart started to speed up. Despite the fact that I still didn't know what had happened the night before with Drake—I was still gathering the courage to ask him about it—my own research about him, plus the opinions of two people I trusted was really starting to change my mind about Dylan Drake. And that was terrifying.

"Speakin' of the Ladies," Ella said, "there was another Facebook status about you last night. Said Drake's car was at your house for a while in the wee hours of the mornin'."

I turned my lips down in distaste. "Yeah, that's what I hear."

She gave me a funny look, but kept going, "You should really be more careful about your affairs, Katie. Have him park in the garage for cripes' sake!"

"Why haven't you added me to the Facebook group yet so I can refute some of the gossip?"

"There's a Facebook group?" Spence asked.

I blew out a sigh. "Unfortunately. They're using it to keep tabs on me."

"That's—" Spence paused, searching for the word. "—dedicated."

"And crazy," I offered. "It's bat-crap crazy. Ella's trying to get me in the group."

Ella shook her head, her face lined with disappointment. "Can't do it. Even if we made you a fake account, you'd never be able to comment. And people can tell who added the member to the group. If it was ever tracked back to me, I'd be on the Ladies' poo list. And I don't want to be there. It's *not* a good place to be."

"Yeah, I know," I said. "I've been there awhile."

"But I came up with a plan." She rubbed her hands together and a twinkle gleamed in her eyes. "I can just keep you updated on the posts. Then you'll know what's goin' on, but neither one of us will get in trouble."

It seemed like that was the only option—for now. "Thanks, Ella. I appreciate it."

Spence saw the notes about the sugar factory on my desk. "Have you heard anything else about the body at the sugar factory?" he asked.

"No," I said. "Bobby's going to call me when they can release the identity. Until then, I'm stuck."

"That fire was pretty darn convenient for Kory Greer," Ella said.

Spence and I both turned to face her. "What do you mean?" I asked.

"The factory's been strugglin' for years. Rumor was he might have to take out bankruptcy."

This was new information. And brought up a lot of other questions since Kory didn't have to lay anyone off after the explosion, and seemed to be doing just fine running things out of their second facility. "So you think the fire was started on purpose for insurance money?"

Ella shrugged. "All I know is that Kory Greer's got more money now than he used to."

Interesting. I wrote myself a note to contact Kory Greer for a follow-up interview, and see if I could figure out if there was more to the story than a simple fire started by vandals or a machine.

Spence got up to answer his office phone, and Ella left for the day. I worked on the community news for another hour or so, and was just about to leave to go home for the day when I saw a large group of people walking down the sidewalk in front of the *Tribune* office. My curiosity piqued, I stood and walked to the front of the building to look out the window. The group had to be over fifty people. They were chanting something and several of them had signs. Then I noticed another group come up on the other side of the street. They were just as large, and also seemed to be yelling out a message. I felt like I was watching *West Side Story* and people were about to break out into angry song. "Spence," I yelled as I ran back to my desk and grabbed my camera. "Do you know what's going on out here?"

He looked confused and followed me out the door.

The chanting from before had turned into full on yelling—from both sides of the road. Signs on one side of the street showed pictures of marijuana leaves with a big red X over them declaring the message *Not in our state!* Signs on the other side of the street showed pictures of children, with the message *Compassion. What Would Jesus Do?*

We were currently on the pro-pot side of the street.

"Did you know this was going on today?" I asked Spence while I lifted my camera to get photos.

He shook his head, taking it in. "No idea."

"We didn't get any warning about it?" Usually when there was going to be an event that the parties wanted media attention for, a news release was sent out—or at least a social media leak campaign was started to cause intrigue.

"No. This is the first I'm hearing about a pot protest."

I shouldn't have been surprised. Utah had recently legalized hemp oil to treat epileptic seizures. The seizures were primarily affecting children, but there was a lot of discussion about the benefits of hemp oil in general, and other diseases marijuana could help treat. With so many states now legalizing pot, including Utah's bordering state, Colorado, it seemed like the nation was headed that way as well. And that didn't sit well with some people in Utah who felt like marijuana legalization was another loss on the nation's moral compass. Those people were still fighting the law.

There had been a vociferous debate about hemp oil in the Utah state legislature, and whether it would lead to an increase in the use of other drugs, as well as the addiction possibilities. Hemp oil as a way to treat seizures was new, and hadn't been vigorously tested yet, but the kids who had been able to use it as a treatment had shown incredible improvements in the number of seizures they had, and in their quality of life.

One of the main people campaigning for the legalization of hemp oil was a Branson resident, John Wilson. His sweet, three-year old daughter Brook had epilepsy, and was currently suffering from more than a hundred seizures a day. He just wanted to be able to give his daughter her medicine, without having to move out of state to do it.

Thanks to differing laws between federal regulations—where marijuana was still an illegal substance—and state regulations, like in Utah where the oil had been legalized, some of the patients who desperately needed the oil, still couldn't get it. There were problems with how it was being prescribed and controlled, as well as how to transport the oil since it was illegal for it to cross state lines from Colorado. Having a child with a disability like that and feeling helpless would be horrible. Feeling helpless and knowing the cure was only a state away and currently tied up in red tape must be absolutely aggravating.

Branson's proximity to the state border between Utah and Colorado made it a target for the illicit marijuana trade. Marijuana, and the legalization of hemp oil, and had been the subject of several city council meetings in the last few months. People on both sides had expressed their opinions—those against it were worried about the moral implications and that hemp oil legalization would lead to legalization of all drugs. People like John Wilson were for it because it would save his daughter's life.

John was a well-respected, church-going Republican, so his support of something like this had thrown a lot of people into a state of confusion over their own beliefs. Personally, I thought it was a good thing. I was all for people stepping out of their comfort zones and being forced to look at something in a new way. Judging by the supporters on the pro-pot side of the street, it had changed some opinions. But the angry "no pot" people on the other side of the street were still firmly rooted in their stance.

"How is this supposed to help?" I asked Spence, gesturing between the two sides of the street. I didn't really understand protests. All it did was let the world know people were displeased. It didn't enforce the change either side was looking for.

A small, perky woman with bright red hair and green eyes answered me instead of Spence. "Protests are taking place all over the state today at the same time."

"They are?" I asked. "No one sent information to the media about it. Why are they fighting a law that already passed?"

She shifted the sign in her hands. "Some people want the law repealed, and they're trying to make it as difficult as possible for the people who need hemp oil to actually get it. The protest was all organized online. Every city participating needed a pot protest leader." She pointed across the street. "Lydia Ackerman volunteered for Branson. She's been fighting against hemp oil legalization for months."

Of course Lydia had volunteered to lead the protest. I didn't know her well, but I knew enough to put her in the same column as the Ladies when it came to self-righteousness.

The redhead went on. "When John heard about it, he decided to organize a counter protest to let Lydia— and everyone else—know that he wasn't going to let this happen without people seeing both sides of the debate."

"Good for him," I said, sincerely. As a reporter, I had to remain objective, but personally, I thought it was ridiculous marijuana hadn't been legalized decades ago. Alcohol was more addictive than pot, and fit the definition of controlled substances far more than marijuana. I thought the war on drugs was a complete waste of tax-payer money, and fueled the problem. There were drug kingpins worth more than entire countries because we were fighting so hard not to let people get it. When someone says something is unattainable, people want it even more.

I went over to speak to John. "Hi, John. I'm Kate Saxee with *The Branson Tribune*." I was pretty sure he already knew that, but felt the need to let him know I was there as a reporter.

"Hi, Kate. Thanks for covering this."

He was wearing a shirt with a photo of his daughter on it. Above the photo it said, "Hemp oil could save her life. Please…don't kill my daughter." My heart constricted in my chest at the thought of his little girl suffering needlessly. As far as opinion changing campaigns went, I thought his shirt was a pretty effective one. And anyone fighting against them must have a heart of coal.

"To tell you the truth, we didn't even know about it until I saw people marching past our front door. I know Lydia spearheaded the protest here, but who's in charge of it statewide? And what other cities are involved?"

Lines formed at the corners of his eyes in frustration. "It was all organized online. Lydia has been one of the most vocal anti-hemp oil protesters in the state. She's just the leader of the Branson protest, though. There are at least fifteen other protests taking place around the state right now. They were organized by a marketing company in Salt Lake City."

"Do you know who hired the marketing company?"

He closed his eyes briefly and shook his head. "No. It could be any number of people. There were no shortages of citizens who disagreed with the hemp oil bill. We were lucky that we had some strong supporters like Dylan Drake in the legislature to help us get it through. His connections with people in Salt Lake—and especially at the children's hospital—really helped us. I don't think it would have passed without him."

I didn't know Drake had helped with that. The bill had passed before I moved back to Utah. I had just been around to see the angry fallout since. Drake's help made sense though. He didn't like to brag about his work with charities, but I already knew he was on the board of trustees for the children's hospital, and philanthropy work was important to him. He wouldn't have let John's daughter suffer if there was anything at all he could do to help. I really admired that about him.

John pulled me out of my Drake thoughts. "Even now that the bill has passed, these special interest groups are still trying to get the law reversed. And they've made it extraordinarily difficult to get the medicine." His statement echoed what the red haired woman had said too.

I shook my head in frustration. "I'm sorry, John. I can't even imagine how you must feel. Is there anything you can do to get the oil?"

"We've registered for hemp oil cards, but since the oil still isn't being produced in Utah, we have to wait for out-of-state vendors. It takes a long time to grow the strain and make the oil. There's a long waiting list of parents with kids who desperately need it. And then there's the additional risk of transporting the oil across state lines."

"You can't be prosecuted under state law though, right?"

"No, but it's still illegal federally. Meanwhile, my daughter sits at home, having seizures every couple of minutes. This isn't a game. It's not politics. It's a little girl who needs medicine to save her life, and people on a high horse who think they know better than everyone else trying to make decisions for the world. They don't know what I go through. I'd dare any one of the protesters or special interest groups to watch their kids go through that kind of hell and still stand back and fight against the only thing that would help them. They wouldn't be able to do it unless they had no soul."

I doubted many of them did have a soul, but I agreed with John. No one should have to go through that, and the people fighting against the use of hemp oil should have to stand in a room and watch what they were making his daughter—and all kids like her—go through. "I don't understand why people are protesting it. It's not even marijuana. It's an extract of the oil. It can't get people high."

John shook his head. "Most of the public is severely uneducated about what hemp oil is and how it works. That's the problem. The protesters across the street think it's going to make everyone who tries it a drug addict. It won't."

"Well, I'll do what I can to help. I'll explain the differences between hemp oil and marijuana in my article."

Some of the lines on his face smoothed. "Thanks, Kate."

I walked across the street to talk to Lydia so I could make sure I presented both sides of the story. She was wearing a checkered black and white dress with a white cardigan over the top, and black belt secured around the cardigan. Her butterscotch blonde hair was twisted at the back of her head in a tight bun, and her face had fine lines around her eyes. I guessed she was in her forties. I introduced myself again, even though she already knew me, and asked some questions. "How did you get involved with this protest, Lydia?"

"I've been working with several anti-marijuana legalization groups for years. When I heard about this one, I volunteered."

"Who organized the protests?"

She shrugged. "I'm not sure. The call went out from a marketing firm, Saffron Star PR. The protest information was posted in several of the online groups I'm part of. I contacted them and said I'd like to lead the Branson Falls protest."

Who led, or went to, protests organized by groups they knew nothing about? "Why are you against the legalization of hemp oil?"

She gave me a look like she thought I was the dumbest person in the world. "It's not just hemp oil. It's all drugs. But especially pot. If we allow one thing to be legalized, all of the rest of the drugs in the world will follow."

"Any drug can be abused, even prescription drugs. How is this any different?"

"Because it's illegal."

"Studies have been done showing that alcohol fits the controlled substance definition better than marijuana."

"If I had my way, we'd outlaw the devil's drink, too."

All righty then. I knew where she stood. She was like a dog with a bone, only hers was a cause she believed in, and no amount of rational thought was going to change her mind. That's the way it was with opinions—unfortunately.

I went back across the street and jotted some notes down for the story. I'd work on it later tonight. I said goodbye to Spence, then stopped to pick up dinner on my way home.

The Devil Wears Tank Tops

The grilled cheese, French fries, and fry sauce were delicious, but my favorite part was the Oreo shake. Every time I had one, I thought of Hawke. The shake was yummy all by itself, but it was even better with the memory of Hawke eating it, and practically having sex with the spoon. I smiled, thinking about it, and almost jumped when my phone starting ringing to the tune, "Play Me." My thoughts must have conjured him up.

"Hey," I said, answering.

"Hi, Kitty Kate."

"Are you back in town?" I asked.

"Not yet."

"That's too bad," I said, taking another bite of my ice cream, "I have an Oreo shake, and I'm willing to share."

"Hmmm," he said. I could hear the smile in his voice.

"Hmmm what?"

"I'm having a serious debate about whether this contract is worth it, or if I should get on a plane and fly home to you right now."

My stomach fluttered. "I'd vote for home."

I heard him sigh. "I might."

"Are you okay?" I asked.

"I'm fine, I just wanted to hear your voice."

I smiled, thinking that was sweet—and unexpected. "I'm glad you called."

I heard a loud noise in the background that sounded a lot like the blades of a helicopter. "I have to go, Kitty Kate, but I'll see you soon. And we'll finish what we started in the corn field."

"Be careful," I said, as he clicked off.

I put my phone back on the table, and licked the Oreo shake off the spoon slowly. I ate the rest of my treat thinking about Hawke, and what he'd do with the ice cream if he were here.

Chapter Ten

I changed into a comfortable, thin cotton cami and matching shorts then started researching the marketing company that had set up the protests, Saffron Star PR, before I fell asleep on the couch. It was early, but it had been a long day and I still couldn't remember the night before.

I woke sometime around dawn to the sound of something falling in the kitchen. I sat straight up and noticed a light on in my kitchen. I never left lights on. And if this was a robber, he needed better burglar training. What kind of thief shows up to rob someone without a flashlight? This was the second time in the last few months someone had broken into my house. I really needed to get an alarm system. Drake had threatened one, but there'd been a massive argument about him overstepping boundaries and he hadn't followed through. Now I kind of wished he had.

I scanned the room for a weapon. The best things I had, and the heaviest, were the remote controls for my ceiling fan and phone docking station. I grabbed them, and crept through the living room to the doorway of the kitchen. I peeked around the door jam, and saw a large silhouette of a man, back toward me. I hurled my remote at him, aiming for his head. I missed.

"Ouch!" he said, rubbing the middle of his back and turning around. His eyes ran over me, taking in my short shorts and barely-there cami. I wrapped my arms around myself, and made a mental note that next time I thought there was an intruder in my house, I should put some clothes on before investigating.

"Drake? What the hell?" He was still holding the knife—and using it to spread jam on his croissant.

"I brought you breakfast," he said, gesturing to the bag of food on the counter.

"And broke into my house?"

"I didn't break in," he said, taking a bite of his buttery roll. "I knocked, but you didn't hear me, so I used your hide-a-key."

"Hey!" I said, my tone full of outrage. "How did you know where my key was?" I'd spent a very long time in the hide-a-key aisle of the home improvement store where a teenager had assured me no one would ever find my secret rock. Then I'd spent a lot of time finding the most inconspicuous place for it in the flower garden under my front window.

"It's the only rock in your whole flower bed," Drake explained. "It kind of stands out."

I wrinkled my nose, and made a commitment to go rock hunting and add to my collection as soon as possible.

"I'll fix that," I said, rubbing my eyes and trying to wake up. "I can't believe I didn't hear you knock." I'd been pretty exhausted the night before, but it didn't say much for my Scooby Senses that I'd slept through an intruder—especially one the size of Drake. A clumsy wallaby would have been less noticeable than him.

"Me either. I saw your car in the driveway, so I knew you were home. After I knocked three times and you didn't answer, I thought something might be wrong. I wouldn't have used the key otherwise."

I cocked a brow. "Good to know you have limits."

"Occasionally," he said with a smile. He held out a bag for me and I took a croissant.

I stole a glance at him as I cut the croissant in half, and spread some sweet strawberry jam on it. He was in jeans and a tight, dark blue t-shirt that highlighted his gorgeous sapphire eyes. He looked like he'd just stepped out of the shower, and smelled like the mountains in summer. I mentally shook myself out of the do-Drake trance. Yeah, he was tall, dark, and looked like great sex, but I couldn't let those little things distract me. He was also arrogant, pretentious, and all alpha male. I wasn't a good match for men like that. The sex was great, but we'd spend the rest of our lives fighting.

"Why the visit to my house?" I asked, taking a bite of my food. In my heightened adrenaline-induced state,

I'd briefly forgotten about the lingerie humiliation with Drake that I couldn't recall. I remembered the whole situation now, though, and wasn't pleased. Although he *had* sent me flowers. I tilted my head to one side in concession; point to Drake. Then I thought about it a little more and frowned. Flowers that indicated I might have done something wildly inappropriate and he still hadn't told me what that was. Point revoked. "You certainly didn't stay yesterday morning."

"I wasn't here that long," he said. "I left after I knew you'd fallen asleep."

My eyes widened and I seriously considering shoving the croissant right up his— I stopped, trying to regain some control. I put the knife down so the potential weapon would be harder to reach. "How thoughtful of you to sneak out after taking advantage of me. If this is how you treat all women, no wonder you have the reputation you do."

His brows pushed together and he looked completely confused. "How did I take advantage of you?"

I grunted at his stupidity. "Are you kidding me? I woke up in my sexiest lingerie, wearing my silk robe. Are you telling me you didn't take advantage of me?" If he hadn't, I was a little insulted. And yes, I realized that was a contradiction. I would have been upset either way things had gone down. Sometimes I felt bad for the men in my life.

He studied me, realization slowly coming over his face. "You don't remember what happened." It was a statement, not a question.

I pursed my lips, unhappy about the entire situation. "No. I don't."

He grinned.

I wanted to punch him.

Right in his perfect stomach.

He took a drink from his glass of orange juice, and then took a bite of his food, savoring every moment. Now I wanted to punch him in the stomach *and* the balls.

"So," I said, my voice impatient.

"So what?" he asked with an innocent lift of his lips.

I was completely exasperated now. I was a reporter who investigated things and got facts. There was one person in the world who could fill in my memory holes, and he was being a douche canoe about the details. "What the hell happened?"

Drake grinned and tilted his head in what I hoped was an acknowledgment that he was done torturing me. "After the party at Annie and Rich's house, I went home. About an hour later, you called me."

"No." I shook my head fervently. "I didn't."

"Yes. You did."

"I checked my cell when I got up. I didn't call, text, or even Facebook anyone."

"You're on Facebook?" He looked wounded. "Why aren't we friends?"

I pointed at him with my croissant. "Stop trying to change the subject."

"You didn't call me from your cell number. You called me from your house."

I made a disbelieving noise. I never used my home phone. I only had it as a backup in case my cell phone wasn't working, or there was some other emergency and I had no other way to make a call. My mom insisted on it in case an electromagnetic pulse hit. She'd been watching too many episodes of *Doomsday Preppers*. She didn't seem to understand that landlines wouldn't survive the apocalypse. "Why would I call you from there?"

He shrugged. "I have no idea. But you did."

"What did I say?"

He gave an unapologetic smile. "I don't dare repeat it, but suffice it to say that an invitation was extended."

I flushed, sure I'd said something—maybe several things—mortifying. "So I propositioned you, and you came right over?" I frowned and looked down at my plate. "That sounds like the Drake I've heard so much about."

His tone was tight. "I came over because you didn't sound like yourself. When I got here, you opened the door wearing the robe, started to untie it, and then tried to lure me back to your bedroom."

I snorted. "I'm sure that took *a lot* of convincing." My voice was thick with sarcasm.

"I thought you might be drunk, or high."

"I wasn't either."

"But you don't remember anything that happened?"

I pressed my lips together again. "I think I might have been drugged or something."

Drake's expression was a mixture of anger and concern. "By Annie and Rich?"

I shook my head repeatedly. "No." I waved him off. That didn't matter in respect to the current conversation. Getting info about my lost night did. "What happened after I tried to seduce you?"

He poured more orange juice in his glass and took another drink. "You told me the Saints and Sinners Cookies were better than your mom's."

I sucked in a sharp breath. "No," I breathed out. "I didn't."

"You did."

I shook my head, eyes huge. "Don't ever tell her that. Ever. We'll both lose our lives."

"Noted." He took another bite of his food. "Then you almost passed out on the floor. I carried you back to your room, tucked you in, and stayed for a couple of hours to make sure you were okay. Once I knew you were, I locked your doors and left."

Okay, so it wasn't as humiliating of a situation as I'd initially thought. Thank the goddesses for that. And he hadn't seen me in my alluring lace bra and panty set, so that also made it to the win column. The situation was still embarrassing, though. I hadn't had a night of memory loss since my sophomore year of college. It wasn't something I'd wanted to repeat then—or now.

"I guess I owe you a thank you."

He smiled. "No need. I'm happy I was in town, and that I could help." He changed the subject. "I heard about the hemp oil protest yesterday."

I rolled my eyes. "It's ridiculous. People don't even understand what they're angry about. I'm going to put an explanation of the differences between hemp oil and pot in my article about the protest."

"I've been trying to help John as much as I can."

"He mentioned that. He said the bill wouldn't have been passed without you."

Drake lifted a shoulder like it wasn't a big deal. "I wasn't the only one who made it happen. I just wish things were moving faster and they didn't have to deal with the crazy anti-marijuana groups."

"The protest was organized by a marketing company called Saffron Star PR. Do you know anything about them?"

Drake furrowed his brow. "I've heard of them, but I'm not really familiar with their clients. I can look into it if you want."

I nodded. "That would really help me out." The information I'd found about them online included a very sleek and professional website, but little information about their clients or the types of marketing and advertising campaigns they offered.

He sliced his head down once. "Consider it done."

I smiled at him. I appreciated a man who took charge and paid attention to details. I had no doubt that with Drake's connections, he'd be able to help me get the information I needed.

Drake leaned back in his chair and watched as I started a pot of coffee. "Do you want some?" I asked, holding up the container.

"No thanks, I have orange juice."

The Devil Wears Tank Tops

I arched an eyebrow as I grabbed a clean mug from the dishwasher. "I forgot. You're not allowed to drink coffee," I said, pouring milk and creamer in a glass while I waited for the pot to finish brewing.

His lips ticked up. "There are other vices I'd rather break rules for."

I made a tsking noise. "That's not helping your reputation."

"Not much does," he said, his voice resigned.

I poured my coffee, and ate the rest of my food while Drake watched. He looked like he wanted to say something, but he didn't speak up.

"What's on your mind?" I asked.

Drake just stared at me, running a finger over the rim of his glass. Finally he answered, "I want to know what it will take to have a chance with you."

If it was possible to drown from drinking coffee, I almost did it. I bent over, my chest constricting as I coughed, trying to get air again.

"Are you okay?" Drake asked, standing up and rubbing my back between my shoulder blades. His light touch, concern, and declaration that he was interested in me sent unauthorized warm feelings to several of my body parts. When I regained full lung capacity, I answered back, "I want to know why you want a chance with me?"

He sat back down in the seat across from me. "Because I've known you for a long time, Katie." He met my eyes and held them. "You're the girl I've never been able to forget."

He'd said that before, but didn't back it up with any additional info. I rubbed my head, feeling a slight headache coming on—either Drake induced, choking induced, or maybe I was still feeling the aftereffects of whatever had taken my memory. "Drake, you didn't even know me when we were younger."

"Yeah. I did."

"That's right," I nodded. "You remember patting me on the head after a football game. Great. Glad I made a lasting impression."

He shook his head slowly. "That's not the only thing I remember."

"What else then? You acknowledged me maybe three times."

He leaned forward, resting his arms on my table and getting closer to me. My table wasn't used to arms like his, and my insurance didn't cover muscles. "I knew you, Katie. And I used to see you around town when I came home from college on breaks. The last time I saw you, you were still in high school. Then you left for college and I was in law school. I knew what you were up to though because your mom was always putting notices about you on the society page of the *Tribune*. When you graduated, I read your freelance work."

I stared at him, the word "liar" on the tip of my tongue. I didn't believe him for one hot second. "You did not."

"Wanna bet?"

I nodded as I raised my brows. "Yeah, actually, I do. "

"Fine," he said, his face giving nothing away. "I'll prove I read your articles if you'll go out on a real date with me. One that's not interrupted by another man, a crisis news story, or your mom."

"The crisis news story and my mom are usually one and the same."

"Still. No interruptions. That's the deal."

"I can't guarantee that."

"Were you interrupted on your dates with Hawke?"

I winced, thinking about it. "Frequently."

Drake's eyes narrowed at the information. I could tell he wasn't pleased, but if he didn't want to know, he shouldn't have asked. "Fine," he said finally. "A day you're not on call then."

I nodded. I was sure Drake had no idea what he was talking about, so it was easy to agree to his terms. "Fine. What do I get if you don't prove it?"

He shrugged. "I'll sell my Hummer."

My eyes widened. "Seriously?" I hated that thing. It was an environmental terrorist masquerading as a vehicle, and the Big Bird yellow color made it easy for everyone in town to find him when he was at my house.

"Seriously."

"Deal," I said, putting out my hand to shake on it.

Drake took it, and his hand lingered as he gave me a slow, smug smile. "What should we start with? The article you did about the homeless teens in Chicago? Or the one about the debt crisis in Greece?"

Shiiiit.

Chapter Eleven

I don't like losing. And I'd lost. Now I was being forced on a date with a man I had seriously conflicted feelings for—feelings that were just becoming more and more blurred. The fact that he'd really kept track of me and read my work was half flattering, half stalkerish. I still didn't know what he saw in me, though, or why he was interested. It's not liked we'd even dated when we were younger. He was far too old for me then. Maybe he'd give me more info on the date.

Drake left after breakfast, and I stewed. I came to the conclusion I needed to take control of something in my life, and went for a run to try to work off my recent cookie and doughnut eating *Guinness Book of World Records* attempt.

I jogged past the high school, trying to put all of my worries out of my mind and relax. I was able to do that for about ten minutes until my phone buzzed. I took it out and saw that I had a text message from Ella.

Facebook update said Drake was at your house this morning. Everyone thinks he spent the night. Amber said you must have ensorcelled him with your super Satanic ways.

My initial reaction was surprise that anyone in that group—let alone, Amber—knew the definition of 'ensorcelled' and had used it in the proper context. My next reaction was anger. My blood was already pumping from my run, but I felt it ratchet up even higher. Maybe I was better off not knowing the things being said about me.

Another notification popped up as I was holding the phone. The familiar little head and half-body with a plus sign indicating I had a Facebook friend request—from Dylan Drake. I took a deep breath and slid the notification to the side. I couldn't deal with the implications of accepting that right now.

I started walking the rest of the way home to cool down, thinking of Amber Kane's before and after nose job picture, and how much it would make me feel better if those photos were on the front page of the *Tribune*. It would be completely unethical, but even the thought of her reaction made me smile like a kid on Christmas morning. I was lost in my nose-reveal daydreams when I heard a familiar voice.

"Hey, Kate! Nice morning."

I smiled as I looked at Michelle, holding the leashes of two beautiful dogs. "It is. Are these your dogs?"

"Yeah. This is Bono," she said, pointing to a black and white Border Collie, "and Ringo," she pointed to the brown and black German Shepherd. Both had tongues hanging out of their mouths as they wagged their tails.

"Can I pet them?" They looked friendly, but I knew it was always smart, and polite, to ask a dog owner first.

"Sure. They're friendly."

I reached down, giving both dogs the backs of my hands. When they licked me, I knew I'd been accepted, and ran a hand over their heads, scratching behind their ears.

"Have you given any more thought to adopting?" Michelle asked.

I had, in between everything else that was going on. I really wanted to take Gandalf and have my own little canine wizard, but I just wasn't sure if my lifestyle would be that great for a dog. "I have, and I want to adopt him, but I'm still thinking about if I can make that commitment. I don't want him to be unhappy."

She nodded, understanding. "Well, I'll let you know if anyone else wants him before I let them adopt him."

"Thanks," I said, really meaning it. "It's a big decision, and I just want to make sure I'd be a good puppy parent."

"You would, but I understand."

Ringo was tilting his head to the side as a hint for me to scratch lower. I moved my hand down and rubbed his tummy. His tongue hung out even further in delight, making him look like he was smiling.

"Are they both rescues?" I asked.

"Bono was, but we got Ringo while I was helping scent train several dogs for K9 units in Salt Lake. He got hurt during training and couldn't continue."

My eyes went wide. "Really? I didn't know you helped with that type of training."

"Yeah. Dogs are such a huge asset to the officers. Ringo was almost finished with training before he got hurt. We're more than happy to have him, though," she said, reaching down and rubbing his back. "He's a great dog."

Michelle pulled a bowl from the bag she was carrying, and gave the dogs some water. Then she pulled out some treats that looked a lot like cookies.

"I didn't know dogs could eat cookies."

She shook her head. "They're special treats I make at home. I don't like the processed treats at pet stores, so I make my own."

"That's impressive!" I said, surprised. I could barely make cereal. "For a minute, I thought they were getting the same cookies as everyone else in town."

Michelle laughed. "No. Ringo hated them."

It seemed Ringo hated Saints and Sinners Cookies as much as my mom. I rubbed both dogs behind the ears again one last time before standing up. "Well, they must just like your treats best."

She laughed and emptied the bowl of water, shaking it out on the park strip grass we were standing next to. "I wish my kids thought I was that good of a cook. It's not too much of a self-esteem boost, though, considering the plethora of horrible things I've seen

Bono and Ringo eat." She put the empty water bowl back in her bag. "Have a good day, Kate."

"You too," I said, and went home to get ready for work.

I edited some stories when I got to work, then answered emails. After that, I placed a call to Bobby.

"Hey," I said when he answered. "It's Kate."

"I know. You're in my caller ID."

Good to know. "Have you heard anything else about the body yet?"

"Nope. Still tryin' to identify it."

"It's been more than a week." Not much more, but still. Things like that usually moved faster in Branson because the town was small and there weren't as many major crimes or strange deaths to process.

He snorted. "It was pretty unidentifiable, Kate."

That conjured up an unpleasant image, and I was a little sorry I'd pressed. I decided to switch topics from the burned remains. I wondered if Bobby had heard the same rumors as Ella, and if those rumors were being investigated. "Ella said the sugar factory wasn't doing well, and Kory Greer was having financial problems."

"That's what we heard, too, but Kory said that's not the case."

So they'd already talked to him. "Did you believe him?"

"The investigator seemed to."

"Okay, thanks Bobby."

"I'll call you when I know more."

I rifled through the notes on my desk for Kory Greer's number, then called him. His assistant put me right through.

"Hi, Kory. It's Kate with *The Branson Tribune*. I'm just following up on the fire. Have you received any more information yet?"

His voice was smooth and calm on the other end. "Not yet. They said the investigation could take several weeks, especially because of the body that was found."

Dead bodies did tend to complicate things. The answer gave me an opening to ask about the sugar factory's finances, though. "That has to put you in a bad financial situation since you probably can't rebuild until the investigation is closed and the insurance money comes in."

"It would have," Kory said, "but we got some new contracts a few months ago that have really helped us out. That's why we were buying the new machines. We were planning to expand production and try to take on more new clients. We're still able to fulfill our current contracts with our satellite facility, so we'll be okay until things get settled, and we can rebuild."

Huh, that answered that question. Even if they'd been in financial distress before, the new contracts must have been enough to keep them pretty far in the black, even with the explosion.

"I'm glad to hear it. Thanks, Kory. I'll probably call back again once the police know the identity of the body."

"That sounds fine. I'll talk to you then, Kate."

I hung up, and noticed the message light on my voice mail blinking. It was from Annie asking me to call her back as soon as possible. I picked up the phone and dialed her number. "Hey, Annie, it's Kate."

"Hey!" She sounded rather perky. "Sorry about the other night. Rich didn't know about your history with Drake, or he wouldn't have invited him over."

I leaned back in my chair and fiddled with a paperclip on my desk. "It's not a big deal. I have to deal with him all the time. I'm getting used to it." And now I had to deal with him on an actual date.

"Still, I felt bad. I didn't want you to be uncomfortable and never come over to my house again. You're one of the only normal friends I have in Branson."

"I feel the same way about you, so you don't have to worry about that. You'll probably get sick of me and eventually ask me to leave you alone."

"Won't happen."

"We'll see."

"Trust me, it won't. There's another reason I was calling you, though."

"Oh yeah? What's up?"

"Opie Vargis—the clown who crashed at the parade—his blood work came back. I heard about it from one of the nurses."

Hmmm, I was sure that crossed some sort of privacy line, but I wasn't going to question it when she was sharing the information. "What did the nurse say?"

She paused for a second like people do when they have important information to share...or when a reality TV show is about to reveal the winner. "Opie had high levels of THC in his blood."

I dropped the paperclip, and immediately picked up my pen. "Does he smoke pot?" That seemed unlikely given the prominent religion Opie was a member of. Drugs were a definite no-no.

"Nope," Annie said, her tone confused. "The doctors asked him about it, but he said he's never had anything worse than Lortab after a surgery five years ago. He doesn't drink, smoke, or do any drugs. And he's not around anyone who does."

Lines formed between my eyes. "How did the THC get in his system, then?"

"No one can figure it out." Her voice sounded perplexed.

"Is it possible Opie's lying because he doesn't want people to know about his drug habit?"

Annie paused like she was thinking. "I don't think so. I've known Opie for a few years. He was pretty distraught when he heard the news about the pot. He even called his bishop to repent for somehow getting it in his system."

"How else could it have gotten there?" As far as I knew, you either had to inhale or ingest it. It didn't sound like Opie had done either.

"I'm not sure," Annie said, "but I thought you'd want to know about it."

"Do you think the THC had something to do with his crash at the parade?"

"Yeah," she said. "He had heart problems anyway, and marijuana can increase heart rate. It put him at a greater risk for a cardiac event."

Huh. I was baffled about how the THC got in his system if he hadn't smoked it—or even been around people who were smoking it. I wanted more information about it, though. I'd have to pay a visit to Opie. "Do you know when Opie will be released?"

"Probably sometime in the next few days. They just have to make sure he's stable."

"Okay, I'll try to stop by and see him. Thanks for the heads-up, Annie. Having an EMT friend sure is handy."

"Especially considering who your mom is."

I laughed, thinking she hadn't had anything crazy happen in the last few days—so she was probably due for an event. It was kind of like waiting for a volcano to blow: you knew it was coming, you just didn't know when, or how bad it would actually be. It wasn't a comforting feeling. At least I had Annie to mend her, though. "I couldn't agree more."

I hung up and went back to work until I was called out to the scene of a stand-off.

With a deer.

That's right, a deer. I didn't believe it when I heard the call come in over the scanner either. When I got to the campground in the mountains ten minutes outside of Branson Falls, Officer Bob was already there. I looked around at the campground in complete disarray. Food, mostly junk food, was spread out all over the table and the ground. Chips littered the dirt like potato confetti. The birds and wild animals in the area would appreciate that. I peeked into the back of the ambulance and saw George Tuttle being treated by an EMT.

I walked up to Officer Bob. "Hey, Bobby. What in the world happened here?"

Bobby hiked up his pants, then rested his thumbs in the belt loops. "More crazy people."

"More than usual?"

"Shoot, Kate! Usually the only crazy person in town we have to deal with is your mom. We've been dealin' with crazy on an even higher level for the past few weeks. On the Catasophie meter, we've hit save-your-families-and-get-outta-Dodge."

I arched a brow. "I didn't realize things were so serious."

He took a deep breath and kicked at some of the food on the ground. "All emergency responder staff's been puttin' in overtime. Everything from weird phone calls and disturbances, to more car accidents and health problems."

"That's weird. What do you think is causing it?"

"Satan, probably."

Yes. Because it couldn't be something rational. "What happened here then?" I asked.

He rocked back on his heels. "George Tuttle tried to wrestle a deer."

I blinked, not sure I'd heard right. "I'm sorry, did you just say George tried to *wrestle* a deer?"

He nodded his head definitively. "Sure did."

"Why?"

"Who the blazes knows?" Bobby said, throwing his hands in the air. "We tried askin' him, but he's got even less sense than usual right now."

"Were there witnesses?"

"Nope. Near as we can figure, George stalked the deer for a good hour. The deer 'round here are used to people. They feed 'em, so the deer aren't afraid of humans. George used that to his advantage. He jumped on the deer's back and tried to wrestle him to the ground."

"How did that go?" Not well, I'd imagine.

"Deer broke two of George's ribs, fractured his arm, and kicked him in the eye."

"Good for the deer," I said, meaning it.

"We'll have to ask him more questions again when he's awake," Bobby said.

I nodded, thinking I'd have to follow up with him when he was more coherent. I couldn't figure out what would have possessed him to try to wrestle any animal, especially one that was wild with pointy horns.

I took some more notes while I talked to Bobby, asked the EMT's when George would be feeling well enough for me to interview him, then drove back to the office to finish work for the day. I couldn't help thinking about what Bobby had said, and all of the strange news stories—my own strange behavior the night of the lingerie, included. Something was going on, I just couldn't put my finger on what.

Chapter Twelve

Hospitals freaked me out. They always had. Even as an adult, I had to wait until after my annual physical to have my blood pressure taken or the doctors would try to admit me immediately. They called it white-coat syndrome. I couldn't believe it actually had a name, but I was happy I wasn't the only one to suffer from an irrational fear of stethoscopes.

Still, I avoided hospital visits for myself whenever possible, but occasionally, I had to go there for a story. Which was why I'd spent the last fifteen minutes lost in a maze of hallways before finding the right room and knocking. I heard a low voice tell me to come in.

Opie looked a bit less clown-like without the wig and makeup he'd been wearing during the parade, but his welcoming smile indicated he was kind. I hoped he'd also shed some light on the mystery THC.

"Hey, Opie. I'm Kate Saxee with *The Branson Tribune*."

"Heya, Kate."

"I'm glad you're feeling better. I'm working on a story. Can I ask you some questions about what happened at the parade?"

He shifted in his bed, and used the remote to move it so he could sit up. "Sure."

I sat on the chair across from him and pulled out my notebook and pen. "I heard that THC was found in your blood, and it could have contributed to your heart attack. Do you have any idea how it got in your system?"

He shook his head and seemed completely befuddled. "Nope. I feel horrible about it, too. I've sinned and I didn't mean to." He looked sincerely horror-stricken. "I really didn't."

I believed him. I had the urge to tell him I wasn't his bishop and didn't need to hear a confession, but figured he just needed to get his story out. "What were you doing before the parade?"

He folded his hands in his lap, thinking back on the day. It probably wasn't a pleasant memory. "I was at the fair. I was one of the judges."

"What were you judging?"

"Baked goods."

My eyes widened at that. That made him one of the people on my mom's "doo-doo" list. She really had a list. It was hanging on her fridge. "How long have you been a baked goods judge?"

"Five years." He winced. "I heard your mom was pretty upset about the cookie results."

I nodded slowly. "I don't think she'll get over it any time soon."

"Well, I've voted for her every year for the past five years, but the Saints and Sinners Cookies were just too good not to recognize."

That interested me, because I'd had them, and really didn't think they were great at first. But then during my memory lapse / fit of blasphemy, I'd apparently declared they were better than my mom's. "How does judging work?" I asked. The judges couldn't possibly eat all of the food entered. If I did that, I'd have to run a marathon every day for a month.

"There's a team of judges for every food entry. I was judging cookies with four other people. Each cookie entry is rated on appearance, then it's sliced into pieces, and we all rate the taste of each entry."

"How many entries do you usually have?"

"Around two hundred."

I took back my previous estimate. I'd have to run a marathon every day for five months. "That's a lot of cookies to sample."

"Yeah. We judge them over the course of two days."

Silently, I questioned the wisdom of a patient with known heart problems eating two hundred cookie samples over the course of two days. "And you only take one piece of each of them?"

He blushed slightly. "Well, usually. But if they're real good, sometimes we have more."

"Whose did you have more of this year?"

"Your mom's are always popular. But this year, everyone was taking multiple pieces of the Saints and Sinners Cookies."

"Who were the other judges?"

Opie rattled off a list of names, one of which I recognized from recent events: Fred Young, the ill-fated hot air balloon pilot. Ryan Miles was another name, and one I remembered from my mom's rant during her cookie tirade. I needed to call the other judges and see if they'd had any side effects from the Saints and Sinners Cookies as well.

I flipped my notebook shut and put my pen back in my purse. "Thanks for talking to me, Opie. You've been really helpful."

"No problem."

"When will you get to go home?"

"Probably tomorrow. My wife's home with the kids right now. It's kind of nice to have some peace and quiet."

I smiled. I couldn't agree more. I cherished my alone time. "I totally understand. I'm glad you're feeling better."

"Thanks, Kate. Let me know if you need anything else."

As I walked through the waiting room, I noticed it was much busier than usual. Some people were bent over, clutching their stomachs. Considering how much a few of them were sweating, they looked like they were on a tropical island with two hundred percent humidity. Others had blood shot eyes and looked like they hadn't slept in days. It seemed like the flu was going around. Regardless of whatever they had, I didn't want it. I got out of the hospital fast.

I went back to the office to call the other judges. The more I heard about this situation, the more I thought there was something fishy about Saints and Sinners Cookies.

I called Fred Young first. I already knew he'd had problems with the cookies since he'd stolen—and crashed—a hot air balloon, then danced around like a fairy and chortled like a hyena. "Hey, Fred. This is Kate Saxee with the *Branson Tribune.*"

"Oh…uh…hi, Kate."

He seemed like he wanted to talk to me about as much as he wanted a colonoscopy. He probably thought I was going to ask him why he stole a hot air balloon while laughing like a wild animal. "I'm working on a story about the fair," I said, trying to ease his fears—though I really did want to ask him what in the world he'd been thinking when he'd done his thievery— "and I was hoping you could answer some questions for me."

"A story? About the fair?"

"Yeah. About some of the food entries. I understand you were a judge?"

His voice took on a tone of relief. "Yes. Yes I was."

"I'm specifically wondering about the cookie entry that won. The Saints and Sinners Cookies."

"Ahhh, the cookies." His tone took on a wistful, loving tone. "They are amazing."

"Did you have a lot of them?"

"Well, I had the ones that we judged, then I went over and bought a couple of bags."

"A couple?" I asked, trying to keep the surprised tone out of my voice. Who could eat that many cookies?

"I ate a lot of them. I shouldn't have, but I did. They made me so happy, I didn't even keep track of how many I'd had. Before I knew it, I was up in a hot air balloon. It was glorious."

The people involved in the traffic accidents his unauthorized balloon flying had caused probably didn't think so.

I thanked Fred for his help and hung up to call the other judges. Ryan Miles had gone to the hospital after having an anxiety attack, and another judge had also felt fatigued, but not bad enough to seek treatment. The last judge wasn't affected. He must have eaten less than everyone else.

The Devil Wears Tank Tops

An idea had been percolating in my head ever since I found out Opie was one of the cookie judges. I'd spent a lot of time thinking about the other night at Annie's and what I couldn't remember afterwards. There was only one other time in my life that I'd had a memory lapse—and subsequent amorous reaction—like that: when I'd tried marijuana in college. I'd apparently propositioned my roommate's life-size cut-out of Henry Cavill—which I'd also done completely sober when she wasn't around; Henry was hard to resist—and then passed out on my bed.

I knew pot affected everyone differently, but I'd decided right then never to try pot again because I didn't like being that out of control. I should have put two-and-two together earlier, but I hadn't smoked anything, and certainly didn't think I'd been drugged with something like pot in my food. But the theory was starting to make sense. I opened my notebook and wrote down a list of things supporting my theory.

The entire town had gone bat-crap crazy over the dumb treats. I'd eaten them like there was a sugar shortage, even after admitting that my mom's cookies were far better. And a lot of the strange things happening around town could be attributed to side effects of pot use. Plus, Ringo, the super sniffer dog that had been scent trained to find drugs with K9 dogs hated the Saints and Sinners Cookies even more than most dogs hated vacuums. I felt like that discovery alone was a huge point in my pot cookie theory.

I decided I needed to find out more information about the cookies, what was in them, and the company that made them.

Chapter Thirteen

I started with a search for Saints and Sinners Cookies, and pulled up their website. The site listed all of the cookies they offered with mouth-watering pictures and descriptions, and the option to order the cookies online. The About Us page showed a happy couple wearing matching aprons, and a story about how the cookie recipe had been passed down for generations, going as far back as the pioneers. That was quite a family cookie legacy.

When I'd first been made aware of the cookie fervor at the fair a week and half ago, I'd called Saints and Sinners to talk to them. I'd tried two other times since, and still hadn't gotten an answer. I decided to try one more time. I got the voice mail and left a message—again. After some research online, I found out Saints and Sinners was actually owned by a company called Makhai, LLC. But the information trail stopped there.

The name was strange, and I'd heard it somewhere before. I did a quick Google search that jogged my memory. The Makhai were two-headed spirits of battle from Greek mythology. Interesting choice for a company name. I wondered who Makhai, LLC was doing cookie battle with—other than my mom.

I sent an email to the private investigator we had on contract, and asked him to check into Makhai, LLC. I copied Spence on it, and blew out a breath. I still had no idea why someone would be putting pot in cookies and trying to get an entire town high. It didn't make sense.

It had to be someone trying to prove a point. But what?

I stretched my arms over my head, and moved my neck from side to side, a pop sounding with each tilt. I didn't know the answer yet, and staying in the office after such a long day wasn't going to help me think. I packed up my stuff and drove home.

I decided to take advantage of the beautiful, early September night, to weed my flower beds in the back yard. I rented the home, and could only afford it because this was small town Utah where rent was just a little bit more than my cell phone bill. My landlady was awesome, and my neighbors were fantastic.

I pulled on my gloves and started weeding, letting my mind wander into quiet oblivion. I really enjoyed working in my yard. I loved the sense of accomplishment that came from a project that let me see the results of my hard work. Before and after shots were my favorite parts of home improvement shows.

I was straining to unearth a horrible weed the size of a tree, fighting it while I cursed up a storm. It would probably get me in trouble with the Ladies if they heard, but I felt like swearing made every hard job easier— there just hadn't been a study on it yet to confirm my theory—and I needed all the help I could get for the weed tree.

"Looks like you could use some help."

I snapped my head up. Hawke was standing behind me, and every part of my body knew it. I hadn't seen him since the hot air balloon crash when he said he was going out of town for a while for work. My eyes moved over him. He was wearing black cargo pants, black heavy-duty boots, and a grey t-shirt that clung to his muscles like water—or a horny woman named Kate. My pulse jumped just from his proximity—and he was still five feet away.

He walked over to the lightly stained wood patio table and put a paper bag on top of it next to a bottle of wine. "What's that?" I asked, standing up and brushing dirt off of my knees.

"Dinner."

I raised my eyebrows. "That was nice of you."

He gave me his heart-stopping smile—which would have been comforting if people hadn't been having pot induced heart attacks lately. I went inside to clean up and came back out with silverware and glasses.

Hawke took the lids off the take out boxes and handed me one. It was a manicotti smothered in a deep red sauce—my favorite kind of sauce. Tomato, but thick, pureed tomato with savory flavors, not chunks of the fruit that tasted way more like a vegetable. He opened another box and handed me a golden breadstick dusted with spices. It smelled fantastic. I took a bite and it was even better than it smelled.

"This is amazing! Where did you get it?"

"A little Italian place." He uncorked the wine, a rich, dark red filling the glasses. Then he handed me a glass.

We didn't have this kind of food in Branson, though Hawke had made me an amazing Italian dinner at his house recently that I still thought about and lusted after. It had almost gotten him laid right on his kitchen table—and anywhere else he wanted. If it wasn't for the take out boxes and bags, I would have thought he'd made this meal, too. "What Italian place?" I wanted to know so I could go there myself.

"A place in Salt Lake."

"Salt Lake?" I was a bit dumbfounded. The food was still warm. Salt Lake City is two hours from Branson. "Did you warm the food up in the microwave before you got here or something?"

He took a sip of his wine. "I fly fast."

I blinked. "You fly?" That confirmed it: Hawke really was Superman.

He nodded.

I made an obvious observation. "Since I don't see your superhero cape, I guess this means you have a plane, too?"

He grinned. "The cape's at the cleaner."

"I don't doubt it," I took another bite of food. "So do you keep your plane in your garage? Because I've never noticed it in the driveway."

He shook his head. "No, I store them at airports. I have more than one."

I managed to keep my mouth from falling open. Sheesh. There was a lot I didn't know about Hawke. "So you're back from your adventure—that you took in a plane I didn't even know you owned or could pilot— is anyone dead?"

His full lips slid into a slow smile. "I'm a private person, Kitty Kate. I've let you in more than any other person I can remember, especially considering we've only known each other for a few months. That's a huge compliment to you. It will take me time, but I'll get comfortable sharing more. I promise."

That really was a compliment. I imagined it wasn't easy for someone like Hawke, who lived his life in shadows, to open up. I tipped my glass toward him. "I look forward to that happening." I took another drink. "How was your trip?"

"Good. Uneventful, so that's always nice."

"I imagine."

"What's been happening around here?"

I snorted as I ate my delicious dinner. "A lot of strange stuff, actually. The sugar factory caught fire from a sugar dust explosion, then they found a body in the wreckage. They're still identifying the person. Opie Vargis's heart attack at the parade wasn't what it seemed and he actually had THC in his system that caused it, but no one could figure out how the THC got there. My mom hallucinated that mice were attacking my dad's Mustang and she drove it into a pond. An ambitious farmer tried to wrestle a deer, and weird accidents in the past few weeks have gone up significantly. The entire town is obsessed with some cookies, but I think they're actually spiked with pot. Oh, and there was an incident with modest clothing being Photoshopped onto girls in the senior pictures. I got blamed for starting a tank top trend." I didn't add that I'd also tried to have sex with Drake. One, it wasn't Hawke's business, and two, Hawke might have been off committing murder, or at best, assault, so I thought it prudent not to mention my strange horny streak.

Hawke narrowed his eyes. "That's a lot. Maybe we should take it one thing at a time."

I understood how he must be feeling because it was usually how I dealt with my mom. I frowned, not liking that connection. I lifted a shoulder and motioned for him to go on.

"Sugar dust is explosive, and it would be easy for someone to get caught inside if something ignited the dust," he said, pausing to remember my list. "Heart attacks happen all the time, though the THC is strange unless Opie is lying about using it. Your mom's situation is pretty par for the course, though the hallucinations are new. Deer wrestling seems out of the ordinary, but then again, this is Branson, so nothing is ever too strange. And the tank tops…that's just classic Utah insanity." He lifted his glass and took a drink of wine, processing all of the information. "But, taken all together, tank tops aside, I'd say you could be right that there might be more going on than just the random craziness that comes with living in Branson."

"What do you mean?"

He took another drink. "Increased heart rate, hallucinations, paranoia, increased appetite, lack of focus and control of motor skills. Those are all symptoms of drug use. Marijuana, specifically. I think your hunch might be right."

I dropped my fork and stared. "You think I'm right? Everyone in town is on drugs?" It was just a working theory, and one I hadn't told to anyone except Hawke. I thought I was right about it too, but I didn't think anyone would back me up without a lot more proof.

He shrugged. "Sure sounds like it. And it doesn't seem like people know they're taking it. I bet they're getting it from food like you thought, so your cookie theory makes sense."

No. People didn't know they were taking it. And by people, I meant me too. Having Hawke confirm my suspicions that pot could have been responsible for my decision to try humping Drake made me feel infinitely better about the situation. At the time, I probably would have humped a cactus.

"I knew it was those damn Saints and Sinners Cookies!" I said, slapping my hand on the top of the table. "They were the most popular item at the fair. Did you even get a chance to go to the fair?"

"Not this year."

I took another breadstick and broke it in half. "Well, there was a cookie craze. I'll have to check, but I bet every person who's been in an accident or incident lately had those cookies."

Hawke nodded. "That sounds like logical reasoning."

I tapped my fingers on the side of my wine glass. "Do you know someone who could do a drug test on the cookies, and get me the tests back fast?"

"How fast?"

"As fast as possible. I'd like to get a story out right away, and get those cookies off the shelves. It's one thing if people are using pot willingly, but it's another if they're being tricked."

He nodded. "I'll take care of it."

Just "I'll take care of it." No information about where he'd get the cookies, how the test would be done, or who it would be done by. Just a promise that he'd make it happen. Regardless of what he did for his living, or his means of getting information, Hawke sure was handy to have around. "I'll owe you."

He arched a brow. "And I'll collect."

My stomach tightened and my mouth went dry at the thought of what his required form of payment would be. I wet my lips and swallowed so I wouldn't sound like a frog with laryngitis. "I'm willing to pay."

The Devil Wears Tank Tops

His eyes moved over me in an appreciative way. He reached over and hauled me against him. His arms enveloped me, and his chest broadened with the movement. His lips pressed hard against mine, his tongue wrapping around my own. His hands moved inside my shirt and my body shuddered against him. I thought we were going to have sex right in the middle of my weed pile when he let me go.

I sputtered a ridiculous protest in a language that even I didn't know. The translation was something to the effect of "let's get inside and get naked."

Somehow, Hawke managed the translation. He must be fluent in nonsensical. "That will take some time, and I don't have enough of it tonight."

Well, that was disappointing. "Still have some people to kill?"

His lips stretched into a slow grin as he deftly changed the subject. "Aside from all of Branson getting accidentally high, has anything else interesting happened?"

My current state of mind, combined with Hawke's question, made thoughts of my sexy lingerie and attempted Drake seduction flash through my mind. I tried to hide my wince. "Nope. Nothing. Boring as ever."

"Your life is rarely boring, Kitty Kate. And that explanation sounded suspicious."

It was hard to lie to a man who dealt in liars frequently, and was probably an expert himself.

I decided to go on the offense. "Drake did stop by."

There was an almost imperceptible tightening of his jaw. "That's not a surprise."

"He thinks everything about you is fake. Even your name."

Hawke gave a sly smile. "I have a lot of aliases."

"Is Ryker Hawkins one of them?"

"It's the name I use professionally."

"But is it your real name?" I asked.

His eyes held mine in an assessing gaze. I wasn't sure what he was about to say next, but my stomach started fluttering and I felt a combination of panic and anticipation that he might decide to let me in a little more.

"I don't know what's real, and what's not about you," I said. "It's hard to have a relationship with a ghost."

"I don't let a lot of people in, Kitty Kate. It's the nature of my job. But you've made me have to start reconsidering some things."

"I have?"

"You have."

He got up and gathered his food, throwing it in the paper bag he'd brought our dinner in. He drank the last of his wine, then walked over, leaned down, and rested his hands on each of my chair's armrests. He pushed his lips against mine and kissed me hard, the taste of wine still on his lips. He stepped back, grabbed his keys and started to walk away.

"You didn't answer my question," I yelled after him.

"Not this time," he said over his shoulder. "But someday I will."

Chapter Fourteen

"Have you heard anything about Makhai, LLC from the private investigator?" I asked Spence when he came back from an errand.

After Hawke's concurrence with my theory, I told Spence about the pot-spiked cookie suspicions as soon as I got into the office that morning. Spence had immediately called the investigator and told him we needed the information on the company as fast as possible.

Spence nodded in answer, and moved his mouse, opening something on his computer. The printer started to run. "I just got an email. Makhai, LLC is owned by a dummy corporation that's owned by another dummy corporation, etc. Our investigator was able to follow the rabbit hole down until he came to an actual name."

I sat down in the chair across from his desk. "Who?" I asked, curious. I had just as many questions about this as I'd had after the series finale of *LOST*. I hoped I'd be less frustrated with these answers, however.

"A guy named Isaac Handler."

I'd never heard the name. "Who is he?"

"Our guy is still looking into that, but so far, we know he has ties to the Brigham Smith Group."

I snorted a laugh. "Seriously? That's the name?" Brigham and Smith were very recognizable names in Utah. They represented two of the most well-known prophets of the Mormon Church: Brigham Young and Joseph Smith. It didn't seem like the organization had spent much time considering their name choice, however. "They realize their initials are B.S. Group?"

"I'm not sure they really thought that through."

I'd heard of them, but couldn't quite place them. "Why does Brigham Smith Group sound familiar?"

"Because they're a group of lobbyists and investors. They have deep pockets."

Lobbyists and investors? That was strange. "Were they investors in Makhai, LLC?"

"That's what it looks like."

"What do you think their involvement is in this? Did Brigham Smith know Isaac Handler, and the company they'd invested in, were spiking cookies with pot?"

Spence shrugged. "No idea," he said, dropping the papers he'd just printed on the desk in front of me.

"There's all the info our investigator found. You should look it over and see if anything jumps out at you."

"Thanks," I said, already scanning the paperwork on my way back to my desk.

"If you have questions, Drake would be a good person to ask. He's had dealings with the Brigham Smith Group a lot."

Considering his job, that made sense. "Good dealings, or bad?"

"Depends on the issue."

Great.

I went through all the information and found out the Brigham Smith Group was a lobbyist organization that routinely campaigned for what they viewed as moral, conservative causes. They invested in companies with similar beliefs as well. I had no idea what their involvement was, but I was pretty sure getting everyone in Utah high on pot cookies wasn't on their mission statement. The only thing I could think of was that maybe someone was trying to discredit Isaac Handler or the Brigham Smith Group by spiking their cookies with pot.

I was taking notes on the information when my phone rang with Neil's song, "Glory Road."

"Hi, honey."

"Hey, Dad. How's it going?"

"Well, your mother hasn't sunk any of our cars lately, so I guess I should be thankful for that."

Clearly, he was still stinging over the mouse-tie, mustang-boat excursion. I would be too.

"I'd put that one in the win column. It's the little victories, Dad."

He sighed. "When I have a heart attack, you can tell her it's her fault."

"She'd make you cookies to say she's sorry. She'd probably even invent a no sugar and no butter recipe for you."

"Well, that wouldn't be much of an apology then, would it. She recently switched our milk from whole to skim with no warning at all. Said it was a simple change to make us healthier and live longer. Her disasters have a far worse effect on my health than whole milk. Skim milk is like drinking colored water. If living longer means drinking that, I want no part of it. I've been sneaking out to get my milk fix."

"And no one's told on you yet?" Sheesh! My whereabouts were constantly reported on Facebook and Twitter. How had he managed to stay under the radar?

"The convenience store manager owes me a favor."

I doodled a flower on my notes while I talked, "You better hope Mom never finds out. You'll get the evil eye." My mom had this look she got when she was really mad about something where her eyes almost rolled completely back in her head and you could only see the whites, no iris. Eyes weren't made to move that way unless demons were behind them. I was sure she was stretching something that absolutely shouldn't be stretched.

"If she finds out, I'll remind her about the Mustang and all of her other adventures, and tell her the least she could do would be to allow me the simple pleasure of decent milk."

I laughed.

"Speaking of your mom, that's why I called."

"What's up?"

"After her situation with the Mustang and the mouse, I took her in for a doctor appointment. They ran some tests, and there was an interesting result."

I wasn't sure whether to be intrigued, or scared. "What was it?"

"They did blood work to see if there was something strange in her system, and there was. THC."

Now my eyes were doing things they weren't made to do. I gasped, "Mom too?" I should have put two and two together earlier, but my mom's antics this past week were pretty normal for her, so her level of crazy wasn't a good baseline measurement. I'd only taken notice of the crazy things that were unusual for *most* Branson residents. Now that I thought about it, though, her hallucinations being induced by the Saints and Sinners Cookies made perfect sense. She'd eaten bags of them in a very short time period, trying to figure out the secret ingredients.

There was a pause on the other end, then, "There are others with similar test results?"

My mind was racing. Hallucinations were a side effect for some pot users, and it seemed my mom was one of them. "So far, only one other person, but I haven't checked for other patients with the same issue, yet." It was on my list of things to do today.

"What do you think is causing it? The doctors had no idea."

I brushed some hair back, away from eyes. "Well, THC comes from people who smoke pot. But since mom and the other person who had it in their system aren't pot smokers, I think they've been ingesting it."

I'd done some research on ingestible pot this morning to see if the symptoms matched what had happened to Opie. People who ingested pot got high thirty to sixty minutes after eating, and their high typically lasted four to six hours—longer if the pot was high strength. The high also lasted longer than someone who'd smoked the pot. In Opie's case, if he'd been eating the cookies all day, he would have stayed high all day. It surprised me no one else had noticed the change in his behavior. Also, if the cookies were spiked with pot, it would be easy to eat too much and not know it...which is what probably happened to my mom. She was determined to replicate the ingredients.

"Where in the world would she have eaten pot?" My dad sounded completely perplexed—which was new for him since he'd stopped trying to figure out the whys and hows of my mom's life a long time ago.

"I think it's in the new Saints and Sinners Cookies. Don't let her have any more of those!"

My dad muttered something about cookies under his breath. I caught the hint of a swear—and not an imitation one.

"I'm still doing some research, but as soon as I have proof, we'll publish the story about it, and the cookies probably won't be available much longer."

"Good. Until then, I'll make sure your mom doesn't get any more. She went crazy trying to figure out their recipe."

"I know. Don't let her keep trying. She doesn't have the proper ingredients, and the last thing we need is her trying to track down a drug dealer to get pot for her baking."

I could practically feel my dad's blood pressure rising at the thought. Lord only knows what she'd get herself into if she tried. I didn't think drug dealers would be too interested in her charms, or her attempts to get out of trouble by offering treats.

"I'll take care of it," he said. "Be careful investigating, sweetie."

"Thanks, Dad."

I hung up the phone and called Annie.

"I need your help with something. It might get you in trouble."

She laughed. "Trouble is my middle name."

"Can you find out if anyone other than Opie has been admitted to the hospital recently with THC in their system?"

"Sure. Is something going on that I should know about?"

"Something might be going on that everyone should know about, but I need more information first."

"Okay," she said. "Let me make some calls and I'll get back to you."

I hung up with Annie, and immediately called Hawke.

"I hope you're calling to tell me you're at my house and naked," he said instead of 'hello.'

I smiled at the thought. "Unfortunately, no."

"That's sad for both of us."

Yes, it really was. "I have some information I thought you might be interested in. My dad took my mom to the hospital after she tried to sink his Mustang. They just got the test results back, and she had THC in her blood. The closest she's ever come to marijuana is when she watches *Locked up Abroad*. Thanks to that dumb show, she won't travel anywhere."

"Well," Hawke said with a smile in his voice, "people are probably safer if she stays confined to Branson."

"That's the truth."

"She'd be fine as long as she didn't try to smuggle anything on her trip."

"This is my mother we're talking about. If it can go wrong it will. It's best to use whatever scare tactics we have available to keep her chaos-causing to a minimum. She wouldn't do well in jail."

"I'd save her."

Hawke and my mom had developed an interesting friendship in the last couple of months. Maybe it had to do with their mutual interest in me, but I wasn't entirely sure. I think my mom liked having Hawke around because she liked his danger factor. I couldn't blame her. I found that rather appealing as well—for a different reason than my mom...I hoped. And I had no doubt about Hawke's abilities to do any saving needed.

He'd probably fly his plane into the prison yard and rescue her himself.

"Don't tell her that. She'll be even more reckless than usual if she knows she's got you as a trump card."

He laughed.

I moved the subject back to the cookies. "I think other people who had the cookies will have the same blood results as my mom."

"Do you have someone helping you get that information?"

I tapped my pen on my desk, dotting my notebook with little specks of ink. "Yeah, for the hospital results. How long do you think it will be before you hear back from your lab about the cookies?"

"Not long. I'll call you as soon as I know."

"Thanks, Hawke." I hung up.

Chapter Fifteen

I was typing up notes from my conversations when Annie called me back.

"I have some info for you," she said.

"Hit me."

"I couldn't get names for the results, or even *all* of the results—I don't have those kinds of favors to call in—but I was able to confirm that in the last three weeks, several people in Branson have had blood work done where THC was found in their systems."

I knew it! "How many is several?"

"I don't have exact numbers, but more than twenty."

Surprise crossed my face as I scribbled down notes. "That's a lot." And those were just the people who sought out medical help. That would be good information to use in the story, though I'd have to cite

172

Annie as a secret informant. I didn't want her to get in trouble for helping me.

"I also have another interesting bit of info."

"I'd love to hear it."

"The ER has been overrun with sick people, and it started about three weeks ago. The EMT shifts too. The hospital has called extra staff in, and all of the employees are working overtime." I remembered Bobby had said the same thing about the emergency responders. "Everyone seems to have similar symptoms: sweating, increased heart rate, vomiting, fatigue, hallucinations. Those symptoms can be indicative of a lot of problems, but specifically heart attacks, food poisoning, and the flu. We've been seeing the same symptoms on a lot of our EMT calls as well."

Based on the research I'd done this morning, they were all also symptoms of ingesting too much pot. People in Branson *really* liked their cookies. "That is *very* interesting. I can't thank you enough, Annie. That helps me out a lot."

"No problem. Anything else I can do?"

"Not right now, but I might have some questions later. And I owe you dinner for your help."

She snorted. "I think you just asked me out on a date."

"I did. Wait until the Ladies hear about that. Prepare yourself, because you're about to become a lesbian."

"You'd be my first choice if I switched teams."

I smiled. "I'm flattered."

She laughed. "Call me if you need an orgasm."

I was still laughing as I clicked off.

At this point, I was one-hundred percent certain the cookies were spiked with pot. I didn't have the final test from Hawke yet, but I was excited about what I knew so far, and I wanted to be able to run with the story as soon as possible. A current of energy ran through me; it was almost as good as mainlining espresso. I loved the feeling of an investigation finally falling into place, and getting to write the story about it.

I got out my notes, and wrote the article as if I had the test results, and would just need to make a few changes when Hawke gave me the information. I cited anonymous sources in the article to protect my sources, and left another message at Makhai, LLC. Our private investigator had given me Isaac Handler's phone number, and I tried to reach him as well, but only got a voice mail. They really needed to hire someone to answer their phones, or at least to return calls. I left a message, and hoped Isaac Handler would call me back before news about the pot was revealed and his cookie company became enemy number one.

I spent the rest of the day writing and re-writing the story. I finished the article and leaned back in my chair, stretching. It would need Spence's editing eye, and I'd have to make changes once I had Hawke's results, but I was happy with it. I still didn't know why the cookies had been spiked with drugs, or how, but I'd write follow-up stories once I knew more. Right now, the public needed to know what was going on. I had no problem with pot, or food infused with pot, but I knew a lot of people in Branson would, and would prefer to know if they were ingesting it. Plus, there were people like Opie who could have serious health repercussions from eating pot. They needed to know the ingredients as soon as possible so they could regulate the amounts. Also, getting the cookies off shelves would probably help decrease the crazy going on around town.

I was packing up my stuff to leave for the night when I heard my computer bing with an email notification. I glanced at it as I put my notepad and camera in my bag. The address wasn't one I recognized, but a lot of news tip emails came to the *Tribune* accounts from addresses I didn't know. So while most people would have ignored messages from strange addresses and sent them to their junk folder, I actually had to open mine. The subject line made me think it was spam. It said:

WARNING.

I pushed my brows together and clicked to open the email. It was short, only a few lines. It said:

Stop investigating Saints and Sinners Cookies. The next warning won't be as friendly.

My lips flattened into a line as I glared at the screen. A surefire way to make a reporter investigate a story with reckless abandon was to tell them they had to stop. We all harbored visions of cracking a huge story and winning a Pulitzer. I'd been threatened before—this wouldn't be my first threat situation, or my last. Still, the email didn't make me thrilled. I thought back to the people I'd talked to about the cookies and THC so far. All of the baked goods fair judges, Annie, Hawke, Spence, my dad…and they could have slipped and mentioned it to anyone. That didn't help me narrow down the threat.

Whoever was sending the message was keeping track of my investigation, and knew exactly what I was doing. I decided I should probably tell Spence.

I called him over and explained the situation. He leaned his hands on my desk and read the email. Judging by the vein pulsing in his neck, and the tight muscles in his forearms, he wasn't pleased. "Are you still taking self-defense lessons?" he asked.

I'd had a rather memorable self-defense lesson with Hawke this past summer, but I was pretty sure the moves he taught me would be more beneficial in a someone-wants-to-kiss-my-clothes-off setting, and wouldn't help me out much in a someone-wants-to-kill-me situation. Though I wasn't averse to learning any of Hawke's skills. Not at all. "I remember the basics."

"And you still have the alarm on your house?"

"The one that Drake threatened to install without my permission?"

He nodded.

"No. I made the installer stop, then had an argument with Drake about it." I didn't like being managed. However, having people constantly going into my house without my knowledge made me regret my decision. I should probably call an alarm company and have them install one for me.

"I don't like this, Kate. I don't want any of my employees in danger, and since you came back to Branson, you've already been in danger once. It's happening again."

I shrugged as I picked up the slinky on my desk and started moving it from one hand to the other. "And it will probably continue to happen. I tend to piss people off. If you didn't want me in danger, then you probably should have hired another editor, because there aren't many things I'm afraid of."

"I know. That's what worries me."

"It's fine. I'll be okay."

He breathed out a sigh. "Just be careful," he said, "and if anything ever seems fishy, call me—or someone—to come and be your backup."

I nodded. That, at least, was something I could agree to.

"Hey," I said, changing the subject from my possible impending death. I liked living in denial. "Where's Ella lately?" I hadn't seen her for a couple of days, and hadn't had any Facebook updates either. She only worked a few days a week, but she was often in the office a lot more than that because she liked the company.

"She's been sick. She said she's feeling better now, though, and she'll probably come in tomorrow."

"Oh." I frowned, wondering if she was okay. I didn't like the idea of our cute archivist being sick. "I didn't know. I'm glad she's feeling better."

"Me too. Ella sick, you being threatened, the whole town on drugs. It's enough to give me an ulcer."

"At least your life isn't boring."

"Is that the rationale you use for dealing with your mom?"

I gave a surprised look. "How did you know?"

"It rolled off your tongue like you'd said it before—frequently."

I laughed, and went home for the night.

I looked through my fridge and cupboards for food. I barely even had pantry staples. It wasn't just because of money—though that was definitely a factor. Small town newspaper editors make less than teachers. My lack of groceries was also because I could rarely find time to go to the grocery store. It seemed like I was always being called away on stories and would have to abandon my milk and ice cream. And the stupid store wasn't open on Sunday, the one day of the week I usually had more free time because people were in church and didn't cause as much news. I scrounged together some bread, butter, and cheese, and made myself a grilled cheese sandwich. Dinner of champions.

I sat down to watch TV when I heard a knock. I opened my door and my lips lifted at the familiar, sculpted jawline and smile that stared back at me.

"Can I come in?" Hawke asked.

He was not someone I'd turn away. "Always."

He smiled, and stepped through the door. He settled on the couch, then patted the cushion next to him. "I have some information for you."

I sat where he'd patted. He handed me a folder with lab test results. Geez, he was efficient! "How did you get this so fast?"

He smiled. "You said you wanted it right away, and I know people."

"Who own drug testing labs?"

"It's useful in my business."

I lifted a brow, wondering what other totally insane professional services he found useful in his job.

"When Colorado legalized marijuana, they created a food safety system to regulate food products infused with THC," he explained. "Colorado can actually trace pot sold in the state back to the bud."

"So people can't just go and buy the legal pot, put it in their brownies, and eat up?" I asked. That's how I'd always thought it worked.

"They can, but just like the FDA regulates foods to make sure they're safe, Colorado is attempting to regulate food being sold with pot in it from actual edible pot distributors like pot bakeries. They're doing an extremely thorough job so far. They could track an outbreak of salmonella in a batch of pot brownies better than the FDA can track disease outbreaks in food from grocery stores."

I raised a brow. "I had no idea it was that controlled."

"Not everywhere, but as marijuana is being legalized in more and more states, Colorado is setting a good example for the rest of the nation to follow."

I flipped through the pages of test results. "So you used one of Colorado's labs to get the Saints and Sinners Cookies tested?"

"Yes. I overnighted a sample. The lab I use is fast, and excellent. I like to work with the best."

"Me too. That's why I asked you."

He grinned.

"What did they find?" I asked, trying to decipher the results and having little success.

Hawke took the folder and pointed to some numbers. "The cookies had a very high concentration of THC. Three times what would normally be used for making baked goods."

My eyes widened. "Three times? So someone had no clue what they were doing?"

"Maybe," Hawke said, pausing. "Or it could be they knew *exactly* what they were doing."

I pushed my brows together, confused.

Hawke saw the look and went into more detail. "Consuming edible marijuana can have different effects than smoking it. It's important for a person to know their proper dose going in. Otherwise, it can make people sick. People who eat too much have a substantially increased heart rate, they sweat profusely, are often fatigued, and they can even vomit."

I nodded. I'd read about that while doing my research. "Those are the some of the same symptoms people have been complaining about at the hospital during the last few weeks."

Hawke thought about it for a second. "Makes sense. The more potent the strength of the marijuana plant used, the bigger the high. And if you ate too much of it, there's a good chance you'd think you were dying."

I shook my head, still not understanding. I'd had one experience with marijuana—well, now two—and had decided I never wanted another. "I can't imagine someone wanting to feel that way on purpose. So it seems like it would have to be someone who had no clue what they were doing or how to mix pot with food, don't you think?"

"That's one option, but infusing food with THC is a lot harder than it seems."

I snorted. "How hard can it be? You buy some pot, dump it in your cookie batter. Poof! You get a sugar *and* pot high."

Hawke shook his head. "That's what most people *think*, but the high is more potent—and less noticeable in the food—if the weed is prepared properly."

I lifted a brow, totally amused. "You're teasing me."

His lips lifted in a seductive smile. "If I was teasing you, it wouldn't be with words."

Heat rose in my cheeks. "Okay, then," I said, changing the subject, "tell me about the preparation."

"If weed is prepped correctly before being added to food, the body can absorb the THC into the blood stream faster. If you just throw a bunch of pot in a recipe, it will look like your food has some weird spice in it, you'll end up eating stems and leaves, and the experience will be unpleasant. There's also some debate about how high you can actually get by mixing a bag of pot into a bowl of food, so there's a chance you'll waste *a lot* of pot."

My lips lifted in amusement as I nodded. "I bet that mistake has disappointed a lot of people."

"Undoubtedly."

"So, how do you prepare it?"

"There are two ways commonly used. The first, and less popular way, is to make cannabis flour. The stems and leaves are removed, and the remaining powder is ground to a flour-like consistency before being added to recipes. THC is fat soluble, not water soluble, so it's important to use a recipe that has a fat, like oil or butter. The other, more popular preparation method is to make cannabis butter. You put the pot and butter in a sauce pan, and heat it on low for almost an hour, then strain the pot out, leaving only the bud butter."

"Bud butter," I started to giggle.

Hawke smiled. "That's really what it's called," he said. "The heating process infuses the butter with THC. You put it back in your fridge and then use it in your cooking just like you'd use normal butter."

"How did you become a pot preparation expert?"

He gave me a side-long look. "I have an eclectic line of work."

That he did. "Seriously, though" I said, totally surprised. "I thought I had a pretty liberal college experience, but I had no idea pot needed special preparation to be used in food."

Hawke stretched out his legs under my coffee table, and crossed his feet over each other. "Most people don't, which is why I'd be surprised if the Saints and Sinners Cookies are an amateur organization. They're producing too fast, and too well, for this to be some college kids in their frat house kitchen."

"Plus, they're making mass quantities of it," I said, "which means they have to be getting their supply from somewhere."

"Or growing their own," Hawke suggested.

I nodded, thinking.

Hawke got up. "I need to check some things out, but I'll be back in a couple of hours. Until I figure out where your email threat came from, you need to be careful, and I'm not comfortable leaving you alone all night."

I gave him a strange look. "How did you know about that?"

"Because I know everything, Kitty Kate."

I didn't even try to argue. I nodded, and watched him lock the door and leave, silently wondering how much he knew about what had happened between me and Drake. I hoped it wasn't much.

I opened my laptop and added Hawke's lab test information to my article before sending it to Spence. He edited it and sent me back changes with a note that he was rearranging the paper layout to get the story in this week. It was a fast turnaround. Our deadline was tomorrow, but I already had most of the article written before I'd talked to Hawke. After a few hasty emails back and forth, and some phone calls, it was all settled. The pot cookies would be revealed to Branson residents tomorrow night. I sprawled out on the couch and fell fast asleep.

I woke up in my bed, and couldn't remember how I got there. Which wasn't comforting considering the last time that had happened, I thought sexy times had gone down and couldn't remember who they'd gone down with. This time, however, I'd had no cookies or baked goods, and was pretty sure I hadn't been drugged. I'd just been really tired.

I threw my robe on and shuffled down the hallway, bleary-eyed. I needed coffee to remedy this situation, immediately. I sniffed and every one of my senses perked up. It smelled like coffee was already brewing! Holy snipes! I had a coffee fairy!

I moved a little faster to the kitchen—I didn't want to miss the magical coffee making being—and found Hawke, dressed in jeans and a red t-shirt, different clothes than he'd been wearing last night, sitting at my kitchen table. So, it wasn't a coffee fairy, but it was just as good. He was eating an apple—one he must have brought from home because the produce I owned was currently colonizing something in my refrigerator's crisper—some toast, and drinking coffee out of my favorite blue mug with a flower on it that I'd painted at a ceramics class.

"Morning, Kitty Kate," he said with a smile.

He licked some butter off his lips, leaving them wet and shiny. I had a hard time convincing myself to look away. Breakfast had never looked so delicious. His lips slid up in a confident grin like he knew exactly what I'd been thinking, and his eyes sparkled with amusement.

"Morning, yourself." I poured myself a cup of coffee, and some cereal. "Interesting mug choice." I nodded toward the flower mug.

"I think it's cute."

"It was a failed attempt at arts and crafts."

He looked at the design I'd attempted to freehand. "I like it."

"I like it too because its ginormous and I can drink an entire barrel of coffee from it." I sat down at the table and mixed creamer and milk into my much smaller mug. Hawke seemed to be drinking his black—like a boss. "I sent the cookie article to Spence. It's coming out tonight."

Hawke looked at me over his coffee mug. "It will be interesting to see what everyone's reaction is."

I nodded as I swallowed a sip of my steaming caramel and cream flavored drink. "I don't think it will be pleasant."

He made a mmm sound in agreement.

"Where did you sleep?" I asked.

"I took you to your room, and then I slept on the couch."

"Well," I took another sip of my delicious coffee, "that's disappointing."

"I agree. But you were so out of it that I figured not even Chris Hemsworth could wake you."

Since Hawke looked quite a bit like Chris Hemsworth himself, I begged to differ on that point. "Lost opportunities," I said over the rim of my cup.

"I'm keeping a tab."

Now it was my turn to look amused. "Where did you go last night?" I asked, changing the subject.

"To see if I could figure out who was sending your emails."

"How did you know about that?"

He cocked a brow. "I think we had this discussion already."

"We did, but you didn't answer. Are you spying on me or something?"

"I don't have to. The whole town is doing it for me."

I frowned and he laughed.

"Well, did you find out anything about the emails?"

"Not yet."

I shrugged. "I'm sure it's fine. I'm working today, so I'll be at work or in public."

"Try not to go anywhere alone. And if you think you might be in danger, call me immediately."

I nodded. "I'll do that."

My phone buzzed with a text from Ella.

Facebook update about a motorcycle in your driveway. Amber suggested it belongs to the devil. Jackie thinks you're trying to set a record for doing it with a whole motorcycle gang at once.

I sighed, and closed my eyes.

"What is it?" Hawke asked.

"The Ladies. They're stalking me and posting information in a Facebook group. Maybe you should start parking in the garage when you come over so they can't see your bike or car."

He winged a brow. "Garage space? That's a serious commitment."

"So is staying off the Ladies' radar."

"That's never going to happen, Kitty Kate. Even if you died, they'd probably have someone watching for your ghost."

"Thanks a lot."

He grinned.

"They're stalking me!" I said, exasperated. "And making it easy for other stalkers! I tried to access the group but I have to be invited, so I can't. It's private, and no one will let me in. Ella's keeping me informed, though. She's the only friend I have there."

Hawke's lips slid into the slow, secret smile I loved so much. "Not the only one."

My eyes went wide. "Ella said none of my friends have been approved to join."

"They haven't."

"Then how did you get in?" If he had access to the group, he definitely knew about me spending time with Drake. I guess it said something about his confidence that he hadn't quizzed me on it. Or maybe he just trusted me. I immediately felt guilty over the cookie blackout…and my conflicted feelings for Drake.

He shook his head. "Nothing is private anymore, Kate. I have my ways." He got up and put his dishes in the sink, then threw his apple core away. "I'll check in with you tonight."

"Sounds promising."

He grinned. "Maybe we'll start taking advantage of some of those lost opportunities."

I smiled back and locked the door behind him, then went to my room to get ready for work.

Chapter Sixteen

I'd been at the office a total of two hours before I got a text from my mom.

EMERGENCY! COME TO THE HOUSE! FAST!

Huh. She'd figured out how to use the caps lock on her phone keyboard. Considering her lack of technological talent, this called for a celebration of some kind. Then again, all of the words were capitalized, so maybe she'd turned it on by accident and it had just gotten stuck. That was a far more likely scenario.

Most children would probably be concerned at a text like that from their parents. But with my mom, the situation could be something as simple as she ran out of flour and didn't have access to a car. A distinct possibility after the mouse-tie incident. I didn't want to know what she'd had to do to get back in my dad's good graces—or if she had yet. As far as I knew, the Mustang was still being aired out.

My mom was waiting on the porch when I arrived. She looked frazzled. "My computer is possessed!"

I revoked my previous call for a celebration of her technological prowess.

"Did it start speaking in tongues?"

"Yes!"

"I was joking."

"I'm not!"

"Well, then the first thing we need to do is get the demon's name." She was watching me with rapt attention. I was surprised she hadn't grabbed a notebook to write down instructions in case it happened again. "Because the only way to perform a proper exorcism is with the evil spirit's true name."

She nodded, eyes wide.

"Then we have to do a ceremonial dance."

She frowned. "I'm not a very good dancer."

"Well, you'll just have to do your best. If you half-ass it, the demon won't go away."

She nodded, and I knew she must be really worried because she didn't even react to my swear. I tried to keep myself from laughing.

We walked into their home office and her desktop computer was sitting on one desk, the laptop on another. I flipped them both on, but the desktop took forever to start. When it finally did, I realized my mom wasn't lying, there really were strange characters all over the screen and the mouse was a jagged blinking arrow as it moved instead of a solid, smooth glide. "How long has this been going on?" I asked, gesturing toward the foreign language and slowness.

She tilted her head, her eyes going up toward the ceiling while she thought. "A few months, I guess. But it got a lot worse this morning. Today it won't even speak English."

"And you haven't taken it somewhere to have it repaired?"

"Where would I take it? I'd have to go to Salt Lake to get decent computer help. That's why I just decided to move all the files." I remembered the file moving from a couple of months ago. She had enough flash drives to form an army.

I wondered if a cord was loose and maybe that was causing the problem. "Have you checked all the plugs and connections?"

"I bent over and looked at them," she said with a shrug. "They seemed fine."

Coming from my mom, that wasn't much reassurance. I knelt down on the floor and climbed under the desk that smelled like oak and always had. Even when I used to hide under there as a kid, it had smelled like I was sitting in a tree instead of on the floor. My dad had built it after my mom's truck had shifted into gear while she was talking to a friend, and crashed through the plate glass window of a ceramics shop. Most people categorized life events by age; I organized mine by my mom's disasters. And her computer seemed to be another one.

I heard a loud thump and saw my mom stomping her foot on the ground, swinging her hips, and raising her arms in the air. "Are you doing Zumba?" I asked, dumbfounded.

"Yes! It's the only dancing I know. I need my computer to work again."

As amused as I was that she'd listened to my demon exorcism instructions, the thumping was distracting. "I think that should be enough," I said. She stopped, but looked ready to wiggle again at any moment.

I checked the plugs first—they were all fine—then I moved out from under the desk to check the tower of the computer. The tower was sitting on a stand next to the desk. I leaned it toward me to look at the connections on the back of the computer when I felt my hand hit something hard stuck to the side of the computer tower. I looked at what I had just hit and pulled it off—with effort. It was a magnet the size of a candy bar and attached to the massive clothespin I'd had to make in junior high wood shop. It was holding up a bunch of coupons and papers. "Mom!" I yelled, waving the clothespin at her in one hand and the papers in another. "Why in the world did you mount this on your computer?"

Mom smiled and took it from me, her fingers running over the wood. "Isn't it nice? You did such a wonderful job staining it. I wanted it somewhere I could see it."

"It was meant to go on a fridge, not a computer!"

She frowned. "It fits perfect on the computer, though. And I hang coupons and notes on it. Look at that nice one from your dad telling me he loves me."

She pointed to a neon pink sticky note. I glanced at it. He'd have to love her to put up with the chaos she caused.

"Mom! Magnets are death for computers. You stuck this on the same side as your motherboard. No wonder it stopped working! You're lucky you got any files off of it at all. I don't think even the smartest computer technician in the world could fix this! You can take it to a repair shop to get it looked at, but I'm pretty sure the computer is trash. You'll have to buy a new one, or just use your laptop."

"Okay," she shrugged like it was no big deal.

"You're not even concerned that you destroyed your computer?"

She waved a hand in the air like she was pushing the worry away. "All the files are on my little color-coded sticks. I'll just make sure to keep the magnets away from them." Unlike every other person in the world who called them flash or thumb drives, my mom called them "sticks." She had her own language for a lot of things. It was hard to follow sometimes.

I pinched my nose and closed my eyes. "Great. Glad I could help. Now get me your "sticks" so I can show you how to transfer the files onto your laptop."

Thirty minutes later, we were sitting in the kitchen with a plate of fresh chocolate chip cookies on the table, two glasses of milk, and the clothespin magnet that had done all the damage. I thumbed through the coupons the magnet had been holding, stopping on an ad for carpet cleaning. It had a very happy couple in white clothes, sitting on their white carpet, playing with a baby and a dog. Something about the ad seemed off, but it was probably the fact that the couple had a kid and a dog, but were sitting on a bright white carpet. Sane people chose carpet colors that covered stains.

I picked up a cookie. "Mmm," I said, closing my eyes to enjoy the rich flavors of chocolate, and the nutty taste of the browned butter she'd used to make them. "These are so much better than the Saints and Sinners Cookies."

I froze, realizing I'd said that part out loud. I squeezed open one eye to gage my mom's reaction. She didn't seem murderous—which was a surprise. But she didn't seem giddy, either.

"I never did figure out what was in the darn cookies. Your dad made me stop trying after the Mustang died." I liked how she said "Mustang died" as if she had nothing to do with the process of killing it. And my dad had made her stop trying because I told him to keep the cookies away from her no matter what. Who knew what other hallucinations she would have conjured up.

"Well, I have some news about that," I said after taking a drink of cold milk.

Her eyes widened in anticipation. "What?"

"The judging wasn't really fair. The cookies are laced with THC."

Her brows pinched together in confusion. "Is that a new flavoring? Do I have to get it from a bakery supply store?"

I sighed at my mom's innocence, and shook my head. "No, Mom. It's marijuana."

She gasped and almost fell right off her chair. She righted herself, but couldn't stop shaking her head. "Those lying little cookie monsters! I knew they were hiding something. I *knew* it! No one's treats are better than mine, especially those stupid Saints and Sinners Cookies. They weren't even moist!"

I wasn't sure what the proper moist ratio was for cookies, but apparently it was important. "Well, now you know."

A vindicated look crossed her face. "Yes. Now I know. And I'll be talking to the County Fair board as soon as possible to rectify the situation. That grand prize ribbon is *mine!*"

Her eyes were getting a little crazy and I thought the opportunity for vengeance might be going to her head. "You should wait until the story comes out about it in the paper tonight. That will be all the leverage you'll need."

"Oh," she said, nodding her head. "I'll wait. I'll wait."

She was scaring me a little, and I wasn't completely convinced that my joke about a demon living in her computer had been off. I thought it might have jumped straight from the computer to her. The dancing must not have scared it. I heard the garage door go up and knew my dad was home. I could safely leave my mom—demon harboring or no—in his hands.

"In the meantime," I said, putting my glass in the sink, "don't eat any more of those Saints and Sinners Cookies."

I don't think she even heard me. She was still staring out the window, a wicked, pleased little smile on her face as I left the house.

I had no doubt a plan was forming in her head—and that I'd probably be hearing about it at some point on the police scanner.

I was walking into the office when I heard a loud rumble on the street. The engine sounded expensive. I turned my head to see a bright red Ferrari convertible. My eyes almost glazed over in envy. As the car passed, I recognized the driver. Kory Greer. He waved as he went by, and I tried to keep my mouth off the ground as I waved back.

Kory's sugar factory had been in financial trouble less than four months ago, and now he was driving a brand new Ferrari? That must have been one hell of a contract he got to absolve all of his debts, and buy him that kind of car. I only knew of one other person in town who could afford a car like that—Hawke—and there was a good chance he killed people for a living. I made a mental note to check in with Bobby about the body, and see if I could find out more about Kory Greer.

When I went inside the office, Ella was sitting in the chair in front of my desk, eating a doughnut. "Heya, Katie!"

"Hey, Ella. Are you feeling better?"

She looked like she'd lost a little weight, but her eyes were bright, and she seemed like her normal, spritely senior citizen self.

"She looks a lot better than she did a few days ago, that's for sure," Spence said, coming out of his office to get a doughnut too. He'd gotten a few salted caramel flavors today. They were my second favorite next to the chocolate frosted with salty peanuts on top. I grabbed one too.

"Yep! All better," Ella said as we sat around and ate our food.

"How did you get sick?" I asked.

"Not sure. It was the flu, I think. Didn't want to eat for a couple of days," she said around her bite of doughnut. Her appetite seemed to be back, at least. "I'm okay now, though."

Knowing what Hawke had said about the symptoms of consuming too much pot, and my own research, I wondered if her diagnosis was actually the flu, or if she'd been eating too many cookies like most of the people in town. She was definitely a good Saints and Sinners customer. "Did you go to the doctor?"

"For the dang flu?" Her face scrunched up, making her look twenty years older than she was as she made a psshh noise. "Heavens no! Who goes to the doctor for somethin' that can be taken care of with a little home remedy?"

Ella was a bit eccentric in general, so I wondered what her version of "home remedy" consisted of. "What do you make to get rid of the flu?"

"Hot toddy," she said, taking another bite of doughnut. "My neighbor told me about 'em and made me some. Calmed me right down. I've been drinkin' 'em all day for three days. Had a few before I came in."

My eyes widened at the same time as Spence's. If she'd been eating the cookies—and based on the huge bag that my mom had destroyed at the fair, I guessed that she had—mixing marijuana and alcohol wasn't a good idea. Granted, she didn't know about the pot, but given that she was Mormon, I was surprised she'd been willing to try a hot toddy as a remedy. "You know what's in a hot toddy, right?"

She wrinkled her nose. " 'Course I do. Honey and lemon."

Spence winged a brow. "And rum."

Her mouth dropped and she made a noise that sounded distinctly like an engine trying to start. "*Rrrrruuuuum?*"

I nodded.

"That's not possible," she said, shaking her head.

"Yeah. It is. Though it could have also been brandy or whiskey, depending on your neighbor's alcohol preference."

Ella kept shaking her head like it was on a motor. "No. I would've tasted the alcohol."

"Because you're an expert on what alcohol tastes like?" I said mildly.

She narrowed her eyes. "I've lived an excitin' life, Katie. There's a lot a things I've tried."

I raised a brow. "Still, the drink is designed so you don't taste the alcohol. Who gave it to you?"

Her expression immediately shifted from aghast to angry. "That *wicked* little Thelma Bart." Her eyes narrowed. "Oh, I'll get her for this. She better watch out. Good thing it was medicinal alcohol, or I'd have to tell my bishop."

Ella turned and headed for the door.

"Where are you going?"

"Home. To plan my revenge."

I shook my head and made it to the door in front of her. Which wasn't hard since she was practically eighty, and was swaying from the toddy. "You're not driving like this."

She stared at me like she couldn't believe I had the nerve to tell her what to do. "I'll do whatever I darn well please!"

"You're a hazard to society when you're driving sober, Ella. I'm not letting you drive drunk."

"I'm not drunk," she said as she stumbled into the wall and pretended she was rearranging the pictures. "Okay. I suppose it wouldn't hurt to get a ride home."

I smiled and took her keys.

After I made sure Ella was safe at home—and threw away the bags of Saints and Sinners Cookies I found all over her kitchen—I went back to work. I'd finished editing all of the stories I had so far for next week's paper, and started the layout. I was enjoying the calm before the storm. I knew as soon as the article came out tonight and people realized they'd been duped into being doped, they'd go nuts.

My phone buzzed with a text message. I looked at the number. Drake. Great. The Ladies had probably informed everyone of Hawke's overnight at my house, and now more rumors would be spreading like crazy. I was surprised my mom hadn't mentioned it when I stopped by earlier. Surely, someone had called to tell her of her daughter's evil ways, and berate her parenting skills.

I opened the text, fully expecting to get Drake's rage. Instead, it said:

I can't stop thinking about how beautiful you are.

My mouth fell open and my stomach started a little fluttering that wasn't authorized at all. What the hell was wrong with him? This wasn't our normal interaction. Usually there was banter, some innuendo, and we each left with a heightened state of awareness of each other and both mostly unsatisfied. This? This was...*nice.* What had possessed him to send something non-antagonizing? I could deal with snarky, arrogant, asshat Drake. Nice Drake was a lot harder to handle. Nice Drake made me melty.

Maybe he hadn't heard about Hawke staying the night yet, and that's why he wasn't fuming. I wasn't sure how to proceed. I sat staring at the text for a good ten minutes before finally texting back.

Thanks. That was...nice.

My phone buzzed again.

LOL! That sounded suspicious.

I smiled.

I'm always suspicious when you're charming.

I'll have to be charming more often.

I didn't like that thought at all. If he was charming more often, my hormones couldn't handle it.

The Devil Wears Tank Tops

I got dinner—a sandwich from the deli down the street—then went home and watched TV while I ate. Copies of the *Tribune* would be at the grocery store any minute, so I expected cookies were about to hit the fan.

I didn't have to wait long.

"Forever in Blue Jeans" started blaring from my phone. "Hey, Spence."

"The paper was delivered ten minutes ago and there are already fights breaking out at the grocery store."

"Fights?" I didn't expect people to fight over the newspaper. There were plenty of copies available.

"Over the cookies."

I blinked. I wasn't prepared for that reaction at all. "I thought people would be upset that they'd been eating cookies laced with drugs!"

"Some of them are, but I think a lot of people are upset with you for exposing the problem. People *really* liked those cookies."

Sheesh! "I thought I was doing a good deed!"

"You know what they say about that."

I rolled my eyes and shook my head. "Yeah, yeah, yeah. I've seen *Wicked*. I know how it goes."

I picked up my keys and bag, and checked to make sure my camera was inside. "Okay, I'm going to the store now. I'll let you know what happens."

"Hopefully they won't try to melt you."

"Funny," I muttered, and drove to the store.

I could barely find a parking place. I hadn't seen the store this crowded since Twinkies died. Oddly, there wasn't nearly as much interest when the Twinkies were resurrected. People just wanted to stock up once they realized there was a chance they might not be able to get them again. I expected that was the case now as well.

I walked into the store, noticing the mostly deserted aisles until I came to the one the Saints and Sinners Cookies were usually stocked on. It was utter mayhem. There were so many people crammed in the aisle yelling and shoving each other that I couldn't distinguish one person from the next.

I stood on my tip-toes, trying to get a better vantage point. Shelves of the cookie aisle were completely bare, and cookies of all kinds were scattered all over the floor—cookie collateral damage. People were pushing and shoving each other, ripping bags of Saints and Sinners Cookies out of each other's hands. One bag broke apart, and an entire group of people scrambled to grab them off the floor. They looked like wild animals descending on their prey.

Police officers were trying to quell the cookie riot with little success. They were being pushed around as much as everyone else, and I saw Bobby get slapped in the face with a macaroon. A bag sailed through the air, and frosted animal cookies rained down on the crowd. I stared as one woman used her purse to slap a guy upside the head. He staggered, but held onto his Saints and Sinners Cookies. She hit him again and he finally dropped the bag. She immediately grabbed the bag and ran out of the crowd to the check-out line. It said something that her moral compass didn't seem to have a problem with treat-beatings, but running out of the store during a riot without paying was unacceptable.

I couldn't believe my eyes as I watched the mayhem. This wasn't a scuffle. This was snack-pocalypse.

I stepped back and started snapping photos, then taking notes. I wanted to talk to the police, but they were a little busy.

"There she is!" someone screamed.

I looked around for who they might be yelling at, and realized they were pointing in my direction. About two seconds later, I realized their target seemed to be me. Like zombies that had just found dinner, the crowd paused, then started moving toward me at a rapid rate of speed, moving as one. Unfortunately for me, the crowd seemed to move at *World War Z* zombie speed, not *The Walking Dead*.

"Oh shit," I muttered under my breath. I started backing up toward the door as I reached into my purse, searching for my keys and phone.

Within seconds, I was surrounded. Some people were hitting me, others were pulling my hair, arms, and everything else. I was screaming for them to stop, and trying—unsuccessfully—to fight back. I remembered some of the self-defense moves Hawke had taught me, but those moves were typically only useful with one or two opponents, not an entire town.

I became vaguely aware of a roar coming from somewhere in the group around me. Then people started getting pushed and pulled away from me. Suddenly the whole wave of people stopped and everyone quieted. It was like the world had calmed. Either that, or I was dead...a distinct possibility. I couldn't figure out why there'd been a decibel change until I saw Hawke step up behind me. He wrapped me in his arms.

"Let's go, Kitty Kate."

I nodded absently, and let him pick me up, and carry me out of the store.

"Are you okay to drive?" he asked, still holding me as he took me to my car.

I nodded again.

He put me down and took my keys from my purse, handing them to me, and then helped me into my Jeep. "I'll follow you to your house." I looked in the rearview mirror and saw him waiting for me to pull out of the parking lot before he got on his bike. Several people stood behind him staring at me with angry looks on their faces.

I shook my head as I drove away. The attack had been unexpected, and I knew I'd be sore tomorrow, but really, I was more stunned than hurt. I called Spence and told him he'd have to go cover the story because everyone in town seemed to want me dead. I suggested he wear body armor.

Hawke followed me into my house and went into the kitchen. I sat on the couch, still completely stunned. "I can't believe they were mad at me," I mumbled. "I really thought I was doing a good thing by exposing the pot cookies."

Hawke came back and handed me a tall glass of orange juice and a pill. "You were. People will realize that eventually. They're just upset they know about the problem now. Ignorance is bliss."

I took the pill without really thinking about it, the sweet and tangy flavor of the orange juice rolling over my tongue. It was good, and I needed the sugar. "Now I'm going to be threatened by the entire town."

Hawke winced. "I would have taken you to my house, but I thought it would be better if we were here so people would know you're home—and I'm home with you—so they shouldn't do anything stupid."

"Yeah, you being home with me is going to cause problems. It's probably already been posted on the Ladies Facebook page."

He grinned. "It has. Along with speculation."

"Maybe we should make some of those things a reality." I wiggled my brows.

"If I thought you were in your right mind, and you weren't covered in bruises, I wouldn't hesitate."

"Hey!" I said, defensive. "I'm not crazy." I couldn't argue about the bruises. I could feel them welling under my skin on my arms, legs, and face.

"No, but you've just been through a traumatic experience. I'd like to get that resolved before we deal with the matter of you wearing too many clothes."

I smiled at his flirting and thought back to the fight at the store. "You stopped that situation pretty fast."

He lifted a shoulder. "People fear what they don't know."

"Maybe you should sit on my front porch tonight so people who come over and try to burn my house down might reconsider."

He smiled. "I can do that."

I started to feel a little sleepy. "I'm tired all of a sudden."

"I know," Hawke said, helping me stand up. "The pill will help you sleep. I knew you'd be up worrying all night. That won't help anything, and I need you alert tomorrow to deal with all of these people, and whoever the email threat is coming from."

I was vaguely aware that the news didn't make me particularly happy, but Hawke was right. I needed to sleep or I'd make bad decisions. I fell into bed. The last thing I remembered was being tucked in by my hero.

Chapter Seventeen

"I heard Hawke tore through the crowd like an avengin' angel," Ella said, awestruck.

Ella had accosted me as soon as I walked into the office that morning. It wasn't a surprise considering the things that were being said about me on the town social media pages. There was now a "Hate Kate" Twitter account. I'd avoided it—and all other social media—after reading some rather unkind comments about my nosy butt.

I wasn't going to argue Ella's comparison regarding Hawke, however. "He probably kept me out of the hospital. Everyone was acting completely insane—way more insane than usual."

"Greta Simpson said she thought he'd killed a few people tryin' to save you."

That I hadn't heard. Good hell. Hawke had stayed mostly out of the rumor mills and limelight in Branson because people were terrified of him. Now they'd be even more scared, but he wouldn't be immune to the gossips like he had been in the past. "Greta needs to get her eyes checked. He might have hurt some people trying to get to me, but they probably would have beat me into a coma without him." I'd heard about groupthink and studied it a bit in my college psych classes. People do a lot of insane things when they think they have support. It's too bad that energy couldn't be channeled elsewhere.

Spence had texted me early in the morning to say an emergency town meeting regarding the cookies had been called for six PM. Thanks to Hawke staying at my house all night, nothing was vandalized, and I wasn't injured even further. He left early, though, for his own job, and I wasn't comfortable being home alone, so I'd come to work instead. Spence still wasn't in the office because he'd been out late covering the cookie riots.

Ella had come in about an hour after me, and was telling me all of the gossip about the previous night.

"Bishops are being overrun with phone calls and meetin' requests from members," Ella said.

"Why?" I asked.

"Because everybody ate the cookies and they think they need to repent!"

When Mormons do something wrong, they have to confess to their ward bishop. The bishop then tells them what needs to be done for the person to atone for their mistakes. Doing drugs is on the sin list, but I didn't think this qualified. "Is it really a sin when they had no idea they were doing it?"

Ella shrugged. "Best to check just in case. You don't wanna get to the other side and find out that's the thing knockin' ya out of the celestial kingdom." She stood up and stretched. "Just a piece of advice" she said. "Be careful. You're number one on people's poop list for exposin' the cookies, and getting' 'em banned. They were great cookies, even if they were evil."

I exhaled deeply. "I was on those lists a long time ago. I don't imagine another reason will affect me much."

"Yeah, but the Ladies' Facebook Group about you got *a lot* of new members in the last twelve hours. The cookies have already been added to the document about your sins in the group."

My mouth gaped. "There's a document?"

She gave me a look like she thought I was crazy. "Course there is! Gotta keep things organized. Amber Kane blames you for her takin' the job sellin' the cookies."

My mouth fell open and I couldn't even form words. She blamed me? I swallowed, and picked up my stress ball, squeezing it repeatedly. It was the only alternative to punching my desk. "How in the hell did I get blamed for that? I didn't make her take the job!"

"She said you were askin' about the cookies at the school. Figures you knew about the pot in them for weeks, and just kept it a secret so everyone in town would be as sinful as you. Says if you'd told people about it earlier, she would have quit the job immediately."

Her logic was astounding. And the fact that she was blaming me for something I had nothing to do with at all irked me to no end. One of my biggest pet peeves was when people didn't take responsibility for their actions. People like Amber were great at not accepting blame.

"That's the most ridiculous thing I've ever heard. I published the article as soon as I knew about the marijuana because I wanted people to be aware of it. I don't care whether people are pot users or not, I just wanted them to have all the information before they ate a bag and got sick, or worse, had a heart attack like Opie."

"I know," she said. "Amber just doesn't like bein' wrong."

I muttered a string of swears under my breath, totally annoyed.

Ella got up from her chair and started down the hall. "I'm gonna go work in the archives. See ya in a little bit."

I shook my head in disbelief and stared blankly at my laptop screen, wondering why I'd ever thought it was good idea to come back to Branson Falls. I was having my love life dissected by the entire town, people were being added to the Ladies' Hate Kate Facebook group left and right, and now I was being blamed for things I had absolutely nothing to do with. The more I thought about it, the more agitated I got. I decided I needed to stop thinking, and distract myself with something productive—like work.

My email inbox was full, and getting fuller. About half were threats, the rest were people either on the fence about my investigation, or thanking me for exposing the cookie drugs. Most of the threats were from Branson residents who had no problem identifying themselves. Some called me a liar, others said I should have left well-enough alone. Still no word from the original email threat makers, however. Maybe now that the cookies had been exposed, they'd decided there was no reason to try to hurt me. The damage was already done.

My phone rang. It was Officer Bob. "You need to come up to the B.F. sign on the hill."

"Why?" I asked. The last time I'd been up there it was to change the B and F to the last two numbers of the year of my graduating high school class. It was a tradition for all seniors. I'd ridden in the back of the truck of some drunk cowboys—who I didn't know were drunk at the time—and sincerely believed I might not live long enough to ever see the fruit of our labors.

"Someone changed the sign on the mountain to say POT."

"What?" I asked, my voice thick with disbelief. "How?" There were only two letters. Did they create their own?

"With garbage sacks. Black ones to block out areas of the B and F they didn't want seen, and white ones to make new lines and the letter T."

"Oh, geez."

"I thought you might want to get some pictures before they start takin' it all down."

"Thanks, Bobby. I'll be there soon."

On my way to witness the POT sign, I drove by the old abandoned steel factory that was frequently painted with welcome home signs for Mormon missionaries, and notes asking people to prom. Today, it was covered in pictures of pot leaves. I shook my head, wondering who had done that. A bunch of hilarious teenagers with some extra paint, I was sure.

When I got to the mountain, it did indeed spell the word POT. I had a feeling this was also the work of some teenage pranksters. "At least they're creative," I said to Bobby.

He snorted. "Yeah, they could've been far more destructive."

I noticed his cheek was a little red from the night before. The macaroon must have hit him hard.

"Have you recovered from the riot last night?"

"Have you?" he asked.

I blew out a breath. "Yeah, I'm fine. I just wasn't expecting that reaction."

"Us either. Next time you publish somethin' like that, do me a favor and give us a heads-up. We didn't even have time to get our riot gear outta storage."

"Sorry about that," I said sincerely.

He lifted a shoulder. "It could've been worse."

I snapped some photos.

"I was gonna call you about this, but since you're here, I'll just tell ya," Bobby said.

I paused and looked over at him.

"We got an identity on the sugar factory body."

I froze. I'd been waiting to hear on that. "You did?"

"Guy named Juan Carlotta. He was an illegal immigrant and had no ties to the sugar factory. We think he was just tryin' to rob the place, and did somethin' to set off a spark."

"You're sure Kory Greer didn't know him?" I asked. The whole situation still felt off.

Bobby nodded. "We got photos from Juan's family, and Kory had never seen him before."

"You believe that?"

"Yeah. We questioned Kory and he didn't act strange at all. He showed no recognition of Juan."

I nodded, and scribbled Juan's name down in my notebook to check on later. I went down the hill to get some more photos at a distance before going back to the office.

The people who changed the sign worked fast. When we'd done it in high school, it had taken half the senior class and about four hours. The paper was delivered to the grocery store around eight PM. The POT sign makers must have heard about the article, and gone immediately to the hill and started their work.

It was a fast turnaround, I thought, as I parked my Jeep and went in the office. When I walked in, a brown paper bag was sitting on my desk.

Ella poked her head out of the back office. "That came while you were gone. Some kid dropped it off."

I picked the bag up and pulled a note off of it before setting it back down on my desk. I opened the note.

You were warned.

It took me about two seconds to make the connection…just long enough for the bag to explode.

"Holy fudge!" Ella yelled.

Not the choice of words I would have used, and in fact, the ones I'd said in my head had been much more representative of the situation. I'd jumped back when the explosion happened and rolled on the floor, covering my head with my arms. Now I stood slowly, looking around at the damage. There was a black mark about the size of my palm on my desk, but other than that, nothing else seemed hurt. I looked at Ella. She'd been standing on the other side of the room, so aside from the scare, she seemed fine. "Are you okay?" I asked her.

She nodded slowly, a little dazed. "Are you?"

I checked myself. I was covered in what appeared to be Saints and Sinners cookie crumbles, but I still seemed to have all my fingers, toes, and both my eyeballs. "I think so."

I picked up the phone and called Spence to tell him what had happened then I called Bobby. "Are you still on duty?" I asked him.

"Yeah."

"Can you come to the *Tribune* office? Someone just tried to explode me."

Complete silence came from the other end of the phone.

"Bobby?"

"I'm here." More pausing. "I used to think your mom kept us busy, but things sure have gotten a lot more interestin' around here since you came back to town. I'll be there soon."

Bobby was there in about ten minutes, followed by Spence.

"What in the world?" Spence said, walking in and surveying my desk. Even though I'd been so scared I'd almost peed my pants, the explosion had been relatively contained to an area less than a foot wide. It was clearly meant to scare me, not do serious damage.

Bobby looked over the desk, took photos, and wrote some notes. "You said a kid dropped it off?" he asked.

I nodded. "Ella saw him."

She looked up from where she was sitting in her chair, a glass of water in her hands. She was still a bit shaken. "He had dark brown hair, a ball cap, and sunglasses. Weird marks on his arm and face like scars. I didn't recognize him, though."

Bobby turned to me. "Have ya pissed anyone off lately?"

I gave him a disbelieving look. "You were at the cookie riot last night, right?"

"I mean anyone ya know about? Were you bein' threatened?"

"Actually, yes." I pulled up the email I'd gotten before the pot cookie story came out, and showed it to Bobby.

He pursed his lips, displeased. "Why didn't you come to us with this earlier, Kate?"

I shrugged. "Because it's not the first time I've been threatened. They usually don't turn into anything, and I didn't want to waste your time."

"In the future, we'd rather be kept informed." He shook his head and blew out a long-suffering sigh. "You're going to be as big of a problem as your mom."

I took offense to that, but considering the black marks I now had decorating my desk, I didn't really have a lot of room to argue.

Bobby asked some more questions about the situation, and I showed him the bag the cookies had come in. "Be careful, Kate," Bobby said. "Until we know who these people are, I think you're probably going to be in danger. I'll put a patrol on your house so you have someone drivin' by at all times. And we'll probably have more questions for you as we investigate."

I nodded, thankful for the extra protection, and annoyed I had to deal with it at all. Considering the threats I was now getting from Branson residents, too, though, I thought it might not be a bad idea to have the police on my side.

Bobby took the bag and cookie pieces for testing, and left. Spence echoed the same thing as Bobby. "I don't like this at all, Kate. I don't want you to get hurt, and things just seem to be escalating."

I shrugged. "They're escalating because I'm on the right trail."

Spence shook his head. "You're going to give me a heart attack one of these times."

I smiled. "I'll get you a hot nurse."

He tried to force it back, but his lips lifted in amusement, undoubtedly imagining the man of his dreams in a doctor's jacket, and nothing else.

I was still covered in cookie dust so I went into the bathroom to attempt cleaning up. There were even cookie crumbles in my hair. When I came back out, Drake's familiar build was occupying my office chair. He was staring at the burn marks on my desk with an unhappy expression on his face.

"Hey," I said, tentatively.

He looked me up and down, his eyes sticking on the cookie pieces still embedded in parts of my clothes and hair. I'd tried to get them all off, but there was only so much I could do with the sticky sugar. The heat had turned it to glue. "You look good enough to eat," Drake said, the innuendo clear.

I flushed. I was surprised he hadn't started with a tirade against the dangers of my job.

"What are you doing here?" I asked.

"I was in Salt Lake for some legislature meetings when I heard about the riot. I left as soon as I could this morning to come back and check on you."

That was nice of him. "Thanks."

A muscle moved at his jaw. "Then I got here and found out you'd been sent a bomb."

I scrunched up my face. "I wouldn't classify it as a bomb, exactly. More like a mini firework that shot out sugar."

His eyes widened and his expression turned to disbelief. "Did it explode on your desk after you were given a warning to stop your investigation?"

I narrowed my eyes and glared at Ella and Spence, who were standing in the corner eating cupcakes that looked like they'd come from out of town. Clearly, they'd been bribed by Drake's treats, and he'd had time to summarize the entire situation while I was cleaning up. "It was a *little* explosion," I said with a wince.

"Then it was a bomb," Drake said, taking a deep breath like it would calm him down. "Are you okay?"

I sighed. "Yeah. I'm fine."

His eyes scanned me, searching for wounds. "Do you need to go to the hospital?"

I looked down. "I don't think you can be injured with sugar shrapnel." After all, it wasn't as lethal as sugar dust.

When Drake was convinced I seemed okay, he asked, "Did you go to the hospital last night?"

"No," I said, instinctively touching my arms. I'd had a few bright bruises bloom on my arms and legs overnight. I'd worn jeans and a three-quarter length shirt to cover them up. "They didn't get many punches in before Hawke showed up."

The line of Drake's jaw hardened and the room fell into silence for several seconds. Whether he was mad that I'd been saved by Hawke, or upset he wasn't the one to do the saving, I wasn't sure. Drake's voice was soft when he spoke, "I wish I'd been there."

I gave a short laugh. "I wish I hadn't."

The Devil Wears Tank Tops

His lips lifted in a smile that didn't touch his eyes. "You're pretty infamous at the moment."

"I know. The entire town either thinks I'm a hero for singlehandedly bringing the evil pot cookies down, or they hate me for getting rid of their fun treat."

"It's a bad place to be in."

I nodded. "You're not kidding."

He studied me for a moment. "Maybe I could help take your mind off of it?"

I lifted a brow in interest. I couldn't wait to see what this proposal would be.

"I believe you owe me a date," he said.

Ah. I'd almost forgotten. "I wondered when you were going to collect."

"Tomorrow night at six?"

"If no one's killed me by then."

He gave a forced smile, like he didn't want to even entertain the thought. "I'll make sure of it." He stood up and met my eyes. His gaze was soft with what looked like concern. "I'm glad you're okay. Be careful, Katie, and call me if you need me."

The request surprised me. In the past, he'd just storm over and take charge. A request wasn't like Drake. He usually dealt in commands. "I always am," I answered.

Drake's lips lifted in a slight smile that indicated he didn't believe that at all. "I'll pick you up tomorrow at six."

I nodded, and watched him walk out the door.

I smiled as I sat down. The thought of going out with Drake and not having to worry about anything except possible arguments with him for a few hours was nice. I needed some time to let my mind clear, and not be concerned about someone vandalizing my personal belongings, or trying to hurt me.

"Woo—eee!" Ella chortled in a sing-song voice. "Drake and Katie, sittin' in a tree—"

"There are no trees involved," I said, cutting her off. "No kissing, either."

"Not yet."

I shook my head. "I have enough to deal with in my life right now without adding romantic entanglements to it."

She chuckled. "You've been in romantic entanglements since you moved back here. I don't think it's gonna stop any time soon."

I frowned. She was probably right, but I had other things I needed to concentrate on at the moment.

"I heard Salt Lake has a bomb squad. Maybe we should hire those guys to follow you around for a little while," Ella suggested.

"That's ridiculous."

"Between you and your mom, that's actually a good idea," Spence said.

"Eh," Ella said, her tone unworried. "She has Drake and Hawke to protect her. She'll be fine."

I had to admit, having those two on my team certainly made me less apprehensive. I'd been threatened before, but never with explosives. I'd exposed the cookies and stopped them from being sold in Branson. Any other sane person would probably stop investigating and let sleeping dogs lie. But apparently, I wasn't sane. Exposing the cookies wasn't the end of the story. I needed to find out who had a cookie vendetta, what they were trying to accomplish, and why I was still being targeted. I had to get more information on Isaac Handler and the Brigham Smith Group.

Chapter Eighteen

The city council room was even more crowded than the grocery store had been last night. People were smashed into the main room—which was small to begin with— hallway, and were even standing outside. News vans lined the street in front of the building. Cookies spiked with drugs were being sold in public locations to anyone who had a few dollars, including kids. The story was big enough to warrant state, and even national, attention. I glanced around at the reporters and saw Karrie Williams, a friend I'd interned with during college at one of the big newspapers in Salt Lake. Karrie and I had worked on a few stories together, and I liked her a lot. I smiled and waved at her across the room. Her mouth spread into a wide grin and she waved back.

The meeting started, and Councilman Mark Brady addressed the mumbling crowd, assuring them all the cookies had been taken off the shelves, and everything possible was being done to figure out how this had happened, and why cookies containing drugs were being sold in grocery stores.

I took some photos, and notes, and listened as people took turns at the microphone, expressing their concerns. Several people brought up the point that if the cookies had drugs in them and no one knew about it, what other foods contained drugs or harmful items. Privately, I thought the answer was most foods, unless they were certified organic. Food ingredient lists were scary, and most contained items you couldn't even pronounce. If I couldn't even sound the word out, chances were high that it wasn't the best thing for my body...which was why I'd never asked for the ingredient list of some of my favorite foods. I'd feel guilty every time I ate them.

The meeting went on for over two hours with the city council and mayor trying to assuage people's fear and anger. After the meeting ended, the crowd dispersed a bit and I went over to talk to Karrie. "Hey!" I said, giving her a hug. "I never thought I'd run into you in Branson Falls."

She laughed. "Me either."

"Don't you usually cover crime?" I asked. I'd read some of her articles, and knew a story like this was out of her usual reporting duties.

"Yeah," she said. "I mean, I guess cookies spiked with pot could fall into that. But I was kind of in the area when we heard about the cookies, and my boss asked me to cover it since I was close."

My bag started slipping from my shoulder so I shifted it and asked, "Were you working on another story?"

Karrie nodded. "Yeah. A body was found in Rowe."

Rowe was a few towns to the south of Branson, about thirty minutes away. It wasn't in my reporting jurisdiction, but I was surprised I hadn't heard of it. Bodies were typically something that got noticed and talked about for miles. "Do they know what happened to the person?"

"A couple of guys were seen leaving the scene. It could have been organized crime, or a drug deal gone wrong."

"I bet the citizens of Rowe weren't happy to hear about that. It always makes people uneasy when a body is found, especially in a small town." People liked feeling safe, and dead bodies, drug dealers, and organized crime didn't help that.

"Definitely. People don't really blink an eye in Salt Lake unless it's a strange circumstance," Karrie said, putting her notebook in her purse. "Speaking of strange circumstances, this pot cookie business is crazy. It's fantastic that you broke the story. Great investigative work."

"Thanks," I said, meaning it. It was always nice to hear praise from other reporters I respected. I didn't add that I'd only started to suspect something was amiss after I'd discarded most of my clothes and tried to seduce Dylan Drake. "Now I just need to figure out who was spiking the cookies, and what their motive was."

We walked out of the building together, skirting the groups of people who were still talking after the meeting.

"Well, if you need any help, let me know," Karrie said.

"Thanks. And let me know if you need any more cookie info."

Karrie got in her car and waved as she drove away. It was a long two hours to get back to Salt Lake. I didn't envy her the drive.

I went back to the office after the meeting, and stayed there working late, a police car driving by every ten minutes or so. Ella and Spence had both left over an hour ago. I couldn't bring myself to go home alone, though, and liked that the *Tribune* office was at least in a more populated area of Branson. As long as I was in public, with other people, I didn't think much about the email or the bag of cookies that had exploded on my desk. But once I was alone, I couldn't stop thinking about it. It wouldn't stop me from doing my job, but the fact was, I didn't really feel safe anywhere.

I couldn't stay at the office for the entire night, though, and I needed to get some sleep. I stretched in my chair, and then started gathering my things. I scrolled through my inbox right before I was about to shut down and noticed a new message from the cookie bomber.

Your Last Warning
Next time, it won't just be your desk.

A shiver ran through me. I hadn't checked my email since before the bag explosion. I looked at the time stamp. It had been delivered one minute after the explosion. I didn't like being threatened, and being threatened by someone I couldn't identify made me even less happy. I glared at the screen. Well, they could keep on trying to scare me away. I wasn't going anywhere. If anything, now I was determined to figure out who they were and what was going on just so I could tell them off in person.

For people who seemed to have access to explosives and drugs, they sure were giving me a lot of warnings.

Still, I found myself looking over my shoulder every three seconds.

I picked up my phone and dialed Bobby. "I got another message from the cookie bomber."

"Dagnabbit," he hissed. "Where are you?"

"The office."

"I'll send a patrol car over to check on you."

I gathered my stuff with shaky hands. "I'm fine," I said, trying to convince myself. "I was just leaving for the night."

"Okay. Can you send me the email?"

"Yeah, but Hawke is already trying to find out who sent it."

Bobby made an ahhh sound. "Well, he's going to have access to much better IP address tracking software than we do, but send it to me anyway so we can have it on file, and check into it."

I clicked on forward, and typed in Bobby's address. "Done."

"And I'd rather not have you alone tonight, Kate. Stay with someone if you can."

"Okay," I said. "Thanks, Bobby."

"Be safe," he said, and clicked off.

I texted Spence to tell him about the email. He texted back and told me to go somewhere safe for the night, too. Part of me—the stubborn bit—felt like I should go home by myself as a way to prove that I could handle things on my own, and wouldn't let the jerks threatening me win. I got in the car and started for my house. My heart sped up the closer I got to my street, and I finally decided that proving myself probably wasn't the best plan, and I wasn't ready to be there alone. It was times like this that I wished I did have a little dog to keep me company. Seeing his happy, wagging tail every day would make it easier to deal with the demons of daily life.

I found myself steering away from my own house, and going to my mom and dad's instead. Nothing felt as safe as home, and since my own home wasn't offering that right now, I thought my parents' house probably would.

I was watching TV with my dad when my phone rang to the tune of "Sweet Caroline." I looked at the caller ID and recognized the number, I just hadn't assigned him a ring tone yet—I wasn't prepared for the commitment. I got up to take the call outside. The night breeze was the perfect temperature, and it was beautiful outside.

I answered. "Are you calling to cancel our date?"

"Never," Drake said. I could almost feel him smile on the other end. "Our date. I like the sound of that."

I was glad he was so confident in his feelings about the subject. Mine wavered like a seesaw.

"I was calling to check up on you. Do you need anything tonight?"

I shook my head. "No. I'm okay."

"Are you home alone?"

"Not right now. I'm at my parents' house."

"I'm not sure if that makes me feel better or not. Your mom is more dangerous than you are."

"She'd bop you on the head if she heard that."

Drake laughed. "I forgot to tell you this earlier, but I found some information on the Saffron Star PR Marketing firm you asked me to look into."

I perked up. Saffron Star was the marketing firm that had organized the pot protest. "What did you learn?"

"They're a pretty big firm in Salt Lake. I looked into some of their clients, and recognized several." He started rattling them off. "Press Automotive Group, Trellis Restaurants, Safeharbor Financial, the Brigham Smith Group—"

My jaw dropped. "B.S.!"

"No, seriously."

I shook my head. "No, that's what I call Brigham Smith because of their initials."

He gave a low laugh. "Only you would think of that."

I was pretty sure I wasn't the only one who had thought of it, but didn't say that.

I tapped my hand against the railing on my parents' front porch. So, Saffron Star had organized the pot protest, and they worked with Brigham Smith. But how were they tied to the Saints and Sinners Cookies? And why? There was a link there that I was missing, I just didn't know what it was yet. "Spence and I were looking into them because of their connection with the pot cookies."

"How are they connected?" Drake asked.

"We're not sure, but think B.S. might have invested in Saints and Sinners. The pot cookies were made under a company called Makhai, LLC. Makhai is owned by a guy named Isaac Handler, and he has some connection to Brigham Smith, probably through the investment side."

I could practically feel Drake's mind puzzling it out on the other end. "Interesting. I've worked with Brigham Smith in the legislature."

"Do you work well with them?"

"Depends on the day. They're lobbyists. Far right."

"How far?" I asked.

"They make Fox News actually seem fair and balanced."

I wrinkled my nose. That didn't bode well.

"So they're active in the Utah political community?"

"Very. Especially when it comes to moral justice. They have a theme song."

I raised a brow. "Seriously?"

"The religious hymn "Put Your Shoulder to the Wheel"."

I snorted. The hymn encouraging people to get to work. Apparently the work of this group was trying to stop anything they thought of as morally dubious.

"Are they affiliated with the Mormon Church?"

"Officially? No."

Ah. "But unofficially, they're there to do the bidding of the Church where the Church can't because if they do, they're apt to get their non-profit status revoked."

Drake's tone softened like he was amused. "I would say that's an accurate assumption."

I rolled my eyes. "You're such a politician. It's not like I'd quote you on that."

"I have to cover my bases, Katie." I still wasn't fond of the name, but the more I got to know Drake, the more I liked that he had a pet name for me.

"When did you work with them last?" I asked.

"All the time, but I don't know why they'd be tied up with a company selling pot cookies. Maybe it was someone trying to discredit Brigham Smith."

"Yeah, that's the theory I had, too. I don't understand the motive. Whoever is doing this can't be doing it for profit. The Saints and Sinners Cookies were each about three dollars. A cookie from Frosted Paradise is two dollars and fifty cents. If you had to cover the costs of production *and* the drugs, you'd want to charge a lot more than three bucks."

"That's true," Drake said, "and pot bakeries do charge a lot for their items. Even a mini cookie at a pot bakery is usually around five dollars."

I raised a brow. "How do you know that?"

He chuckled. "I keep informed."

I wrinkled my brow. This was a side of Drake I hadn't seen before. Like, maybe he was a normal person and not the superman everyone made him out to be. The thought was disturbing because it made him a lot more accessible for someone like me.

"But," he continued, "people go into those bakeries knowing they're getting pot with their chocolate chips. If people didn't know what they were consuming, they wouldn't have been willing to pay the going rate for pot-spiked baked foods."

"And most people in Branson wouldn't have tried them at all," I reasoned.

"Exactly."

"Okay, well thanks for checking into Saffron Star PR for me, and for the call."

"No problem. Let me know if you need anything else before tomorrow."

"I will. I'll be fine, though."

There was a pause on the other end. "I wouldn't have been able to sleep without checking on you first. Have a good night, Katie."

I hung up, and went to find my parents for dinner. My mom was making hand-cut French fries. My favorite.

After hearing about everything that had happened in my day, my parents had insisted I spend the night. I hadn't argued, and felt relieved I had a place to go, and didn't have to ask to stay. I'd spent dinner thinking about the story, but still couldn't figure out how it all tied together. When that had become too frustrating, I'd switched my train of thought to Drake, a man who seemed to care about me far more than I'd believed. Before, I thought his interest in me was just to have another notch on his bedpost. I wasn't falling for that. The rumors about him and his arrogant, overbearing attitude had pushed me away. But now I was seeing another side of him. And it was making me more confused than ever.

The next morning, I was in the kitchen pouring a glass of orange juice when a knock sounded on the door.

I opened it and found Hawke on the porch. His sandy hair was slicked back and he smelled like the beach. I took a deep breath and closed my eyes. Good grief, I loved his Swagger body wash. "Morning," I said. "Did you just get out of the shower?" Hawke had a glorious shower. Gigantic—like him—and it looked like it belonged to a multi-millionaire. It might.

"I had a long workout this morning."

I frowned, wondering who he'd been working out with.

He seemed to read my mind. "I was alone, but it would have been better with you, Kitty Kate."

I flushed and invited him inside. "How did you know I was here?"

He gave me a knowing smile. "Tracker on your Jeep."

"Oh yeah. I forgot that's still there."

"And it's never coming off." His tone was no-nonsense. "I heard about the explosion at the *Tribune* and the new email. I wanted to check on you."

I smiled, not even questioning how he knew about both of those things. "Thanks. I'm fine." I did have a question for him though. "Any news on figuring out who sent me the emails?"

He folded his arms across his chest. "Not yet. Bobby called and forwarded me the email from last night too, though, so I've got my people working on all of them." Ah, so that's how he knew about the previous night's events—well, one of the ways at least.

"I thought it was pretty easy to track IP addresses."

"It is if the sender doesn't know what they're doing. If they don't want to be found though, they can route the address to other addresses in a path that stretches all over the world, and goes on for a very long time. That's what the sender of your emails did."

That sounded complicated, I thought, as I leaned against the door frame. "How do you track that?"

He gave a slow smile. "It's not easy, and not many people can do it. Luckily, I know a few of them."

I chuckled. "Remind me never to get on your bad side."

"Kate?" I heard my mom call from the kitchen. "Who are you talking to? Do they want breakfast?"

I looked at Hawke. "Apparently my mom's up. Do you want to eat?"

"Sure." He followed me into the kitchen. "Hawke's here," I said as I shuffled over the slate tile. My mom turned around and I froze, staring at her, my eyes almost popping out of their sockets. She looked like she'd fallen down the stairs...or something equally as horrible.

"What happened to you?" I was highly alarmed. Maybe all of the blood vessels around her eyes had collapsed. We needed to get her to a hospital immediately!

I caught sight of my dad behind her, shaking his head with wide eyes. I ignored it, and went back to my mom. "Did you get in another car accident this morning? I didn't even hear you leave! Did an air bag do this?" I was already preparing my story and thinking of people to call for interviews and quotes. People needed to be warned about the dangers! I stopped, taking in the various shades of blues and blacks, another possibility coming to my mind. "Or did someone beat you up?" Maybe she'd followed through with her plan of fair-cookie vengeance, and one of the judges had fought back.

"What are you talking about, you silly girl? Nothing happened."

"But, your eyes!" Another possibility sprung to my mind and I pointed at her. "Oh! I told you not to eat any more of those cookies!"

I heard my dad interrupt with a warning cough, and looked at my mom. She seemed a little upset. "There's nothing wrong with my eyes! I'll have you know, this is the latest style. It's called a smoky eye, and you can do it with almost any color. I took a class."

I knew what a smoky eye was, and it certainly wasn't that. "Who taught the class? You look like a gothic grandma!" Her face screwed up into an angry pout. I wasn't sure what made her madder—that I didn't like her makeup, or that I'd insinuated she was old enough to be a grandma.

"It looks lovely, Mrs. Saxee," Hawke said, smiling and taking her hand.

She blushed. "Thank you, Hawke."

"Don't encourage her!" I said.

She turned to me. "See, Kate. That's the proper way to treat someone. At least Hawke has manners." She shook her head, disappointed. "I don't know where you got yours from, but it certainly wasn't me."

"No," I said, folding my arms across my chest in defiance. "Someone who really cares about you will tell you when you look like a raccoon, and not let you go out in public that way."

She huffed, and folded her own arms across her chest, mimicking my stance. "Well, I think you're being ridiculous. It's not my fault you don't keep up with current fashion trends. I'm not changing it."

I shook my head in defeat. That was one thing I loved about my mom, and something I'd inherited from her: her ability to stick her heels in and not move when she'd made a decision. She was as stubborn as an ox, and I was lucky to be her daughter.

I released a deep breath. "You're right, Mom," I said, relenting. "I'm sorry. I didn't mean to hurt your feelings. You should wear whatever makes you feel good, and if that makes you happy, you shouldn't change it."

She beamed. "Thank you, Kate. Now," she said, turning back to her ingredients on the counter, "who wants breakfast?"

I helped my mom make waffles then we all sat down to eat. "What have you been up to lately, Hawke?" my mom asked. "I haven't seen you around for a couple of weeks."

During a recent UFO investigation, I learned my mom and Hawke had been hanging out. The concept of the two of them as buddies was weirder than UFOs.

"I've had some jobs out of state."

"Ooooo," my mom said, interested. "Were you shooting things?"

Apparently my mom was under the impression Hawke didn't shoot people, just things. I, however, knew differently.

Hawke leaned toward her. "If I told you, I'd get in a lot of trouble. But," he said with a conspiratorial smile, "I'd consider it for you."

My mom's grin lit up the room. "Well, hopefully you stay safe. Between the two of you," she gestured between us, "I don't do anything but worry."

Hawke looked up at me. "She's giving me an ulcer, too."

"It's really not my fault," I said, swallowing my food.

My mom, dad, and Hawke all exchanged a look. I recognized it, because it was the same look I usually shared with my dad after my mom had a Catasophie and declared it wasn't her fault. "Hey!" I said, pointing at all of them. "It's really not my fault! I'm just doing my job."

"Well," my mom said in a huff, "I certainly wish your job was a little less dangerous."

"Me, too," my dad said.

"How's the Mustang?" Hawke asked my dad, changing the subject.

"It's in the shop getting the carpets cleaned, and a detail done."

"At least it was something that could be fixed," I offered.

"Exactly!" my mom said. "That's what I tried to tell him."

Given my dad's glare, I had a feeling he wasn't ready to look on the bright side.

I finished my food and put my plate in the sink. My phone buzzed. It was a message from Spence telling me to come into the office as soon as possible.

I looked at my parents and Hawke. "I have to go. Thanks for letting me stay over, Mom and Dad," I kissed them both on the cheek. "And thanks for stopping by to check on me," I said to Hawke. "I'll see you guys later."

Chapter Nineteen

I got another text from Ella as I walked into the office.

Drake's Hummer and Hawke's motorcycle were both at your house last night. Different times. Didn't stay long. Everyone in the group thought you had a couple a quickies, but I told them you were staying at your parents' house.

I blew out a long sigh at the surveillance and reporting, but then smiled a little, thinking Drake and Hawke had both stopped to check on me, but neither one had mentioned it when I talked to them. I shoved my phone in my purse as I walked to my desk.

"What's up?" I asked Spence as I put my stuff down, and flipped on my laptop.

"Billboards."

I arched a brow. "We have those in Branson."

"Not just here. All over the state. They have messages against the legalization of hemp oil, and they use the pot cookies as their reason for the dangers of allowing drugs to be legalized in any capacity."

"How did they get a marketing campaign up that fast?" The cookie story had just come out a couple of days ago.

"They practically went up overnight. Marketing and PR companies are quick. I'm sure some organization jumped on the story, and thought it would be great to use in fear-based marketing. One of the ads has a picture of a little kid's coffin with cookie crumbs all around it."

I wrinkled my nose. "That's morbid."

"The campaign started this morning with billboards, but I just got word that it has spread to TV spots, radio, and it's all over social media. The ads all have the disclaimer that they're paid for by Concerned Citizens for Health."

I opened my browser and did a search for the billboards. Images came up quickly and I started clicking through them. I got to the third photo before I froze. "I recognize the girl in this ad."

Spence looked interested. "Someone you know?"

"No," I said, shaking my head. I'd seen her before though, twice. I did another quick search and soon had my answer. "The marketing company behind the billboards and ad campaign is Saffron Star PR."

"How do you know?" Spence asked.

I gestured toward my screen. "The model was also in an ad for carpet cleaning. I noticed it at my mom's the other day, and thought she looked familiar. I recognized her because she was in the About Us page photo on the Saints and Sinners cookie website." Since the pot-spiked cookie news broke, the Saints and Sinners site had been taken down, but I was able to pull up a cached version with the photo to show Spence.

"Marketing companies use the same models all the time," Spence reasoned. "If Saffron Star was hired to build the Saints and Sinners site, maybe it's just a coincidence."

It was a possibility. Saffron Star had a lot of clients, including Brigham Smith, and if B.S. was investing in Saints and Sinners Cookies, they could have recommended Saffron Star's services to Isaac Handler—who, incidentally, still hadn't returned my calls. But there were too many links to ignore, and my gut told me Saffron Star, or someone involved with them, was playing a bigger role than just marketing and PR company.

I leaned back in my chair, tapping my pen against my thigh. "Can our private investigator look into Concerned Citizens for Health, and Saffron Star?"

"I'll email him right now."

"Thanks, Spence."

I settled into my work for the day, flipping through my notes. Things had been so hectic that I hadn't even had a chance to look up information on Juan Carlotta. I'd meant to, but then cookies had exploded on my desk and a lot of things had fallen through the cracks. I typed Juan's name into our background check service and waited for the information to come up. He was from South America, and had been in the United States illegally—like Bobby had said. He never stayed in one place too long, and seemed to be living out of hotels, if anything. It looked like he used cash most times, so he was hard to track.

It didn't look like Juan had any dealings with Kory Greer, and I probably would have been more likely to believe that if the police hadn't found Juan's arms and legs no longer attached to his body. Bobby had said the force of the explosion caused the mangled remains. But I thought there might be more to it. I picked up my phone.

"What do you know about dismembering a body?" I asked when Hawke picked up.

"Is there someone you need to dispose of, Kitty Kate?" His tone sounded amused.

"Yeah," I said, crossing one leg over the other, "the Ladies are high on that list."

"I could help with that."

"Your "help" is the reason I'm always in so much trouble with them to begin with." I took a sip of the water on my desk. "The body found at the sugar factory no longer had arms and legs attached. The police think they were blown off during the explosion, but it seems weird that only those appendages would have been affected. Is there some reason arms and legs might be chopped off of a body before, or after, the person was killed?"

Hawke paused, thinking. "It's a pretty violent act. Someone who had a vendetta or something to prove. There's a history for that sort of body mutilation in situations related to drug lords and organized crime."

There was? "Cutting off body parts is normal?"

"The specific type of mutilation is like a calling card. It lets people know not to mess with the organization."

"That's disturbing."

"It's even more disturbing to see in person."

I pursed my lips. "Your job scares me sometimes."

"Ditto. Let me know if you need anything else."

I hung up and thought about the body. If Juan was part of a drug ring or organized crime group, why was he killed and dismembered in the sugar factory? And what did it have to do with Kory Greer?

I didn't know a lot about organized crime and drug rings in Utah, but I knew someone who did. I picked up the phone and called my reporter friend, Karrie Williams.

"Hi, Karrie. It's Kate Saxee."

"Hey, Kate! I didn't expect to hear from you so soon."

I didn't expect it either. "I was hoping you could help me with something."

"Sure, shoot."

"You mentioned the body you were investigating in Rowe, and that you thought it might have happened because of a drug deal. Was there anything strange about the body that made you consider drugs as the motive?"

She paused for a minute. "Actually, there was. The body was missing both arms and legs. They'd been chopped off and left to the side of the body."

I knew it! Just like Juan's body in the sugar factory. Minus the arms and legs being left to the side of the body. The explosion likely moved them to a different location. "Have you seen bodies dismembered like that before?"

"Yeah. I've been covering the story for a while. There have been five similar bodies found across the state over the past six months. The body in Rowe belonged to an immigrant who was here on a work visa. He hadn't been into work for more than a week, and then a jogger found his body in a field."

"Do you have any proof that the bodies are related to a drug ring?"

"That's what police think, but we haven't been able to track down much information. That's the problem with drugs," Karrie said with a sigh. "Nothing is documented. It's all done with cash, and it's a pretty secretive business."

Hmmm, that didn't help me.

"There was a witness for the crime scene in Rowe," Karrie said.

My ears perked up at that.

"The witness said they saw two men in their twenties leaving the scene of the crime soon after the time of death. The body was left in some brush next to a jogging trail. One of the suspects was Caucasian, and one Hispanic. The Caucasian guy had bright red burn marks on his right arm and the right side of his face that looked fairly recent."

Burn marks? I'd already been suspicious that the other bodies had a connection to Juan Carlotta's. Now, my mind was piecing information together, forming a lead. The murder in Rowe happened after Juan was killed. If someone had murdered Juan at the sugar factory, there was a chance they might have gotten caught up in the explosion too. They weren't dead, so they must have made it out, but the explosion would definitely explain the burn marks, especially if the marks looked like a recent injury. I had a feeling all of the murders were being carried out by the same two guys.

"What's going on? And if you tell me you have a body in Branson, I might phone slap you. I've already been up there once in the past week; I really don't want to make that drive again."

I sympathized with her. I didn't enjoy the drive either. "We had an explosion a few weeks ago, and a body was found. I think the victim might have been killed by the same men who killed the victim in Rowe."

Karrie blew out a breath. "Fantastic."

"Could you possibly send me a list of the dismembered bodies found recently?"

"Sure, I'll email it."

"That would be great. Thanks for your help, Karrie."

"Anytime, Kate. Call me when your info is drive-worthy."

"Deal."

I still didn't know exactly how the murders were connected to the sugar factory, why Juan had been left there, or who had started the factory on fire, but drug dealing would definitely explain Kory Greer's new financial status, and his Ferrari. I'd go through the list from Karrie as soon as I got it and see if I could make any connections. Then, I'd set up a time to talk to Kory Greer.

Ella came in that afternoon and plopped down in the chair across from my desk. "Anyone try to kill ya today?"

"Not yet."

"That's good."

"I thought so."

"There was another Facebook update about you a few hours ago. Your car and Hawke's bike were seen at your parents' house this morning."

I took a deep breath and closed my eyes. I was either going to have to get used to the gossip, or move away. Otherwise, I was going to give myself a stress-induced heart attack. Who knew The Ladies would be more stressful than cookie bombs and email threats. "I didn't want to be alone last night."

"I don't blame ya, but Hawke should've hidden his hog."

Were bikes even called hogs anymore? "He just came over this morning to check on me. He had breakfast with my family, and then I left for work."

Ella held her hands up. "I'm sure it was innocent as all heck, but people are watchin' and assumin'."

"It's ridiculous," I said, throwing my hands in the air. "I give up. I can't regulate what everyone I know does, or make them park in special spots and sneak in side doors so they won't be seen. I'm not going to try."

Ella gave me a sympathetic nod. "Well, since the cookie debacle, you haven't been as much of a topic as usual."

I perked up. "I haven't?"

"Nope. Now people are mostly fightin' over the pro-pot cookies, and the no-pot cookies. There's even a website where people who still have some Saints and Sinners can sell 'em."

"Seriously? So it's eBay for pot fans?"

"Pretty much. It's called Cookie Crack."

"Creative." Though not really accurate. "It should probably be called Cookie Hash."

"Not many people would get that," Ella informed me as she stood to get a doughnut from the box Spence had brought in this morning. I was surprised she understood the reference.

"I can't believe the site hasn't been found and shut down yet. Now that it's public knowledge the cookies contain pot, anyone caught buying and selling them could go to federal prison for drug dealing."

Ella shrugged. "Guess people aren't too concerned about that since they're makin' buckets of money."

Money that wouldn't be too helpful once they were living out a real-life *Orange is the New Black*. "I'm sure the site will be taken down soon."

Ella took a bite of her doughnut. "So, tonight's the big night, huh?"

I pushed my brows together. "Big night? For what?"

"Deflowerin' Drake!"

I snorted. "Drake's deflowering happened a *long* time ago." Before I even knew him, I was sure. "And definitely not by me."

"Where ya goin'?" she asked.

"I'm not sure." I took a sip of water to try and masque my unease at not knowing the night's plans. I didn't like surprises.

She gave a happy sigh, her eyelashes fluttering. "I betcha it will be somewhere romantic."

"I doubt it. It's just a little date."

Ella laughed. "Honey," she said, patting me on the shoulder, "a date with Dylan Drake is never just a date."

She got up and went to the back room to file. I went back to work. Karrie's email came through and I spent the rest of the day researching information on the other bodies that had been found. They all had similarities, with the arms and legs removed, but none of the others had been blown up. I wasn't sure what made Juan so special—and unfortunate.

As the day wound down, and I gathered my things to leave, I couldn't stop thinking of Ella's statement about my date with Drake. She seemed to think it would be life changing. I had a feeling she was probably right.

The Devil Wears Tank Tops

Drake had picked me up in his yellow Hummer, which I totally disapproved of for its ginormous qualities. We'd discussed it before. Repeatedly. This time though, he'd at least brought me a stepstool so I didn't have to pull a muscle getting into the behemoth.

We'd driven about thirty miles out of town into the mountains. Despite hating his vehicle, I had to admit that I appreciated its ground clearance and shocks on the bumpy mountain roads.

He'd packed a picnic dinner for us, and taken me to a secluded spot by an enormous and gorgeous cascading waterfall that I didn't even know was there.

"This is beautiful," I gasped as we walked up. "I've never been here before."

"Really?" He sounded surprised. "There were always parties up here when I was younger."

I shrugged. "Not parties that I was invited to."

He tsked. "You were popular in high school."

"Not that popular, apparently."

He put a checkered blue and white blanket down and took cheese, meat, fruit, and various kinds of bread out of the basket. We settled everything and started to eat. Drake had piqued my interest in the last few weeks. I actually wanted to get to know him, instead of just relying on what I'd heard about him. I thought now would be a good time to start.

"So," I said, picking up a piece of bread, "tell me how you got the reputation you did." I spread some creamy cheese on the bread before topping it with ham. "I heard about your prowess with girls even when I was a teenager, and I was five years younger than you."

He shook his head and breathed out a long sigh. "What you heard then, and what you keep hearing now is just an exaggeration. I was a popular jock who dated a lot of girls. People jumped to conclusions about me." He paused, taking a bite of his food. "Now, people can't seem to understand why I'm still single. People need things to make sense, and their minds take the path of least resistance to get there. They think I'm attractive, young, and financially secure. They can't wrap their heads around me being alone, and they're looking for a reason to explain why I haven't settled down."

I'd wondered that myself. "Why haven't you?"

He looked at me and held my gaze, hot and intense. "Because I've been waiting for the right woman."

I stopped breathing for at least ten seconds and stared back. I got the distinct feeling he seemed to think he'd found her, and I was eighty shades of confused by it. He hadn't been interested in me when I was younger, why would he suddenly decide I was the one for him? I couldn't even begin to process my feelings. I hurried to change the subject so I wouldn't have to deal with the emotions that seemed to be creeping into my head— and my heart. "If the rumors are wrong, why do you let people keep talking? Why not try to stop them?"

He raised a brow. "You should know how well that works. I tried when I was younger. Refuting the rumors just made more people talk. I decided it was best to keep my mouth shut and eventually, they'd find a bigger target."

The Devil Wears Tank Tops

Judging by how often Drake was the subject of conversation, I thought he should re-strategize. "I don't think that worked."

"Sometimes it does, sometimes it doesn't. You've helped the situation a little bit because everyone is more interested in you than me..." his mouth slid up in a taunting smile, "except for the times people lump me in with the rumors about you."

"Oh, so it's my fault?" I asked, incredulous. "I believe you're the one who's been pursuing me," I pointed out.

"I am." He said it without apology. "And I don't plan to stop."

I cocked a brow. "We'll see about that." I paused and took a drink of the sparkling cider he'd brought for us. "So, Mr.-I-totally-know-you-and-always-have. You've never given me any details about that. Enlighten me about when you think we met."

I knew. It was at a dance after one of the football games. I was thirteen, and every stage of awkward as I stood against the wall, hoping someone, anyone, would pay attention to me. And let's be honest, I was hard to miss: big, permed, frizzy brown hair held in place with crunchy gel and an entire can of Aqua Net; blush that made me look like I'd fallen off a circus truck; and lipstick that had far too many orange tones for my cool complexion. I'd worn my prettiest dress: royal blue with matching lace over the top of the satin.

I'd watched Drake all night, dancing with the prettiest girls, and dreamed of what it would be like to be the focus of all that tall, dark attention. At the end of the night, he'd walked by with a girl who looked like a supermodel. Curves in all the right places, platinum blonde hair falling over her shoulders in soft waves, and huge boobs. She was the head cheerleader. I'd had a cheerleader complex ever since.

I'd lowered my lashes as they passed me, feeling like I wasn't even good enough to look at the gorgeous couple, but Drake had stopped. My eyes had fluttered up in surprise, and Drake had focused his beautiful sapphire gaze on me. I shrank back further against the wall. He'd flashed a stunning smile and said, "You look really pretty in that color." Then he walked away.

Nothing could have done more for my teenage self-esteem than that simple sentence. In less than ten seconds, he'd made me feel like I mattered. Not because he thought I was pretty—though that definitely helped—but because he'd taken the time to notice me when I thought no one did.

From then on, I'd been quietly fixated on him, hoping for another conversation. Another confirmation that someone saw more in me than I did. He'd changed my life that day. And I doubted he even remembered it.

Of course, then I'd grown up and realized I really wasn't that important and Drake handed out compliments more than forty-year old women got Botox because he was charming and good at getting what he wanted.

I'd become a little cynical with age.

"Do you remember an incident at the fair when you were a teenager?" he asked.

The Devil Wears Tank Tops

The question caught me off guard and I frowned. I remembered a lot of incidents at the fair. Including puking on my eleventh grade crush after he convinced me to go on a ride that spun so fast the laws of gravity went AWOL. It was not my best moment. I also peed my pants after a Slushee drinking dare went poorly. And those were the memories I hadn't repressed—none of which I wanted Drake privy to. "Umm, remind me which one."

"There were a lot?"

"I had an eventful childhood."

He laughed. "I'm sorry I wasn't there for them all."

I wasn't.

He leaned against a rock, putting one knee up. "This happened late on the last night of the fair. You were there with some of your friends listening to a concert. During the middle of the concert, some guys in front of you started harassing a boy. He was uncomfortable and tried to move away, but they grabbed him and started pulling him from the crowd. As soon as you realized what was happening, you got a determined look on your face, marched right up to them and told them to leave the boy alone. They tried to make you back down, but you wouldn't. You stood between them and the boy. And they left him alone because of it. Afterwards, you brought the boy over to your group of friends to make sure they wouldn't harass him again."

I remembered the incident. Martin Thomas was autistic. Most of the members of the community and my peers were great with him and tried to include him as much as possible. But the guys at the concert were either drunk, dumb, or both, and had the nerve to try to hurt him. I'd been furious. It had taken a threat to their twig-and-berry area involving my kickass Doc Martens to get them to leave Martin alone, but they had. After it happened, I'd been concerned Martin would face even more ridicule when he got back to school for needing a girl to save him. I was younger than he was, and still in middle school. I'd been worried about him for days. Luckily, that hadn't happened and he'd actually become the manager for the football team. "How did you know about that?" I asked, surprised.

Drake picked up a piece of grass and started weaving it through his fingers. "I was there. I noticed what was happening around the same time as you, but I was further away. By the time I got there, you had the situation handled. I stayed off to the side to make sure everything was okay. When the guys walked away, me and some of my friends talked to them and made sure it wouldn't happen again."

My mouth dropped in complete shock. *Drake* was the reason they'd left Martin alone after I'd told them all off? All of this time, and I had no idea he'd done that for Martin. Other than the night at the dance—which happened after the fair incident—I felt like I'd really only seen one side of Drake. And it was becoming more and more apparent that the side I'd seen was cloaked in rumors and lies—not the man he'd actually been, or the man he'd become.

"I tried to make sure Martin and kids like him were taken care of. I've never liked bullies. I was lucky to be in a position to do something about it. But what really impressed me is that you weren't. You were about twelve at the time, standing up to a group of high school football players who outweighed you by a collective seven hundred pounds at least. And you were fearless." His eyes softened with admiration as he looked up at me. "You didn't have the brawn, or even their age, but you saw an injustice and wouldn't let it stand. I'd never been so impressed—and I haven't been since."

If I hadn't already been sitting down, I would have staggered. He'd been impressed by me? When I was twelve? And he still was?

"I'll never forget Martin saying, 'Thank you, Katie. Thank you.' "

I'd forgotten that until just now. Martin had always called me Katie. I blinked back tears at the memory.

"I learned something about myself that day, Katie. I don't handle weak women well. I loved how strong, independent, outspoken, and stubborn you were even then. I still do."

My heart was racing with a flurry of emotions. I was stunned, moved, and amazed. Three things I never thought I'd feel regarding Dylan Drake. In the span of a story, my opinion of him had completely changed. "Why didn't you tell me this a long time ago?"

"Would you have believed me?" he asked.

Truthfully, I wasn't sure. But I wished I'd known.

"I wanted to wait for the right time," he said. "This seemed like it."

He reached over, his hand cupping my cheek. I thought for sure he was going to kiss me, and I had the sudden realization that I wanted him to—more than I'd wanted anything for a long time. "You're an incredible woman, and I'm lucky to have you in my life."

"Thanks," I breathed.

"Do you think you'd do this again? With me?"

I'd probably do any number of things with him at the moment. I managed to stop that from making it out of my mouth, though. "Go on a date?" I asked instead.

He nodded.

I bit the corner of my lip. "I'd like that very much."

He gave me a wide smile. "I'll start planning it tomorrow." He moved and started packing up our basket. "I know you've had a long week. I just wanted to spend some time with you, and try to take your mind off things. Thank you for trusting me."

I watched him closely, feeling like I was looking at him for the first time. "Thank you for finally letting me see the real you."

He stood and helped me up. The electricity between us was there and pulsing, but instead of kissing me like I'd hoped he would, he took my hand and led me back to the Hummer. My stomach jumped at the touch of his fingers laced through mine, and I wished things had gone further than hand holding. The whole way home I thought about what he'd said, and tried to hide my disappointment that we hadn't kissed. Maybe he just wasn't feeling the connection like I was? Or maybe he didn't want to rush things. It was a bad move on his part because I probably would have agreed to just about anything.

When we got to my house, Drake got out and walked me to the door. He waited patiently as I opened the lock. "Thanks for tonight, Drake. I really did have a good time."

He laughed. "You sound surprised."

"I wasn't expecting it."

"Well," he said, reaching up and brushing the hair off the side of my face, "I like to rise above expectations."

I smiled and opened the door. I turned around to go inside when he caught my hand. I looked up at him.

"Oh, and the first night we met? It was at a dance. You were wearing a blue dress and even then, I thought you were stunning."

He took my face in both of his hands, leaned in, kissed my forehead lightly, and walked back to his Hummer. I stood there, holding my keys and bag, unable to move for at least five minutes.

Expectations exceeded.

Chapter Twenty

"Well, well, well. Look who's got some afterglow," Ella said, examining me with a critical eye. I must have been smiling a little wider than usual.

"That's ridiculous. We just had dinner. We didn't even kiss." Technically. I didn't count a forehead kiss as a kiss kiss.

Ella gave me a sly smile. "But you look much happier than usual."

I nodded as I sat at my desk. "It was a good date." I opened my email, and started clicking through the messages. I was only half-listening to Ella as I sorted my inbox.

"—and then Amber said you'd probably drugged him to get him to sleep with you."

I stopped, looked up at her and blinked. "What?"

"The Ladies saw Drake pick you up. There was a long discussion about it in the Facebook group."

I rolled my eyes. "I'm sure there was. I think maybe you should stop telling me what they're all saying. It's just making me more and more pissed off."

Ella shrugged. "Whatever you want, Katie."

I checked my own Facebook messages, the little head and body still glowing with a red notification, reminding me I had a friend request. I'd thought about the implications of being Drake's friend before now, and hadn't wanted to deal with it. Now that I saw another side of him though, and knew who he really was, I knew I wanted him in my life, and my social media. I clicked 'confirm' on the notification tab, and smiled as the link popped up saying we were now friends.

I went back to my emails. I'd emailed Karrie some follow-up questions about the bodies, and she sent me back information about the locations they were all found in, and the descriptions of crime scenes. Most of the remains were found in random locations outdoors. But several things—the way the bodies had been treated, the police and Karrie's suspicion that they were all drug related murders, and Kory Greer's sudden influx of money—supported my hunch that Juan Carlotta's death was somehow connected to the other murders, and Kory Greer.

I wanted to see Kory's reaction when I told him about the other bodies, and ask him more about where he was getting his money. I put an interview with Kory on my list to do today, and this time, I was going to talk to him in person so I could see his reaction as I asked questions.

Spence interrupted my thoughts. "We just got a press release about another pot protest."

"Another protest?" I asked. The movement had probably gained steam since the pot cookie reveal.

"The protest is on Main Street at noon." Main Street was right outside our store window, so it seemed like they were having it in the same place as last time, which was convenient for me. This time they'd given warning, and would probably have better attendance.

I had a few hours before the protest started, so I decided to take a break and run to the grocery store to make sure I had more than moldy cheese in my house. It was safer to go during the middle of the day. The grocery store was the place that had been the most affected by the lack of pot cookies. Spence told me that after the police got things under control, store employees had to work all night to clean up from the cookie riot, and some people were still bitter with me about it. Going back to the scene so soon after the disaster probably wasn't the best idea, but my fridge was bare and there was only one place in town to remedy that. I'd have to get groceries sooner or later. I knew there'd be less people shopping in the morning though, and thought I could probably make it out with my groceries unscathed.

I ran through aisles, grabbing Cap'n Crunch cereal, milk, bread, cheese, ice cream, chocolate, and I threw in some fruits and vegetables out of guilt. I noticed the cookie section was back to normal, and free of any Saints and Sinners Cookies. I paid, blowing out a sigh of relief that I'd had no cookie confrontation, and was on my way to the Jeep when I heard a familiar voice. "Heeey! It's the reporter lady!"

Keanu—not his real name, but the name I'd christened him with after our first meeting when he'd been drunk, high, and sounded a lot like a character out of *Bill and Ted's Excellent Adventures*—was leaning against an old beat up green Honda in the parking lot with some of his friends.

"Hey," I said, pushing my cart over and stopping by his car.

"Dude," he said, his expression sad as he shook his head, "my friends aren't too happy you told everyone about the cookies."

I lifted my hands in an I-give-up gesture. "Join the club."

"Those cookies were stellar! And *waaaayy* cheaper than buying just weed."

My mouth curved down in sympathy. "I know. Sorry about that. They were making people sick, though."

Keanu's eyes went wide and he looked totally amused. "That's just because people were eating so much at once."

Yeah, that was part of it. "Well, they didn't know they were eating anything but sugar and flour."

He nodded in understanding. "I told the dudes to put a warning on the edibles. Businesses can't survive if clients don't have the proper information."

I froze. "Wait. You told what dudes?"

"The cookie dudes!"

I'd been trying to find someone connected to Makhai, LLC and their production for weeks with no success. All of my phone calls to Saints and Sinners, and Isaac Handler had been left unreturned. I stared at Keanu, wondering if he might actually have all the information I needed. "Where did you meet these guys?"

He studied me with a suspicious eye. "You're a reporter. I might get in trouble if I tell you."

I shook my head, excited at the possibility of the lead. "You'll be my *super*-secret source. I won't tell anyone I heard it from you."

He watched me for a few more seconds before deciding. "*Super*-secret?"

I nodded.

He crossed one foot over the other and lit a cigarette as he answered, "At the deliveries."

I had to fight to keep my chin off the ground. "You were at the delivery locations?"

"Yep," he said, taking a drag. "Word got out that a new company was trying to show people pot wasn't dangerous."

A new company…so was Saints and Sinners behind the pot cookies, or were they being sabotaged like I'd originally thought?

Keanu continued, "They needed help distributing. So, a bunch of us gave the cookies away."

"How long ago was that?"

He pushed his brows together, thinking. "A couple of weeks before the fair. Stores were stocking the cookies within a week of us handing out samples."

The Devil Wears Tank Tops

So that's how they got people interested. A little sample would have made people feel awesome and want more—unless they were like me and the pot had just made them horny and pass out. The crazy incidents and people getting sick got worse over the three week period between when the cookies were first made available, and when I wrote the article. Once the cookies were easier to get, people were being affected more often.

"Did you ever meet the people you were working for?"

Keanu shook his head. "No, just the delivery drivers. They're the ones I told that the cookies needed warning labels. They didn't listen."

The more I heard, the more I thought Saints and Sinners could be the bad guy in the pot cookie scenario, instead of the victim. I wondered if the delivery drivers were part of the scam, or just more minions. It seemed like Makhai, LLC and Isaac Handler were doing their best to hide their trail and not get their hands dirty. I still couldn't figure out what Brigham Smith's role was in this, though. They were fighting to stop drug legalization. Why would they have anything to do with pot-spiked cookies? The only thing that made sense was that B.S. got involved in the cookie company, but didn't know what the ingredients actually were, and maybe someone was using the cookies as a way to cause a scandal for B.S.

Keanu kept talking, "The samples were dropped off in delivery trucks every Sunday, Wednesday, and Friday, and left for us at an old abandoned building outside of town. We each took our cookie share, and handed them out."

I was impressed they'd managed to hand any out and not eat, or horde, all of the supply. "Where did you hand them out at?"

"To friends, and then other people we know. Not little kids, though. That's stepping over a line."

I was glad he had scruples on some level. Clearly, Makhai, LLC didn't. They didn't care who had access to the cookies. Kids with a little allowance money could have walked in the store and bought the pot cookies as easily as a pack of gum. "There was a Saints and Sinners cookie booth at the high school," I said.

Keanu and his friends started cracking up. "It's hilarious! The school was selling hash treats!"

"They're not anymore." I'd heard the school dismantled the booth as soon as the article came out.

Keanu frowned. "I know." His eyes held mine in a bleary gaze. "That's kind of your fault."

I grimaced. "Yeah."

He lifted a shoulder like it really wasn't a big deal. "It was good while it lasted, though. And they asked us to do some fun stuff too, like paintin' pot leaves on the steel factory, and changing the "BF" on the hill to say POT."

My brows went up. "That was you?"

He nodded, pride showing on his face. "Me and my buddies," he gave a clumsy gesture to the group he was standing with. They all nodded or waved in my direction.

"When did the cookie people tell you to do that?"

He took another drag on his cigarette. "They told us what they wanted done a couple of weeks ago, and said we'd just have to be ready with the paint and bags as soon as they called."

I nodded my head slowly as I thought about it. The pot vandalism had occurred within twelve hours of my article coming out. I thought both things had happened pretty fast. They had. Because the whole thing had been planned.

"I wouldn't tell anyone else about that if I were you."

Keanu shook his head. "No way!" His voice turned gentle as he whispered, "But I like you, and know you'll keep our secrets."

I chuckled at Keanu. Despite his constantly drunk or stoned state, he'd been one of my most helpful informants since I moved back to Branson. "You can count on it."

Keanu smiled so wide I thought he might strain something.

I thought about it for a minute, and wondered if anything had changed with the delivery schedule since my story broke about the cookies. "Are you still helping distribute the cookies?"

He shook his head and frowned. "We stopped getting samples as soon as people found out about the pot."

So the distribution had stopped when my story came out. That made sense because the cookies had been pulled and were nowhere to be found. Neither was Isaac Handler and Makhai, LLC. And I wasn't the only reporter looking for them. The story had gone national, and even I was getting calls and emails from other journalists trying to trace the cookie path.

The Saints and Sinners website had been pulled down right after my story came out, the pot vandalism had been organized long before my story was released, and billboards against pot and hemp oil legalization had gone up almost immediately after my story was released. It was like everything had been organized weeks ago, before the pot cookies had even been given to the public. The common thread with all of those things so far seemed to be Saffron Star PR. I needed to go back to the office and see if our private investigator had any information on Concerned Citizens for Health and Saffron Star yet. "Thanks for your help," I said to Keanu as I started to push my cart away.

"No problemo, reporter lady!"

I got back in my Jeep and took some notes about what Keanu had said, then ran home to put my groceries away. It said something about the state of my life that I entered my house with my bags in one hand, and pepper spray in the other, just in case. When I was satisfied I wouldn't have to burn anyone's eyeballs, I put the groceries away, locked up, and went back to the *Tribune* office.

"The grocery store must have been busy. You were gone for a while. I thought I might have to come rescue you."

"Luckily no one accosted me," I said, putting my bag in my bottom desk drawer. "I did have an interesting conversation with Keanu, though."

Spence's brows went up. "About?"

"Apparently, he and some of his friends were helping to distribute the Saints and Sinners Cookies." I explained everything Keanu had told me, and the fact that Saffron Star seemed pretty wrapped up in both the Saints and Sinners Cookies, and the anti-pot campaign.

"That's interesting, because I just talked to our P.I."

"What did he find out?"

"Saffron Star has *a lot* of clients, but their president works frequently with another familiar group: Brigham Smith."

My brows shot up at that.

"And," Spence continued, "Concerned Citizens for Health is heavily funded by Brigham Smith."

"That's a pretty big connection."

"That's what I thought too," Spence said.

"So the common thread isn't just Saffron Star, it's the Brigham Smith Group, too." I just couldn't figure out their motive.

I settled into my desk, thinking about why Brigham Smith would be involved with the distribution of pot cookies *and* an anti-pot campaign, but my thoughts were interrupted when I heard yelling coming from outside. "I think the protest is starting," I said to Spence. I grabbed my bag with all of my essentials, and went outside. Spence followed.

Last time, the protest had been small. Now though, it seemed like half the town had turned up for, and against, pot. Spence and I split up to better cover the area. I was walking around the pro-pot side when I saw

John Wilson. "Hi, John," I said, going up to him. He was wearing the same shirt as last time with a picture of his daughter on it, and passing out information on hemp oil while the crowd behind him shouted, "Save our kids!"

John glanced up at his name. Lines formed at his eyes and he pursed his lips. He did not look happy to see me. "Hi, Kate." His tone was cool, and I got the distinct impression he was trying his best to be nice.

I guess I was just pissing everyone off lately, but I couldn't figure out what I'd done to him. "Is something wrong?"

"Well," he said, passing out more papers to people walking up and down the street, "your article about the cookies didn't help our cause."

My eyes went wide and I was totally stunned. "Oh my gosh! I didn't write it as a way to hurt you. I agree that hemp oil should be legalized. I didn't think it would affect you at all. I just saw a situation where the cookie manufacturer was doing something wrong, and I needed to report on it. People were having health problems because the level of THC in the cookies was so high."

John sighed and looked resigned. "I know. And in truth, it helped make people more aware of the situation, but now the public is even more convinced that hemp oil and marijuana are the same thing. We have a lot more people fighting us now. Before, we were on a wait list to get the hemp oil—and that was hard in and of itself. We have to wait months for the low THC strain to be processed, and then we're on a waiting list with thousands of other families who need it to save their kids. The pot-spiked cookies have caused so much backlash that I'm worried the hemp oil legalization is going to be revoked. I don't know if we'll ever get the oil we need."

I was horrified. I never would have guessed this would be one of the ramifications of the article. "What can I do to help you?" I asked, desperate to right the situation.

He shook his head, looking defeated.

"What if I do a story on your family?" I knew smaller bits and pieces about them had been covered in the Utah news before, but I hadn't seen a full feature. I had friends at the Associated Press, and news stations. I thought I could help his story be seen nationally, and maybe move him up on the hemp oil list.

"That might help."

"I'll get it done for next week's issue." I was determined to right the situation as soon as possible.

"Thanks, Kate. I appreciate it." He gave me the weary smile of a man who'd been fighting—and losing—for a long time. I wanted him to keep fighting, and I'd help any way I could.

"I'm more than happy to do it."

I walked across the street to talk to Lydia Ackerman again. Her side of the protest was significantly larger than last time, and much bigger than the pro-pot side. I winced, realizing I'd helped that to happen. "Why are you protesting today?" I asked her.

She gave me a long-suffering look. "You should know better than anyone, Kate. You're the one who investigated the story. We need to stop the infiltration of dangerous drugs in our culture."

It sounded like something she'd memorized from a pot haters manual.

"Pot is one of the least addictive substances out there, Lydia." I'd said something similar to her at the last protest as well.

"It's dangerous. You know that first hand."

I stared at her. Did Lydia know I'd gotten high from pot cookies? Who told her? "What makes you think that?"

"Because you wrote the article about it, and all of the horrible affects it had on people in our community." She seemed like she was about to follow that statement with "duh," but stopped herself.

"How does the protest solve anything?"

She rolled her eyes. "Don't be obtuse, Kate. It brings awareness to the cause. There are protests all over the state today, and they're all as big as this, if not bigger. I appreciate your article, by the way. Our newsletter subscriptions went up by thousands when your story was released."

Now it was my turn to roll my eyes. I needed to fix this, and fast. I'd get the story about John Wilson and his daughter in next week's paper even if I had to convince Spence to hold the paper from going to press.

I left Lydia and talked to some protesters and Branson residents on both sides of the issue. I noticed Spence in the crowd doing the same thing. I was taking photos when I saw June Tate standing off to the side of the road, watching everything.

"Hey, June!" I said with a smile. I was happy to see a friendly face.

"Hi, Kate."

"What are you doing in town?"

"I came in to get groceries, but wanted to see what all the ruckus was about."

I nodded. "How are things at your house? Are you still having problems with the traffic?"

She nodded, a hopeless look on her face. "It's a shortcut to Colorado, so we get a lot of people who use it. The trucks are the real problem, though. They're big, and noisy."

"Do you know what company they're from? You might be able to file a complaint."

"No. There's not a name on the side. But they're the ugliest shade of green you've ever seen. Luckily, they only go by three times a week."

I frowned. "I'm sorry it's been such a pain for you."

"Me, too. But we'll deal with it."

I smiled, and decided I could use a bit of her positive attitude. "I have to get back to work, but have a good day, June."

"You too, Kate."

Something about the conversation with June stuck out in my head, but I couldn't put my finger on it. I was trying to figure it out when I saw Kory Greer wandering through the crowd. That was fortuitous since I needed to talk to him about Juan Carlotta's body, and Kory's possible involvement in Juan's death.

I started to move toward Kory, but noticed he was acting odd. His gaze darted back and forth among the protesters. Dark circles rimmed his eyes, and his clothes were wrinkled like he'd been wearing them for a while. His hair looked like he'd raked his hands through it repeatedly.

I watched as he moved through the crowd, checking over his shoulder frequently, like he was trying to keep watch on everyone and everything. Suddenly he saw someone in the crowd he recognized and froze, the skin on his face stretching in a masque of terror. I followed his gaze to two large men: one Hispanic and one Caucasian, with burn marks on his right arm and face.

Chapter Twenty-One

Kory turned and ran toward his Ferrari, which was parked down the street near my Jeep. I pulled my keys from my bag and raced after him. I wasn't sure what Kory was caught up in, but if I was right about the guy with the burn mark, the men following him were murderers, and he was going to need all the help he could get. I hoped the two men didn't have a supercar like Kory. The Ferrari would at least give Kory a little lead.

I raced down the road behind him, trying to keep up in my heavy Jeep. I didn't see anyone following Kory and I, so I thought maybe he'd lost the guys.

We drove for about twenty minutes before Kory steered off the road and drove down a long, dirt covered path. I followed at a distance, and watched Kory pull in next to a large, concrete-framed structure.

He got out of his Ferrari, and ran to the front of the building, fumbling with his set of keys as he opened one of the double glass doors. He glanced over his shoulder as he fled inside.

I pulled into an area surrounded by trees so I'd have some cover until I figured out what to do. I looked at the building and recognized the sign above it as the sugar factory's satellite office. Four large, ugly green delivery trucks were parked to the side of the building, and I had an ah-ha moment. I'd passed June's house while following Kory. She'd said the trucks only went by three days a week, and Keanu had said the same thing about when he got cookie samples. The trucks that were making deliveries to Keanu and the trucks that had been going by June's house were one and the same.

I picked up my phone and called Hawke. "I just followed Kory Greer to his sugar factory satellite office," I said when Hawke answered. "I think he might have something to do with the cookies. And I think some drug dealers might be on their way to kill him. I'm pretty sure they're the ones who've been cutting off arms and legs."

"I've got you on the tracker. Stay put. I'll be to you in ten minutes."

"It took me twenty to get here, and that was breaking enough speeding laws to warrant a felony."

"I have my cape," he said, and clicked off.

Funny man, Hawke. Making flying jokes when killers were on their way.

The Devil Wears Tank Tops

Staying put was something I could do. My car was obscured from sight thanks to the trees, and though my view wasn't great, I could still see the factory. Things were fine for about one minute. Then the guys who had been following Kory showed up. They must have known where Kory was going. Or maybe they employed a Tracker on his Ferrari like Hawke used on my Jeep.

They were in a giant black truck with the windows completely blacked out. I frowned, thinking that had to be illegal, then remembered they killed people and chopped off arms, so they probably weren't too worried about a tinting ticket. I was surprised they didn't have an assault rifle mounted to the top of the truck—then again, it was probably inside the truck, where the tinting hid it.

They both got out of the truck and didn't say a word to each other. Their faces were a study in calm as they walked toward the building. The burned guy slid a handgun from his back pocket, and shot the glass door. It shattered into a million pieces. The two men looked at each other, and stepped through the broken door.

I stared at what used to be a glass covered entrance, and started to bite my nails. This was a problem. Kory Greer was inside his building with people I was almost certain were murderers. Did he know them? Did he need to be saved from them? It had certainly seemed like he was terrified of them at the protest.

I looked around my Jeep for a weapon. All I had was pepper spray and my fire extinguisher. Considering what I thought had happened the last time the two guys had been in a sugar factory, I thought the extinguisher might actually be useful. The guys had guns though, and guns were faster than my pressurized nitrogen. But I also had the element of surprise.

I was debating the merits of going in, extinguisher firing, when another car pulled up. Sleek, black, and sexy, it also had dark, tinted windows and chrome trim. I loved cars the same way I loved Frosted Paradise doughnuts, so I was certain the car that had just cruised in was a Maybach. It purred in the way only extremely expensive cars do, and rolled to a silent stop in front of the building. It cost more than most houses, and looked like drivable money.

A man in a white shirt, black suit, and dark sunglasses stepped out of the driver's seat. He opened the back door, and another man, dressed in a perfectly tailored black suit and blood red shirt, stepped out. He was balding, and probably in his sixties. His gaze went toward the side of the building where Kory's Ferrari was parked, then he nodded to the driver and they both walked up the steps of the building. They paused momentarily, looking from the black truck to the shattered glass doors, before going inside.

Now I was even more confused. I'd never seen the man—or car—around town before…and I would have definitely noticed the car. But he walked into the building like he was supposed to be there. Did he know about the two guys inside? Did I need to warn him and his driver? I mulled it over, going back and forth before intuition took over, and told me that with the way the older guy had driven up, and then walked inside, he'd been there before. The guy acted like he owned the place. He knew Kory was here, and had stopped briefly as he walked by the black truck like he was expecting it—and the men's—presence.

As much as I wanted to help Kory, I knew it was far safer for me to wait in the car like Hawke had told me to do. There'd be enough people who needed rescuing by the time Hawke arrived; I didn't need to add to it. I kept my gaze locked on the building, windows down as I strained to hear any noise that might come from inside. My commitment to stay in the car lasted a total of three minutes. Long enough for another car to pull up, and me to see a bewildered John Wilson step out of his rusting, white Toyota.

"Shit," I muttered, unbuttoning my seat belt. I was hoping to get John's attention before he went inside, but I didn't get out of the car fast enough. By the time I was out of the clearing, John was gone.

I wasn't sure where the two scary guys were, or anyone else for that matter, but I couldn't stay outside and do nothing. John, at least, was innocent in all of this. That, I was sure of. I had to help him.

During my attempt to stop John, I'd left the fire extinguisher in the car, but I had my pepper spray, and palmed it, prepared to use it at a moment's notice.

I crept up to the side of the building and peeked through the former glass door. I couldn't see anyone in the hallway. I slowly stepped through the door, being careful about where I put my feet. I didn't want crunching glass to alert people to my presence.

I moved to the first room on my right. The door was closed, so I pressed my ear against it, listening for movement. I didn't hear anyone inside, so I slowly pressed the door open, looking in. It was empty. I inched quietly down the hall, my ear tuned for any errant noise, and finally heard a voice coming from somewhere ahead of me. I pressed myself against the wall as I moved, trying to be stealthy.

I came to a large room with double doors. One of the doors was open, and I peeked around the corner inside. I took a quick inventory of the space. Machines lined the expansive area, and boxes of cookies with the Saints and Sinners logo were stacked in the corner on pallets from floor to ceiling. Kory and John were both tied to chairs and facing the older guy and his driver. The Caucasian and Hispanic guys stood to the side, and appeared to be enforcers, keeping Kory and John in line.

"I was given a card with information that I needed to come here if I wanted help with the hemp oil," John said. "Why am I being held hostage?"

I'd just talked to him less than an hour ago. He must have left the protest and come straight here.

"Don't worry about the ropes. We just used them to make sure we'd have your undivided attention," the older man said. "And we'd be glad to help you with the oil, Mr. Wilson. In exchange for a little help from you as well."

A confused look crossed John's face. "What do you need my help with?"

The Devil Wears Tank Tops

The guy eyed John speculatively. "I'd like to make you an offer."

John gave him a wary look in return.

"How would you like to have all of the low THC strain hemp oil you could ever need? For free."

John's mouth fell open and if he hadn't been sitting down already, I was sure he would have staggered. "You're joking."

The bald man shook his head. "No. I'm not. I have access to it, and I can get it to you. But there's a cost."

"What?" John quickly asked.

"In exchange, you'll stop speaking out in support of hemp oil. As your daughter gets better, you'll go on record saying her new medications were a God-send, and they have healed your daughter."

John stared at the man blankly. "But medications don't work. We've tried for years. Only the hemp oil will help."

The man nodded. "And you'll have as much as you could ever dream of. But no one will know that except us. To everyone else, you'll tell them she's on a new seizure medication combination that's keeping her healthy. You'll say how happy you are that you didn't have to put her on something as untested as marijuana. And you'll campaign in support of the cause to make marijuana—hemp oil included—illegal in all fifty states once again."

John's eyes went wide, his face stretched with horror. He looked like he might not be breathing. "I can't do that. Do you have any idea how many people need the oil? It's not just my daughter being affected.

It's thousands of children! I can't turn on my friends and watch my daughter get better while their kids get worse and die." He looked down at the floor and shook his head. When he looked up at the bald guy again, his eyes were shining with tears. "I can't accept your offer."

The bald guy gave him a smile that wasn't at all reassuring. "You misunderstand, John." The bald guy gestured toward the enforcers. "The hemp oil was an attempt to be nice, but I could accomplish the same outcome other ways." The enforcers each took one of John's arms. "A pro-pot activist being murdered by drug dealers would make a great story for my cause."

John looked stunned, and couldn't even respond. Kory responded for him. "You're an evil man," Kory said, his face bright red with anger. "You gave me a contract to make cookies. You never told me the ingredients included marijuana! Do you have any idea what I've been going through since I found out? I was producing something that made people ill, and I didn't even know it!" His voice got louder with each sentence he spoke. "You wanted people to get sick so you could use the cookies as an example of how dangerous pot is. You're trying to stop people like John from using hemp oil to keep their kids alive. You're the definition of wicked."

The bald guy gave Kory a bored look. "Your sugar factory was going under, Mr. Greer. You came to Brigham Smith, desperate for investors. We gave you the machines, tools, and licenses you needed to branch out into food production. Then we gave you the cookie ingredients—including sugar from your own sugar factory—and a staff to make them. You were also given an *extremely* generous amount of money for your compliance. All you had to do was let us use your building, stay out of our business, and keep quiet about where the cookies were being produced. You accepted without a second thought." He was the picture of arrogance as he stepped forward, looking down on Kory, a distasteful expression on his face. "Unfortunately, you didn't ask about the ingredients at the time, Mr. Greer. In fact, you seemed rather thrilled to have the offer at all. You couldn't wait to sign the contract. You didn't even have your attorney look it over."

"Because I thought I was dealing with someone respectable!" Kory yelled.

"You were. And we were dealing with someone stupid, which was exactly what we'd hoped for."

Kory's face went even redder. "I hope you die a horrible death for what you've done."

The man smiled slowly. "Well, I can guarantee that of the two of us, you'll die first."

At the most inopportune moment, my phone started playing "Forever in Blue Jeans." I muttered a curse—a really bad one—as I fumbled to shut off the ring. I did it, but not fast enough. I had about five seconds before the enforcers found me to realize Neil—and Spence—might have just gotten me killed. At least the last song I listened to would be a good one.

The two guys tied me up in a chair, and put me next to Kory and John. "My, my," the old guy said, coming over to me. "If it isn't the intrepid reporter who was so helpful in our cause."

I'd heard the entire conversation and wasn't pleased with what I'd learned. At all. I held his eyes with a stony gaze. "If I'd known I was being helpful, I wouldn't have written the story."

"We know," the bald guy said. "That's why we gave you incentive. The threats helped push you to find out the truth."

The realization that Brigham Smith used me to push their cause and convince the public that marijuana was dangerous made me spitting mad. If he'd been close enough, I would have kicked him in his fancy, suit-covered shin—at the very least. "Who are you?" I knew he was part of the Brigham Smith Group, but I wanted to know the name of the man who was threatening me and holding me against my will.

"Isaac Handler."

Of course he was.

He gave a slow smile in response. I wanted to punch him.

"So you own Makhai, LLC, and the Saints and Sinners Cookies?" I asked.

He regarded me with interest. "I was the name behind them both, yes. But Makhai was started by Brigham Smith."

"Clever name," I said. "And appropriate since the Brigham Smith Group is two-faced."

He smiled without any hint of humor. "The Makhai were also known for their ability to attract fellow spirits of war, and make them even more formidable. We were using the Saints and Sinners Cookies to build our outraged army."

They were delusional is what they were. "If that was your goal, why did you keep threatening me even after the article came out?"

"Misdirection, Ms. Saxee. It insured you'd continue pursuing the marijuana story, and help to keep the dangers of pot relevant in the media. Every step of this process was planned. We knew once the story was published in Branson, it would be picked up throughout Utah. After that, it would move nationally, and we'd have a bigger base to support our cause and help us fight against drug legalization. Exposure is key, but exposure by carefully calculated manipulation works far better. You helped us achieve that."

I felt anger tightening my stomach. "But you lied about the cookies," I said, righteous indignation showing through. Nothing made me madder than a liar. "You put quadruple doses of pot in them! You made people think marijuana is a lot worse than it really is."

He shrugged like it wasn't a big deal. "It was an end to a means. Things have to be done for the greater good."

The greater good was one of the dumbest, and most dangerous, arguments I'd ever heard. A lot of horrible things had been done in the name of doing what was best for the masses. A small set of opinions shouldn't be able to make that choice for everyone. "Things like murder?" I asked.

"Well…" he said, mulling it over, "that's a rather strong word. We like to think of it as housekeeping."

I'd never seen such a sweet looking old man turn an idea into something so vile. "The bodies found all over the state with their arms and legs cut off, including Juan Carlotta's body in the sugar factory were 'housekeeping' to you?" I wasn't sure how Brigham Smith had been connected to them, but I knew they were.

"Ah, yes. That was an unfortunate incident. One my men are still recovering from." He gestured towards the two enforcers. They stared straight ahead with stony expressions. "They learned their lesson, though. Don't chop off body parts with an ax in the presence of sugar dust."

My eyes went wide. "The ax caused the spark?"

He nodded. "Pity. We'd planned to retrofit two sections of Mr. Greer's sugar factory for our cookie production. The cookie campaign could have been so much bigger, maybe even nationwide instead of just across Utah, if we'd been producing out of two spaces instead of one."

My mouth gaped. He'd ordered the deaths of six men, and was only concerned with how the fire had slowed down his production and ultimate plan to end all drug legalization, regardless of the cost.

"Was Juan Carlotta working for you?"

I hadn't been able to piece that together. "For a time. We have several runners who move the pot for us. Unfortunately, a handful of them knew too much about our operations. We couldn't have them exposing the Brigham Smith Group as the proprietors of the cookies. We had to get rid of them. Cutting off their arms as a calling card and depositing the bodies around the state made it easy enough to set the deaths up to look like a drug deal gone bad."

He said "deaths" like it was something that just happened, not murders he'd been responsible for.

"Why leave him in the sugar factory?" I asked.

Isaac looked toward Kory. "As a message to Mr. Greer. He had started to suspect something strange was going on after he tried the cookies and got high."

I arched a brow in Kory's direction, surprised he had enough experience with marijuana to know that's what he was feeling. Kory lifted a shoulder. "I experimented in college."

"Why didn't you tell me what you suspected when I talked to you?" I asked.

Kory's eyes widened. "A dead body was found in my blown up factory two days after I confronted Brigham Smith about the cookies. I got the message."

I couldn't fault him for that. I also had the realization that if Brigham Smith killed their employees for knowing too much—and those employees likely knew far less than me, John, and Kory—there probably wasn't a good chance we'd be alive much longer. Most people in this situation would have lamented the things they didn't do during their lives and thought about their regrets. Not me. I got pissed because dying would mean I wouldn't get to see how the last season of *Sons of Anarchy* ended. I was not about to let that happen.

Hawke had said he was ten minutes away. He knew me well enough that he probably assumed I hadn't stayed in my car. That meant he would have driven—or flown—even faster than usual, and should arrive any moment, if he wasn't already here. I just had to stall and keep them from the killing us until Hawke made an appearance. "You'll lose everything when people find out what you've done. You broke the law and intoxicated people with drugs that are still considered illegal, even in Utah. You didn't use hemp oil, you used real marijuana."

"A group like ours is breaking the laws for the people who can't."

"That's convenient. Is that how you convince yourself to sleep at night?"

"I sleep just fine. I'll sleep fine tonight, too, when you're dead."

He motioned to his enforcers and they moved to the edge of the room where they uncovered a machine that looked like it had been in storage. The plugged it in, and started it. "Wha…what are you doing?" Kory stuttered out.

Isaac looked around the room, and brushed his hands together, like he was pleased with a job well-done. "You should know better than anyone, Kory," he said. "We're making sugar dust."

As a fine dust started to accumulate in the room, the realization that I was going to die from sweetness didn't please me, regardless of how much I liked sugar.

"It just takes a little spark," he said, reaching in his pocket.

"Two sugar factory explosions within a few weeks of each other is going to look pretty suspicious." I said, trying to reason with him. "And it will look even stranger to have the owner, a local reporter, and a supporter of hemp oil legalization in the wreckage."

His lips slid into a vile smile. "There's where you're wrong, Ms. Saxee. It will make perfect sense when we spin it."

I had all the pieces, I could put that particular puzzle together—even if it was a complete lie. I was sure they'd say Kory Greer was making the pot cookies and working with John to try to prove that pot legalization wouldn't be harmful. I found out they were working together, and came here to confront them both. Something caused a spark, and the factory exploded.

"You won't get away with this," I said. "Enough people know about my suspicions that they'll keep investigating you." Spence, Hawke, and Drake to name a few.

Isaac licked his lips and pulled a shiny, gold lighter out of his pocket. "I wish them luck."

I thought I was done for and I'd never get to see what happened to Jax Teller when Isaac Handler fell to the ground. A dark, red spot was blooming on his chest and getting bigger with each passing second. The two enforcers ran over to him, then immediately took off.

Hawke stepped out from behind a stack of Saints and Sinners boxes. "Are you okay?" he asked, checking me over.

I breathed in a staggered breath, and managed to nod. He untied me, and then wrapped me in a hug, his arms strong and solid around my body. "I'm not happy you came in here alone. At all."

"I had to," I explained. "They would have hurt John and Kory without me."

Hawke's expression softened and he kissed me, a hard press of his lips against mine. It lasted less than five seconds, but it was exactly what I needed at the moment. "Part of me loves that about you, and part of me hates it. Kitty Kate."

"Could you forget about the part that hates it right now. I don't think I can handle an argument."

He nodded, shut off the machine, and went to untie Kory and John.

"The two guys who got away were helping the Brigham Smith group. They murdered at least six people, and made it look like the crimes were connected to a drug ring."

Hawke looked over at me. "They didn't get away. My guys have them out front. The police should be here any minute too."

I sank back down in the chair, exhausted from the ordeal, and relieved to be alive. I was sure my mind would change—soon—but right now, I never wanted to see a grain of sugar again.

Chapter Twenty-Two

"I'm really glad you decided to do this," Michelle said, watching me play with my little ball of fur. I threw a tiny tennis ball that was a perfect fit for Gandalf's little mouth. His tongue lolled to the side as he brought it back to me and waited for me to throw it again.

"Me too," I said, standing up. I'd just finished signing the adoption paperwork. I was still reticent, especially considering everything that had happened to me recently. I didn't want to put an animal in danger. At the same time though, I wanted Gandalf to have a home where he was happy and loved.

I might have a crazy life sometimes, but I could offer Gandalf a family. The thought of having a companion made me happy, and let's be honest, I'd fallen in love with the little guy the moment he'd rolled over and demanded a tummy rub in the booth at the fair. When I'd started recording *The Dog Whisperer* for training tips a week ago, I knew I'd pretty much made my choice. Training would start tomorrow.

Michelle handed me a carrying crate, and a box of Gandalf's toys, food, and some treats. "Let me know if you need anything," she said as I put Gandalf in the carrier.

"I will," I said, and walked out to my Jeep with my new little buddy.

I stopped by my mom and dad's house on the way home from the shelter so they'd have a chance to meet their grandpuppy.

My dad opened the door when I arrived, and my mom greeted me and Gandalf with a lot of unintelligible screeches. I did catch the word "adorable" and laughed when she kissed the top of his head. Repeatedly. She'd known him less than five minutes and I was pretty sure she already loved him more than me.

She kept muttering as she held him and talked in a high, excited voice that sounded a lot like she'd talk to a baby.

"—and we'll get you clothes, and paint your nails, and oh my gosh! Halloween is coming up!" She spared a glance for me. "We have to plan a costume! I think he'd make a perfect little ballerina."

The Devil Wears Tank Tops

Okay, maybe she didn't love him more than me. And I had a feeling he wouldn't be too pleased about any costume, let alone a tutu.

My dad shook his head. "You've done it now. She thinks this is a grandkid." My dad had gotten down on the floor with them both and was playing tug-of-war with Gandalf and a braided rope. He laughed when Gandalf pulled it out of his grasp and growled, running down the hall. He came back after a few seconds, wondering why no one had chased him. My dad got up and ran after him, and then I heard the back door open. Gandalf would have fun playing on their grass.

I smiled, happy that my parents loved my dog as much as I did.

It was only after the initial puppy-reveal excitement that I noticed a new addition to my mom's prized fair ribbons. She'd gotten the grand prize cookie ribbon. I narrowed my eyes. "Mom," I said, my tone suspicious, "where did you get this?"

I wasn't one to place blame, but I didn't put it past her to steal the thing.

She glared at me. "I didn't steal it."

I lifted a brow.

She folded her arms across her chest, defiant. "I didn't!" She got up from the floor and sat on the couch. "After the story came out about the pot cookies, I petitioned the fair board. My cookies had the next highest score, so I won—like I should have won in the first place."

Whew. I thought she might have resorted to threats and thievery. "Well, I'm glad you won, and that you got the ribbon without committing a crime."

Her nose wrinkled up. "Well, I almost committed one, but I stopped."

"What are you talking about?"

She took a deep breath and folded her hands in her lap like she was trying to decide if she should tell me or not.

"Mom," I said with a warning in my voice.

"Oh, fooey! Fine. I'll tell you. I heard that putting Visine in food could make people really sick. I sent the petition to the fair board, but I was still so mad after I found out about the pot cookies that I made some Visine cupcakes. I was going to deliver them to all of the judges, but then I decided it was too mean, and I shouldn't do it. It was a good thing, too, because I got the call about my cookies winning the day after your story came out. See," she said, a big smile on her face. "Everything works out."

I had a feeling her sudden bout of guilty conscious had more to do with the realization that people would think the judges had gotten sick from her baked goods, and her reputation as cooking queen would suffer for it.

"I hear Kory Greer issued an apology for the pot cookies," she said.

I nodded. "He did. Even though he didn't really do anything wrong. The ingredients for the cookies were delivered to his company, and he just made and distributed them. He had no idea what was in them. He vowed to help John educate the public about the difference between hemp oil and marijuana with high THC levels."

"That's so nice of him!" my mom said. "I'm glad something good came from it all."

"Me too."

"Hawke sure is handy to have around." She pursed her lips and shook her head, worried. "I don't even like to think about what would have happened if he hadn't been there."

Neither did I. I wouldn't have seen Jax Teller's last ride, that's for sure. "Me either." Issac Handler hadn't died, but he'd been close. He'd be around to go to trial, but he'd accepted all responsibility for the pot cookies. Which meant the Brigham Smith Group still existed, and their reach was far.

The room fell into silence for a minute as my mind wandered. Though I greatly appreciated Hawke and his ability to keep me alive, his comfort with killing had unsettled me. I felt like there was still a lot I didn't know about Hawke, and I wasn't sure when he'd be ready to tell me more. After he'd made sure I was okay, he'd had to stay at the scene to give statements to the police. Almost killing a man was apparently something that required a lot of paperwork. I hadn't seen him since that night, though he did send me a text to tell me he was thinking of me.

I texted him back a picture of Gandalf. He thought it was adorable, so he got points for that.

My dad came running back in from outside and my mom petted Gandalf as he ran over and jumped against her legs like they were playing tag.

"Oh!" my mom exclaimed. "I need to make him doggie treats!" she stood and started for the kitchen, Gandalf trailing behind. "I'm going to look up recipes right now!"

At least Gandalf wouldn't go hungry. I hoped the treats were also edible for humans so we could both eat.

A knock sounded on the front door and Gandalf gave a little yelp. He'd kindly marked my living room floor as soon as he walked in the house, letting me know he approved of his new home. And he'd done it all with a smile. He was already house trained, so I was sure this was an isolated incident to let any stray animals or bugs know the territory was his.

Gandalf and I both walked across the bright blue rug to the front door. I smiled when I opened it. "Hi, Drake," I said, inviting him in. I left the front door open to get the benefit of the nice, evening fall breeze.

He smiled back. "Hi." Gandalf spun in excitement at the new person in our space. Drake leaned down. "Who's this?"

"It's my new dog. Gandalf."

Drake looked up at me and grinned. "I like the name."

I shrugged. "He looks like a wizard."

"He definitely does," Drake said, scratching Gandalf under the chin. "It makes me feel good to know you have a guard dog, and even better to know he might have magic powers."

I gave him a strange look. "I'm not sure he qualifies as a guard dog. He won't even be ten pounds full grown."

"He can bark and notify you of intruders. That qualifies."

Drake had called me last night as soon as he'd heard about what happened. He was in Salt Lake, but insisted on coming back to check on me. I told him I'd be busy writing the story and wouldn't get to see him anyway. He'd agreed to wait until today to come back to Branson, but he'd sent me a giant bouquet of flowers and some doughnuts from Frosted Paradise. So my swearing off of sugar had lasted about twelve hours. I wasn't going to lie. I ate them all. I deserved it.

Drake pulled something from behind his back. "I brought you a present."

I noticed the bag. Saints and Sinners Cookies. "Please don't tell me that's what I think it is?"

"Last time they made you pretty excited," he said, lifting his brows.

I narrowed my eyes. "You weren't supposed to remember that."

His lips lifted. "They're not really cookies. Look inside."

I opened it and excited surprise crossed my face. "You brought my favorite chocolate covered espresso beans from my favorite coffee house in Salt Lake!" I pulled out another bag. "And coffee! Thank you!" I threw my arms around him in a hug. Then I felt awkward because I'd never really hugged Drake before. He hadn't even been on my potential hug list until recently. I stepped back, and he seemed rather pleased with himself.

"I'm glad it made you happy."

I looked at the coffee. "You made me happy, and I hope no one saw you buy this. You'll be in so much trouble if someone snapped a photo of Dylan Drake buying coffee beans."

"I'd do anything to make you smile, Katie." His voice lowered, the tone more serious than before.

My eyes softened as I looked at him. This wasn't just something Drake was saying to be charming. He really cared about me, and that meant a lot. "I'm corrupting you."

One corner of his lips hitched. "That sounds promising."

I blushed.

"So," Drake said, sitting on the couch, "since I braved the gossips and bought you coffee, can we talk about when you have time for another date?"

I took a deep breath. I'd had some time to think about the date with Drake, and about my feelings for him. They were progressing, and I realized that probably wasn't a good thing. I sat next to him and Gandalf jumped up on my lap, then immediately defected and moved to Drake's.

Because Drake cared about me, and he, and his gestures, meant a lot to me, I had to stop this now before either of us got hurt. Though, I thought I might be too far gone for that outcome myself.

My lashes lifted and I met his eyes. "Where do you think this is going to go, Drake?"

Wrinkles formed on his forehead. "Wherever you'll let it."

I shook my head. "It will never work between us. You have to know that."

A vein in his neck started throbbing and he didn't look pleased. "Why?" he asked, his voice clipped.

I took a deep breath and placed my hands palms down on my thighs, resigned. "Because I'll never be a member of the Mormon Church again." I'd given this a lot of thought, and saw no real way around it. "There's a lot of compromise that happens in relationships, but you can't ask me to change my beliefs. I've been a reporter for four years. I've covered politicians and I know how this works. Your wife, or even your girlfriend at this point, could make or break your career. It's even more of an issue in a conservative, religious state like this. Your job depends on you having a significant other who's willing to stand silently by and let you take the lead in every aspect of your life. I haven't been silent since I was in the womb."

He massaged Gandalf's back and looked at the floor for several minutes, like he was doing some serious contemplation. I knew how he felt. I'd been thinking about it ever since our date. A sour feeling started creeping its way through my stomach. I didn't want to end things, but I didn't see a way around it. I wrapped my arms around myself and studied the light flecks of azure on my blue rug.

Drake's voice made me look up. "I've already thought about that, Katie."

I nodded, understanding. No matter how I'd felt about Drake in the past, the things I'd learned about him in the last few weeks, and the way he'd made me feel, had made me respect him. I was starting to care about him far more than I should.

I knew it couldn't work, and I needed to protect myself, my heart—and Drake. A relationship with him would always be a battle because I didn't fit the mold. Being together would make both of our lives harder, and that's not how a relationship should work. I'd reconciled myself that dating—or anything else— wasn't in the cards with Drake. Hopefully he'd seen it too.

Drake picked Gandalf up and put him down on the rug, then turned toward me and lightly lifted my chin with his fingers. He met my eyes with a determined gaze. "I've thought about it, and I don't give a shit what people think."

My eyes widened as I stared at him. I'd been expecting him to agree with me, and us to end whatever it was we'd started. That wasn't what I got. My stomach started to flutter with nervous anticipation as he continued, "I love that you're independent, and not afraid to speak your mind. I would never change that about you. It's what made me fall for you years ago, and I've just kept falling since." He pursed his lips, then continued, "I want you, Katie. I want you, and not what you, or anyone else thinks you need to be. And I could care less about your religion. People can go to hell if they think I'd lose you for something as ridiculous as that."

He took my face in his hands and bent down. "I was a lawyer before I was a politician. I could easily be a lawyer again. I'm not giving up on you, or us. Not now. Not ever."

His lips met mine, soft, like they'd been waiting years for this. We both had. His smooth tongue traced mine as my mouth opened, and the kiss deepened. His hands moved over my back in a strong embrace, hugging me close to him. It was the kiss I'd dreamed about since I'd watched him on the dance floor as a teenager. The kiss I thought I'd never have. And in that moment, it felt like everything I'd ever need. He pulled back to study me, and I fell against the arm of the couch, licking my kiss swollen lips.

I looked at him, strong, sexy, and willing to risk everything for me. The kiss had done nothing to dim my attraction to him. It had just made the problem a thousand times worse. "We need to talk about this," I said, gasping for breath and trying to clear my foggy head. One of us needed to be rational.

I wasn't sure it could be me.

He gave a slow smile that was full of innuendo. "We'll have time for that later."

He stood up, walked to the front of the living room, and shut the door before turning back to me. "Now, where were we?"

Acknowledgments

Once again, HUGE thanks to my incredible production team! My extremely talented cover designer, Kat Tallon at Ink and Circuit Designs. My fantastic editor, Ashley Argyle, PhD at Inktip Editing. And my amazing formatter, Ali Cross, at Novel Ninjutsu.

For my family and friends who put up with my crazy schedule, and still find time for me—even if it's in the middle of the night. I couldn't do this without you.

Massive thank you to Ashley, who insisted this book was funnier than I thought it was, and kept me writing. Honestly, none of my books would get written without her pep talks and reassurance.

To my mom, for making Sophie Saxee the easiest character in the world to channel and write. The Kate Saxee books wouldn't be possible without my mom and her adventures. After reading this book, she texted me, incensed about Sophie's clothing choices with the following: "When have I EVER worn a PINK checkered skirt?!?" She didn't say anything about the mouse-tie outfit, however, which she did actually wear—and dubbed one of her greatest creations.

Being an author means having insane work hours, talking to people who live in my head, and stopping mid-conversation to write down ideas. One of the most important things an author needs is a supportive partner. I'm so lucky I found that person, and that he loves me as much as I love him. Dan makes me laugh, reminds me to eat, and forces me to step away from the keyboard once in a while. He keeps me sane, and the comments he writes in the margins of my books are hilarious.

And Pippin, Dan's partner in crime, who forces me to take writing breaks by stomping on my keyboard with his four little paws and staring at me until I get on the floor and throw his ball. This book also has a family addition for Kate—a sweet dog named Gandalf. Gandalf was my dog when I was young, and he was my best friend. Putting him in this book has been a wonderful way to bring him back to life with memories.

Most of all, thank you to my amazing readers! One of the biggest compliments an author gets is people continuing to read their books. With every book I release, I'm always amazed by your support and I'm so incredibly appreciative! I wouldn't be able to do this without you, and I wish I could give every one of you a hug. Come see me at an event so I can!

xoxo,
Ang

About the Author

Angela Corbett graduated from Westminster College and previously worked as a journalist, freelance writer, and director of communications and marketing. She lives in Utah with her extremely supportive husband, and loves classic cars, traveling, and chasing their five-pound Pomeranian, Pippin—who is just as mischievous as his hobbit namesake. She's the author of Young Adult, New Adult, and Adult fiction—with lots of kissing. She writes under two names, Angela Corbett, and Destiny Ford.

You can find her online at
@angcorbett
angelacorbett.com

Other books by
Angela Corbett/Destiny Ford

The Devil Drinks Coffee
Devilishly Short #1

Tempting Sydney

Eternal Starling
Eternal Echoes

For special sneak peeks, giveaways, and super secret
news, join Angela's newsletter list!
http://eepurl.com/KhLAn

If you enjoyed reading *The Devil Wears Tank Tops*, please
help others enjoy this book too by lending it,
recommending it, or reviewing it on Amazon, Barnes
and Noble, or Goodreads. If you do write a review,
please send me a message through my website so I can
thank you! www.angelacorbett.com

xoxo,
Ang